HER
MISSING
CHILD

BOOKS BY KERRY WATTS

Heartlands

KERRY WATTS
HER MISSING CHILD

Bookouture

Published by Bookouture in 2019

An imprint of Storyfire Ltd.
Carmelite House
50 Victoria Embankment
London EC4Y 0DZ

www.bookouture.com

ISBN: 978-1-78681-794-5
eBook ISBN: 978-1-78681-793-8

Previously published as *Safe Home*

Thanks, Misty. You were the best x

PROLOGUE

The deafening horn blast from the rusting white van startled her. Her eyes were stretched wide at the sudden sound, but her chaotic mind remained elsewhere. The heavily tattooed driver mouthed his discontent through the window and gesticulated with his fist. This was quickly followed by a close shave with a taxi, which had to slam on his brakes to avoid hitting her.

'Idiot! Watch where you're going!'

The taxi driver's gesture went unnoticed. She ran on past an elderly couple she recognised from the village, but her cloudy mind couldn't recall their names. They gasped as she narrowly missed their neatly groomed bichon frise.

'Watch where you're going, lassie!' The man tutted as his wife clung to his arm, the small dog barking at her as she left them behind.

She couldn't stop. She mustn't. Her mind was racing so fast she didn't notice the man ahead of her until she had already collided with him, sending her to the ground. The man reached out his sweaty hand to help her up. She took it, got to her feet and ran on with barely a backward glance.

That was close.

'You're welcome,' the man growled breathlessly, before pushing his earbuds back in and moving off, muttering something inaudible under his breath.

She ran on, towards the children heading home from school. She narrowed her eyes at them as they passed, laughing and pointing at her. Two young mothers, both seemingly startled by her appearance, frowned in her direction before continuing to fuss with their toddlers, each already trussed up in thick ski suits. The cold wind blew harder, and the wind turbines that sat high above the village in the Ochil Hills spun with gusto as thick white clouds sped across the horizon.

She was dressed only in skinny blue jeans and an orange T-shirt, and damp strands of her wavy auburn hair dangled across her face. But she couldn't stop. On she ran, past the village school, moving against the flow of children and parents all chattering and laughing about their day, all the while repeating the word 'no' to herself.

'Hey, are you OK?' one father called out as he watched her slice through the crowd, but still she couldn't stop. Finally clear of the throng, she headed towards the Moncreiffe Hill woodland.

Hurry up. They're coming.

'I know, I know,' she called out into the freezing air.

She had to get out of the village. It had all happened so quickly. Why couldn't she just have done what she was supposed to do today? If she had just gone there instead, this wouldn't be happening. Her legs burned from running and her toes felt numb in the bitter January chill. Snow had been falling in the village for three days, and forecasters predicted the coldest winter for decades was on its way.

As she passed McCabe's garage, co-proprietor Tim McCabe was alarmed at the state of her. He considered calling out to see if she was OK, but his brother Peter had told him to stay out of sight. Tim watched her cross the bridge and head towards the entrance to Moncreiffe Wood, thinking she looked worse than he'd seen her for a long time. He eyed his van keys on the office table, before deciding it'd be quicker on foot – if he hurried he could catch up to her, no problem. His phone buzzed in his pocket. *Peter.* He answered it.

'Aye, I know. I can handle it,' Tim growled at his brother. 'Just get back here, will you? I don't see why I should be the one taking all the risk.' He hung up and stuffed his phone deep into the pocket of his overalls. *I don't see why he even asked me if he doesn't trust me*, Tim thought, as he watched her figure disappear up the snow-covered path between the trees.

Her chest tightened, as if caught in a vice, as she struggled to run uphill. Her heart pounded, and she jumped at the sound of the collared doves scattering above her. Their sudden flight caused snow to fall from the branches onto her already sweat-soaked hair. She ran because she'd panicked. It was just so awful – she couldn't bear it.

'OK, calm down, calm down.' She tried to remember to breathe. In and out. In and out. She couldn't think. Her brain seemed to have locked away her ability to process thoughts and she couldn't find the key, no matter how hard she tried. All she felt was a heavy fog. A cloudy mist floating inside her head where the solution to this horrific problem should be. Why did she have to listen to *them*? Her fists tightened into balls and she hammered them against her thighs. She wanted to cry out. For something, anything to fix it.

'What are you staring at?' she screamed at a passing jogger, who'd simply glanced her way from further up the track while adjusting the handles on her rucksack.

The girl couldn't handle this on her own any longer. They were going to be so angry with her. She sobbed uncontrollably and paced back and forth up the track, tugging on her knotted hair. Her whole body trembled in the freezing cold. Finally, she grabbed her phone and called the only person she knew who could fix this.

'It's me, I've done something terrible. You have to come. I am so sorry,' she cried, her words almost lost in the foam of fizzy tears. 'You have to hurry before anyone else finds out. She can't ever know it was me.'

CHAPTER ONE

Dianne Davidson tightened her blue scarf against the bitter chill, the wind catching her as she rounded the bend at the furthest end of Moncreiffe Wood from the village of Bridge of Earn, parallel to the main Edinburgh–Perth road.

The surgeon had been right. Exercise was great in helping her recover from the hysterectomy. This was a long walk – three miles – and it had taken her and her young Labrador, Benson, a good hour and a half, but it hadn't felt that far at all. The bright winter sun was encouraging, necessarily so, given that Dianne's mood when she got up that morning had been anything but bright. Two years ago to the day, but Dianne remembered *that* morning as if it were yesterday.

She rubbed her gloved hand across the back of her neck, wiping away the stubborn patch of moisture that had gathered under her scarf from the bottom of her short brown hair. It would have been a good idea to dry her hair after her shower, perhaps, but the beckoning sunshine and Benson's barking had made her skip it.

As she reached *her* bench, Dianne pulled the small bunch of white carnations, tied neatly in a pink silk ribbon, from inside the bag and lowered herself onto the bench to rest. Benson stopped to look back to where his mistress had interrupted his walk and whimpered before turning to join her. He sat down close to Dianne's knee and lifted a paw to pat her leg. Dianne smiled at his gesture. He had been more like a therapy pet than just a dog to her these past eighteen months. Dianne had barely been able to cross the front door for six months after it happened. Thank goodness for her husband Colin, too; without him she didn't know what she would have done. He'd lost a child as well, though.

She laid the flowers against the back of the bench and wiped away the single tear that gathered. She promised herself she wouldn't cry today. Instead she would try to remember the happy, warm memories Stacey had created for her. Her first smile. Her first laugh. The way she'd raged with determination to roll over that first time. Her baby daughter had a lot to say for someone so young. Six months wasn't nearly long enough to have had her in her life. It was explained away as a cot death, but Dianne had done everything right, hadn't she? Didn't she try to make sure she followed all the advice? When it happened, she wondered if people would blame her. Were they accusing her with their eyes, if not their words? She knew people were whispering behind her back. It didn't matter how many times Colin tried to reassure her that was not true. She opened the bag again and pulled out the soft blue blanket. She held it close to her face and closed her eyes. That smell. The unmistakable baby smell. There was nothing in the world that compared to the sweet scent of a baby. Her mind filled with a sense of soothing comfort. Benson pawed her once more and whimpered, pulling her out of her trance. He was so in tune with her mood.

'It's OK, silly,' Dianne smiled at him. 'Mummy's fine.'

Benson barked loudly, just once. One short, sharp, deep bark, but certainly enough to startle a young doe, Dianne only catching a flash of the animal as it bolted deeper into the trees. The deer's hurried flight caused a grey squirrel to scamper up the nearest tree it could find – the scaly trunk of a Scots pine. Dianne sighed contentedly, rubbed Benson roughly behind his ears and then leaned down to kiss the top of his big brown head.

'You big softy. You are a silly boy, aren't you?' she teased, and he nuzzled his face deeper into her legs, almost lifting them off the ground with the force of his near thirty-kilogram bulk. 'Hey, hey you, calm down, young man.' She pulled a treat from the pocket of her duffle coat and watched him devour it in one bite.

He really was a tonic. But another, human tonic had crash-landed into Dianne's life six months ago. One that had done more good than any antidepressant or counsellor or hyperactive puppy. Dianne's mouth had dropped open in horror when she saw the tatty white van pull into the drive of the empty bungalow next door. Her horror had deepened when out of it had climbed a young couple, the girl barely into her twenties, covered in tattoos and sporting a nose ring. But what had really filled Dianne with dread was the fact that the girl had been heavily pregnant.

The young couple, it transpired, couldn't have been nicer, but Claire Lucas didn't take to motherhood as naturally as Dianne had, which only increased the bittersweet taste of having a new baby next door. As the weeks had gone by, Claire had been diagnosed with post-natal depression, and Dianne had found herself doing more and more for little Finlay Lucas – things that his mother should really have been doing but wasn't able to. Dianne didn't resent it – she enjoyed every minute of the time she spent feeding, bathing and taking care of this gorgeous baby boy, rediscovering some of the happiness she and Colin had been so cruelly robbed of. Pushing Finlay around the village in his pram felt right. Dianne felt whole again somehow.

But in recent days it was getting harder and harder to give him back. Back to a house that was dirty and chaotic. To a mother who seemed indifferent to him. She wanted to give Claire a shake and scream *Look at your son!* This beautiful boy. Cherish him. Treasure every moment you get to spend with him. Dianne lifted Finlay's blanket to her cheek and rubbed it gently over her skin, inhaling its scent one last time. She smiled. Her racing heart slowed while she folded and tucked the blanket back down into the bottom of her bag. She picked up Benson's lead and stood up from the bench. She kissed the tips of the gloved fingers of one hand and laid them gently on the bench's small silver plaque, which simply read: *For Stacey x.*

Her iPhone buzzed in her pocket and she read the email and grinned. Their plane tickets were confirmed. She hoped Colin would be as excited as she was.

'Come on, Benny boy.' She patted her leg and tossed the dog's ball ahead of them, and he shot after his toy without having to be told twice.

Despite the date, today was a good day. The first day of the rest of their lives. They could finally put the past behind them and start again. She couldn't wait to surprise Colin.

CHAPTER TWO

Darren Lucas was exhausted, and yawned as he pulled into his drive. He switched off the engine and flopped his head back into the headrest then exhaled a long, slow breath before going inside to face her. He wondered what kind of mood she would be in – it was like walking on eggshells these days. On top of that, working for his father-in-law was taking it out of him. As well as taking care of Finlay during the night. Stopping by Maggie's to share a stolen few moments had probably not been a good idea in his already exhausted state. Darren was ready for bed, but knew it would be a long time before his head would hit the pillow. He yawned again and waved to his neighbour, Colin Davidson, who nodded while he dropped a large black bag into his wheelie bin. Darren stared at his own overflowing bin and told himself that he must remember to wheel it out later tonight after missing the collection last time round.

'It's another cold one,' Colin Davidson called out. 'Roll on spring,' he chuckled and blew warmth into his freezing-cold hands.

'Aye, it's bitter the night,' Darren called back, before heading round to the back door. He unzipped his fleece and slung it over one of the kitchen chairs, cursing under his breath at the heat. How many times did he keep telling Claire they didn't need the heating on so high? They were already behind with the gas and electric, among other things.

He called out to her as he tossed his keys onto the hall table, before seeing her slumped on the sofa, surrounded by the debris she'd said she would tidy that morning. He shook his head and grabbed a towel from the pile of laundry on the kitchen table. He needed a shower, needed to wash Maggie off him. Stopping by her place on his way home had become a habit. A habit that helped him deal with the stress he was facing at home. Darren hadn't planned to have an affair. She was Claire's best friend, after all. But it just sort of happened.

He snatched up a clean T-shirt and joggers from another laundry pile in the corner of the bedroom and sniffed them. They didn't smell of washing powder, but they were passable. He switched on the hot jets of water and peeled his sweaty work shirt over his head, then tossed it towards the laundry basket in the corner of the bathroom. He wiped the fog off the steamed-up mirror and glanced at his reflection. He did look tired. More like his thirties than his mid-twenties. He stepped into the shower and stood under the steaming-hot flow, trying to wash away his guilt.

'Thanks babe,' Darren took a huge swig from the mug of tea Claire had made for him while he showered. He'd been gasping for a brew and had quickly sunk more than half the mug in a couple of large gulps. He rubbed at his hair with his towel and sank the remainder of his tea before clicking the kettle on again.

'How's your day been?' he asked his wife.

'There's more in the pot,' she responded, deliberately avoiding his question.

'You're a lifesaver.' Darren moved closer and reached out towards her cheek. He might have even dropped a gentle kiss on it, but she flinched as soon as he got too close. He settled for a smile instead. 'Thanks.'

Claire's half-smile in return betrayed her discomfort.

'Here you go.' Claire handed him the milk.

'Cheers, you want one?' he asked as he poured.

Claire scrunched up her nose and shook her head. 'I'm fine. How was your day?'

There was a time when all he had to do was brush past her or run his fingers through her hair and they would be in bed within minutes. Sometimes they didn't even make it into the bedroom. Perhaps if that was still the case he wouldn't have turned to Maggie. Post-natal depression had ended their sex life months ago. Not that Darren blamed Finlay. Not for one second would he blame his son. He just wished life was different.

'Oh, you know, busy,' he answered with a shrug. He yawned then glanced at the clock. 'The wee man having a nap at this time?' Darren did his best to conceal his frustration. 'He won't go down for ages now.'

'Don't have a go at me, Darren – you're just in the door. I'm the one that's been here with him all day. What if I wanted a bit of peace?' Her defensive response was the default these days. 'It's OK for you. You have a life outside these four walls.'

Darren turned away and rolled his eyes. There was nothing to be gained by pursuing the point. It wasn't Claire that would have to deal with Finlay at midnight or worse tonight. She would have a headache, or she would be too tired. Darren did try to understand what she was going through, he really did. The health visitor had given him enough leaflets on post-natal depression that he could probably tell you everything there was to know about pregnancy and antidepressants and even therapy. He loved Claire and he absolutely worshipped his son, but Darren could do with a good night's sleep, too. He couldn't remember the last time he'd slept right through.

'I'm not having a go, Claire, forget I said anything.'

Claire shot him a glance of indignation before storming out of the kitchen. Darren tossed his mug into the sink, splashing himself with the last drops of tea. He stood by the sink and peered out through the blinds. He could see right into Dianne and Colin's kitchen window. He could see them laughing together. They looked happy. Maybe one day he and Claire would be happy like that. Darren allowed the blind to fall. He needed a hug from his boy. Finlay should be wakened anyway, otherwise it really would be late before Darren could get to bed and he was already exhausted. He couldn't just lie down whenever he pleased.

Darren closed the living room door as he passed, leaving Claire sitting in front of the television. He shook his head gently and sighed as he scratched at his messy brown hair then pushed Finlay's bedroom door open with one finger. He felt bad about waking him from his peaceful slumber, but sometimes we all have to do things we don't want. He moved through the darkness to switch on Finlay's Winnie-the-Pooh lamp on his bedside table. He flicked through a story book he didn't recognise, figuring Dianne must have bought it for him. She was always buying Finlay books. He and Claire were damn lucky to have them around. Dianne had been a godsend when Claire's depression was at its worst.

Darren turned to Finlay's cot and smiled. 'Hey, wee man, Daddy's home and needs a big hug from his baby boy. Time you were—'

Darren's heart thundered in his chest. He grabbed at the blanket and tossed it aside. His son was gone.

CHAPTER THREE

'Claire!' Darren screamed and raced into the living room. 'Claire, where is he?'

Claire frowned and sat bolt upright. 'What? Where's who?'

'Who the hell do you think I mean?' Darren growled. 'Where's Finlay?'

Claire leaped up from the sofa and ran into Finlay's room. She grabbed at the blanket, then threw it back into his cot.

'Where is he?' she roared at Darren.

'I don't bloody know! Is he with Dianne?' He raced out the back door, skidding on the icy path, hopped the fence and hammered on the Davidsons' back door. The support they'd received from Dianne could never be repaid, but it was unusual for her to have Finlay with her at this time of the day. She knew that Darren would be home to take care of him.

Colin opened the door, still drying his hands on a tea towel. 'Darren, what's wrong?'

'Is Finlay here?' Darren shouted, trying to barge past him. 'Has Dianne got him?'

Dianne overheard Darren's panicked voice. 'What's happened, Darren? Come in, come in, sit down.'

'No, I just want to know if he's here with you.'

Dianne stared over Darren's shoulder at the shell-shocked look on Claire's face, the young mother having caught her husband up. Dianne clasped her hands to her mouth.

'No, of course he's not here,' Colin said, pulling his mobile phone from his pocket. 'Why would he be here?'

'Then where is he?' Darren shouted, panic now soaring round his blood. 'Where the hell is he?'

'I'm calling the police,' Colin announced, trying to keep his voice level despite the horror on Darren's face.

Dianne pulled the back door behind her as the group headed back into Darren and Claire's, past the chaos of unmatched shoes that littered the kitchen doorway.

'Let's not jump to conc—' Dianne started.

'Let's not jump to conclusions? What's that supposed to mean?' Darren blasted, his terror reaching fever pitch. 'My little boy wasn't in his cot where his mother left him!'

'The police are coming,' Colin told them. He glanced anxiously at Dianne, who avoided his gaze.

CHAPTER FOUR

Detective Inspector Jessie Blake wanted to put the card out of her mind and just enjoy her evening. It was her fortieth birthday after all, and her colleague Dylan and his wife Shelly had gone to so much trouble over this meal, despite the tiredness that plagued this stage of Shelly's pregnancy. When Dylan's suggestion of drinks didn't suit, he insisted Jessie should at least come for dinner, that she had to celebrate such a landmark. Jessie told herself turning forty was just a number, but the reality was she'd always imagined herself settled with a couple of kids by now. She hadn't dared tell anyone about the birthday card her ex-husband had sent her. She wanted to put Dan's attempt at manipulation out of her mind tonight, because that's all it was. Another way to control her. She was convinced of that.

'Here we go,' Shelly announced when she switched off the dining room light. '*Happy birthday to you, happy birthday to you, happy birthday dear Jessie, happy birthday to you.*'

She placed a delicious-looking chocolate sponge cake on the table with two candles shining on top.

'Remember to make a wish.' Dylan winked and grinned, then sipped from his glass.

Jessie smiled and shook her head before blowing out her candles.

'Thanks, guys, this is so sweet of you. You shouldn't have gone to so much trouble.'

'Nonsense,' Shelly passed Jessie a plate with a large slice of cake and licked the chocolate frosting from her thumb. 'You only turn forty once, don't you?'

Jessie shot an appreciative glance at Dylan.

'Thank you, both of you. I really appreciate everything you've done.'

Jessie wondered if she should tell Dylan about the card.

'Shall we take our cake and coffee to a soft seat?' Shelly suggested. Her hand drifted to her heavily pregnant belly and she winced. 'Ouch! Damn Braxton Hicks.'

Jessie smiled, desperate to ask if she could feel their baby kicking, but resisted. *That would be too weird, right?* 'Not long now, huh?'

'Can't come soon enough,' Shelly announced as another kick hammered inside her. 'I think this might be a footballer we've got cooking in here.'

'I'll start clearing these plates.' Dylan kissed Shelly's cheek. 'Cracking meal, hon. Go through, Jess, and I'll join you both in a minute.'

Just as he said it, their toddler son Jack's cry echoed from his bedroom at the top of the stairs.

'I'll go,' Shelly said. 'You two go and have your cake.'

Dylan laid the plates in the sink, then joined Jessie in the living room.

'It's some view, isn't it?' he pointed out as he stood next to her by the large bay window.

'Aye, you're not wrong.' Jessie looked out at the far-reaching view of the hills, silhouetted by the moonlight in the distance. The tops of the wind turbines seeming to touch the sky.

'Worth every penny.' He smiled. 'We needed something with a decent garden for the wee man.'

Jessie nodded. 'Three bedrooms, too, for the increasing number of Logans.'

A wry smile crept across Dylan's lips before he sipped his coffee.

In that moment, Jessie felt lonelier than she had for a long time. She was relieved to hear her phone ring in her bag on the sofa, but frowned as she checked the display.

'It's the station.' She pursed her lips as she answered. 'Hey, boss. What's up?'

Dylan sank the last of his coffee and laid his mug on the table, watching with concern the growing look of horror on Jessie's face.

'What's going on?' he asked.

Jessie held her hand up to silence him. 'OK, text me the address. We're on our way.' She hung up and waited for the address, then thrust her phone into her trouser pocket. 'A missing baby, Dylan. Come on. Uniform are already on the scene.'

Dylan slipped into his heavy boots then grabbed his thick down jacket from the peg. It was freezing out there, and he didn't know how long he would be gone. He peered round Jack's bedroom door to see Shelly cradling their almost eighteen-month-old son in her arms in an attempt to rock him back to sleep. She lifted her finger to her lips.

'Work – an urgent one. I love you, don't wait up,' Dylan whispered then blew them both a small kiss.

'We'll take my car,' Jessie suggested as he joined her outside. 'Six-month-old Finlay Lucas. Last seen when his mum Claire laid him down for a nap. Father Darren went to get him, and Finlay wasn't in his cot. He went to his next-door neighbours to see if they had him.'

Jessie tugged on her seat belt then started the engine.

'Why would he think the neighbours had him?' Dylan asked. 'Sounds a bit weird.'

'Neighbour helps out a lot, apparently. Takes Finlay out for walks to give the parents a break. Helps in the house. That kind of thing. Not sure, but she might even have a key.' Jessie's wheels spat up the gravel in Dylan's drive before she turned towards the M90.

'Where are we headed then, boss?'

'Claire and Darren Lucas live in Bridge of Earn. Their house backs onto the burn.'

'Shit, Shelly's frae the Brig.'

Jessie turned to face him and grinned. 'The Brig? Since when did you become a yokel, Dylan Logan?'

CHAPTER FIVE

'Hello, Theresa. I'm Carol. I'll be looking after you tonight.'

The smiling face of the overweight, middle-aged nurse didn't put Theresa at ease one bit. Neither did her neatly trimmed fringe and bob haircut. But her mum had said this would be best, under the circumstances. She fiddled with her knotted auburn hair and tucked her knees up to her chin as she shuffled as far back on the bed as she could. *I've let everybody down, haven't I?* Her mum's face as she marched up that hill through the woods towards her was terrifying, but Theresa had had no choice. Who else could she have called? There was nobody else she could have trusted. Not with that.

Say nothing.

'Hello,' Theresa muttered with a fake smile, trying to ignore the voice in her head.

It was always best to smile in these situations. Don't ever give away what you're really thinking. She didn't want to risk having her medication increased by being honest about her thoughts.

Her mum was right. A bit of rest was probably the best thing right now. At least until she could get her head straight. Her mum had promised she would help, and her mum always did as she said she would. She was a woman of her word.

*

Bridget Moran straightened her skirt after getting up from the chair in the nurses' office. She wiped what she thought were crumbs from the back of it. *Disgusting*, she thought. The doctor reached out his hand.

'Once Theresa's medication has been reviewed we'll have her back to her normal self, don't worry.' He smiled with what Bridget figured was his attempt at sincerity.

She accepted his offer of a handshake, wondering how a man with such a weak, wet grip could possibly have reached the role of consultant psychiatrist. She tried to wipe her hand on her shawl without him noticing. It wouldn't do to be rude about it.

'Thank you,' Bridget answered as she lifted her brown leather handbag from the back of the chair, gripping it firmly to her before being led out by the staff nurse.

'Come on, I'll take you to Theresa's room,' the cheerful woman said.

Bridget's face was tired from all the grateful smiles she was giving, bags forming under her large hazel eyes. She'd been surprised and relieved to be able to get Theresa a bed so quickly. Her eldest daughter couldn't be left alone in the state she was in. Bridget couldn't help being angry with Theresa for stopping taking her medication again, but she also planned to complain to the staff at the day hospital's therapy garden – they should have noticed the deterioration in her daughter's condition before it came to this. They were supposed to be the professionals. But, under the circumstances, that was the least of the Morans' problems. Bridget was just relieved it was she Theresa had called and not anyone else. Bridget shuddered at the thought of anybody else finding out.

'Mum!' Theresa sprang up from her bed and hugged her mother with a tight squeeze, then whispered in her ear.

'I know, I know,' Bridget patted her daughter's back and withdrew. 'Everything is sorted. Go to sleep now.'

CHAPTER SIX

As soon as the uniformed officer had shown Jessie and Dylan into the Lucases' bungalow, a frantic young man sprang towards them.

'You have to help us!' he exclaimed. 'My son…' He paced up and down the living room, rubbing his hand across his untidy brown hair. 'Someone's taken my son. I can't believe this is happening.'

Jessie glanced past him to the emotionless figure slumped on the sofa.

'We'll be next door, Darren.' This from a man slim and balding, his arm around the shoulder of a haunted-looking woman, ushering her towards the door. *Colin and Dianne Davidson*, Jessie thought. *The helpful neighbours.*

Dylan nodded to them. 'Mr and Mrs Davidson, correct? I'll be through in a bit to talk to you, so don't go anywhere, will you?'

Colin Davidson closed his eyes and nodded before leaving with Dianne. Jessie heard the back door shut behind them and strained to hear what their muffled voices were saying. She narrowed her eyes, struggling to take them off Claire Lucas. *How can she be so calm? Her baby son is missing.*

Jessie turned to the young man pacing the room. 'Mr Lucas, my name is Detective Inspector Jessie Blake and this is my colleague, Detective Constable Dylan Logan. Is it OK to call you Darren?'

'Yes, of course. Darren's fine. That's my wife, Claire. Please, you have to help. We don't know where Finlay is. I went to get him up and he wasn't there.' Darren was begging, his voice tormented by terror. 'God, please, you have to do something.'

'OK, OK, first things first. Tell us exactly what happened.' Jessie spoke quietly and calmly. She wasn't going to get any facts from him until Darren was able to focus properly.

'I've already told you!' Darren roared. 'My son's gone!'

Jessie wasn't surprised by the panic he was showing but she needed more detail.

'Darren, could you take me and DC Logan to your son's room? Show us his cot. Could you do that for me?' Her eyes drifted towards Dylan. 'OK?'

'Yes, sure, come on,' Darren continued to nibble his thumbnail, which he'd been chewing since the two detectives arrived, as he led them along the short hallway. It was littered with shoes and bags of all kinds: carrier bags filled with what looked like clothes, an open, half-empty sports bag. There was even a tennis racquet leaning against the hall table. Dylan glanced momentarily at Jessie, raising his eyebrows at the mess.

'There, see, empty.' Darren moved to Finlay's bedroom window and ripped open the curtains that Claire had closed for their son's nap. He looked out into the darkness of the garden as the security light was triggered by the cat from the house three doors down. 'I really can't believe this is happening. This has to be some kind of horrible nightmare.'

Dylan pulled plastic gloves from his jacket pocket and lifted Finlay's blanket. He peeled back the mattress, then tucked both it and the blanket neatly back in place.

'Is there anything missing that you can see? Anything out of place?' he asked, moving to the fitted wardrobe. He slid open the mirrored door and flicked through the coat hangers – some held only one pair of tiny trousers; most were empty.

'Apart from my son, you mean?' Darren yelled, his patience wearing thin. 'You won't find my son in there.'

'Is this all of your son's things?' Dylan pointed to the almost bare wardrobe.

'What? Yes – most of it is in the washing basket. I don't know. Why does that matter?'

Dylan closed the wardrobe door and focused his full attention on Darren. 'I want you to take a good look for me. Does anything look out of place in here? Even something small. Anything missing, like clothes, toys, blankets? Anything. Is there anything here that *shouldn't* be here that is? Anything you don't recognise.'

Darren stopped pacing and seemed to be trying to quell the terror that had gripped him. He inhaled a long breath, both hands covering his mouth, and scanned Finlay's room from corner to corner, exhaling slowly and carefully as he did so.

'I c-can't,' he stuttered. 'I just… no, I don't think so. Just Finlay. He's the only thing missing.'

Dylan placed a hand on Darren's shoulder and squeezed, but said nothing.

Jessie gave her DC a quick nod – he was taking control of the situation, and this was an early chance to talk to the missing child's parents individually. She went back to the living room alone and took a seat next to Claire. Jessie noticed the chaos in their home wasn't limited to the hallway. Here, magazines were piled high. Laundry was strewn across several of the surfaces – or had the items been taken off and simply tossed aside? A thick layer of dust covered the television and mantelpiece. Cards celebrating the birth of a new baby were still up in several places. Jessie's eyes and nose itched with the dust particles. She sniffed and rubbed at her nose with the back of her hand, then coughed.

'Hello, Mrs Lucas,' she began. 'Could you tell me what's happened here tonight? When did you realise Finlay was missing?'

Something about Claire's reaction to their arrival had disturbed Jessie. Darren was distraught, naturally, but Claire had seemed scarily indifferent. *Shock, perhaps?* Claire finally lifted her head to face Jessie. Then, suddenly, she frowned and leaped up from the sofa, startling Jessie.

'What do mean, Finlay's missing?' Claire shouted. She raced down the hallway and into his room, with a visibly shocked Jessie not far behind. 'Where is he? Where's Finlay?'

Dylan was confused and looked to Darren, who seemed just as startled by Claire's sudden arrival.

'I don't understand,' Darren snapped, scratching at his head and leaving his hair sticking up in three different directions. He turned to Dylan. 'Claire knows. She was here when I discovered his cot empty.' He turned back to his wife as she screamed and began hysterically ripping their son's cot apart. 'What the hell? Claire, what are you doing?'

'Finlay, where are you?' Claire yelled. She tore open the wardrobe, pulling out every remaining item and tossing the hangers behind her, narrowly missing Jessie.

'Claire, sweetheart,' Jessie moved closer to the distraught woman, who was now clawing at the bedroom's beige waffle carpet.

'Claire,' Darren whimpered.

Dylan gently took hold of his arm. 'Come on, stand back a bit. Let DI Blake—'

'Get off me,' Darren blasted, yanking his arm free and flopping to his knees next to Claire, who responded by turning and lashing out with her fist, catching Darren's cheek and sending him to the floor.

'Where's my son?' she screamed in his face, small drops of spit erupting and landing on Darren's chin.

Jessie moved towards the woman to intervene, but Claire turned and lashed out again, her open palm connecting with Jessie's cheek.

'What have you done with my son?' Claire growled, right in Jessie's face, her blue eyes manically wide.

'OK, come on Claire, that's enough,' Dylan pulled Claire away from Jessie but her distressed state only deepened.

'Get off me!' she screamed, breaking free and ripping the pale blue curtains off the wall.

'I'm calling the doctor,' Jessie grabbed her phone while she rubbed her stinging cheek, hot from the impact of Claire's palm. For a small woman, Claire Lucas could deliver a heavy slap. 'Your wife is going to need help calming down before we go any further, Darren – that might mean sedation.'

Darren rubbed his jaw and watched in horror as Claire clawed at the corner of the bedroom carpet until she had managed to lift it, exposing the bare concrete floor below. Her nails dug deeper, leaving visible scratches on the surface. Several blood droplets left a trail after her nails snagged in places.

'What do we do now?' Darren clasped his fingers together behind his head. 'We can't leave her like this.'

Dylan shook his head and stood in front of him when he attempted to move closer to his wife. Her distress was clearly breaking his heart. Jessie glanced up at Dylan's shocked expression, realising he had never seen anything like this in his life before either.

CHAPTER SEVEN

'OK, I'll be in touch soon,' Dianne whispered, quickly hanging up the phone on the hall table when she heard Colin's footsteps coming towards her. She tried to smile as she intercepted him at the kitchen door.

'There you are,' Colin said. 'I've made a pot of tea.'

Colin handed Dianne a cup of hot, sweet tea. For the shock.

'Thank you,' she whispered, and wiped away the tears that dripped from her cheeks and jaw before tugging the belt of her fluffy dressing gown tighter around her waist.

Colin wrapped his arm around his wife's shoulders and kissed the top of her head, wishing he could think of something constructive or helpful to say, but words weren't Colin's thing. He was more a man who used his hands. Give him a dilapidated shell of a house that others might demolish, and Colin could transform it into a home fit for a king. He often worked with little Finlay's grandad on projects – he too owned a small building firm, and employed his son-in-law Darren. He felt terrible for them, and for Dianne, too. His wife seemed as devastated as if Finlay were her own child. In truth, Colin had been worried recently that she considered the little boy to be exactly that. He had grieved for their daughter for a long time after she died, but Dianne took it much harder, and now the hysterectomy on top of it meant any chance of a family was lost. He knew Dianne would have made a wonderful mother. She had been a fantastic mother to Stacey. Dianne had so much love to offer a child. Losing their daughter was the worst thing Colin had ever been through, and he wouldn't wish it on anyone. They had talked about adoption or perhaps fostering, a while back. And then they'd got Benson, too. That was all before the cancer that had robbed Dianne completely of any chance of having her own baby. But Colin still had Dianne. She was alive, and that was what mattered most to him. He couldn't stand the thought of living without her. Sacrificing any potential pregnancy was a price worth paying to him. Dianne was his world.

'Why don't you finish that and try to get some sleep, eh?' he suggested. 'You can go over and see Claire in the morning.'

'How can I sleep? What a ridiculous thing to say,' Dianne snapped. 'Finlay has been snatched from his cot, for goodness' sake!'

'I know, I'm sorry.' He held up his hands. 'I don't know why I said that, I'm sorry. That was stupid of me. The police are probably going to want to talk to us tonight too, aren't they?'

Dianne tried to sniff back another burst of tears but failed, then whimpered, 'Where is he? Who would do such a terrible thing to an innocent wee baby boy?'

'Come here, sweetheart.' He reached out his hands and pulled her close to his chest. 'I don't know. I wish I did.'

Dianne gripped him tight and sobbed into her husband's shirt, soaking it quickly with her frightened tears. Colin spotted Finlay's blue blanket on the counter behind them and frowned.

'I'm going to take this into the living room.' Dianne pulled out of his embrace then lifted her mug of tea and nodded towards the door. 'Are you coming?'

'I'll be through in a minute,' he answered, and watched her until her back disappeared through the door, which he closed gently after her. He turned and picked up Finlay's blanket, then lifted the kitchen curtain. He peered out and into Darren and Claire's window, where he could see Darren's angst-ridden expression as he was comforted by the male detective. Colin laid the blanket back down and switched off the kitchen light before heading into the lounge.

CHAPTER EIGHT

Jessie opened the front door and ushered in a man who had 'doctor' written all over him: brown corduroy slacks and blazer; black leather medical bag. The only thing missing was a pair of half-moon glasses perched over the edge of his nose, threatening to fall at any moment. Instead, his green eyes were unadorned, other than by the dark circles underneath them, suggesting to Jessie that his day had already been very long.

'I'm Dr David Lambert, a senior partner of the practice in the village. I know the family well. Ouch, that looks painful,' he added, sucking air in through his teeth as he spotted the hot, red mark on Jessie's cheek.

'Yes, watch yourself. She's got a pretty good right hook.' Jessie's attempt at humour didn't go unnoticed, as Dr Lambert smiled kindly. She found herself tidying her hair then smoothing it back down to flatten the bumps.

'Will do, detective.' He grinned again and wiped his feet on the doormat before following her inside.

'Claire is in that back bedroom and Darren is in the kitchen with my colleague. I'm DI Blake, by the way.' Jessie held out her hand to shake his, pleasantly impressed by his firm grip. He looked like he could handle this situation. 'Go straight through.'

Darren appeared from the kitchen. 'Dr Lambert, thanks for coming so quickly. She's just flipped. I've never seen anything like it.'

'Darren, it might be better if you wait out here until I've examined your wife. Is that OK?' Dr Lambert suggested.

'I dunno, maybe I should come with you?' Darren seemed unsure, until Dylan stepped forward and placed a comforting hand on his shoulder.

'Come on, let him do his job.' The DC spoke quietly, and Darren went back into the kitchen with more ease than he seemed to have anticipated.

Jessie scrunched up her nose and nodded her thanks, and Dylan answered her gesture with a wink of one of his brown eyes before he pulled the kitchen door behind them. She turned her attention to the doctor, who she could see was listening at the closed bedroom door. All Jessie could hear now was a series of whimpers, accompanied by occasional bangs and cracks on what she figured must be the bare floor.

'Wish me luck,' Dr Lambert said, his hand gently pulling on the door handle.

Once he was inside, Jessie rested her head on the door and listened for a moment, long enough to be immensely impressed with Dr Lambert's calm manner.

David Lambert smiled as he popped his head round the kitchen door.

'That's me off now, Darren,' he announced. 'I've given Claire some diazepam, and here are a few more, just in case she needs them. They're fine to take with her other medication, don't worry. How are you holding up?'

Other medication? Jessie mused, her interest piqued instantly.

Darren shrugged as his fingers curled around the tablets. He sipped on the coffee Dylan had made. 'Thanks for coming.'

'I'll be back in the morning to see her.' Lambert's hand dropped onto Darren's shoulder and he squeezed.

Jessie nodded to him before he closed the front door behind him, eager to quiz Darren on the other medication the doctor had referred to.

'What other medicines does Claire take?' Jessie asked Darren directly. 'What are they for?'

'Erm, she takes anti-epileptics, although she hasn't had seizures in years, and antidepressants for post-natal depression. It's been hard for her since Finlay was born. She's found it tougher than she imagined, becoming a mum.' He flopped down onto one of the kitchen chairs and grabbed his head in his hands. 'Oh my God, what's happening? Where is he? He can't have just vanished, for goodness' sake. Babies don't just disappear.'

Could Claire's depression have something to do with Finlay's disappearance? Jessie struggled to get her head around it. The young mum's behaviour was strange. Was it the shock, or was something more sinister going on here?

'I know this is hard for you. I understand—' Jessie began. It proved a poor choice of words.

'You understand?' Darren scoffed. 'Exactly how many of your children have been stolen, Detective? How can you possibly say you understand?'

CHAPTER NINE

The bed creaked as Calum McBride dropped his six-foot-two, muscular body down next to his wife. His job as a personal trainer kept him in great shape. Maggie was flicking through her running magazine; not really reading it but trying to distract herself from the thoughts spinning around inside her head.

'I am so ready for bed.' Calum yawned and tugged the duvet around his shoulders. 'Come here and warm me up,' he teased, and reached his cold hands out to hug her.

'Calum, stop it,' Maggie shot him a glare and slapped his arm away. 'Your hands are freezing.'

'Sorry, babe,' Calum laughed, his deep-set blue eyes dancing. He rolled over to face the other way. 'My first client isn't until ten tomorrow, so we could maybe have a long lie? We haven't done that for ages, have we?'

Right then Maggie could think of nothing worse than a romantic lie-in with Calum. Lying to him was troubling her more every day. Her increasing guilt made the sight of him irritate her, as if in some twisted way he was to blame for her feelings. She slid out of bed without answering and stepped into her slippers.

'I can't sleep. I'm going to make myself some hot chocolate,' she said, without looking at him.

Maggie found herself staring out of her kitchen window at the frozen ground. The car would take some scraping in the morning, she feared. Probably be quicker to get the bus to the gym rather than drive. The pavements around their street could be treacherous in winter – the gritter wasn't really able to get to the minor roads and paths up here. Maggie decided she would pull on her good hiking boots and walk to the bus stop instead tomorrow. The sound of the kettle clicking off startled her out of her daydreams. As she made her hot chocolate, her hand drifted over her stomach.

'Hey, you, I'll have one as well.'

'Shit, Calum, you scared me.' Maggie put a hand to her chest then turned back to the kettle.

She switched it on again, not turning to face him. Instead she continued to sip her drink as she stared out of the window. Then it just happened. She didn't know the tears were there until the first one burst out and trickled down her cheek, then dripped off her chin. Her emotions were all over the place recently, thanks to her hormones.

'Maggie?' Calum moved forward and spun her round to face him. He tilted her head towards him and wiped her tears away with his thumb. 'What's wrong? Has something happened?'

Maggie nestled her face into his chest and he held her close while she sobbed, soaking his bare skin. She listened to the increased rhythm of his heart. She had clearly worried him. 'I'm sorry,' she whispered, unsure whether he had heard.

'It can't be that bad. Tell me, babe.' Calum kissed the top of her head.

Maggie sniffed and rubbed her face with the back of her hand and stared up into her husband's soft blue eyes. She swallowed back a tear and smiled. 'I'm pregnant.'

CHAPTER TEN

Jessie pushed Claire's bedroom door open with caution. She didn't fancy getting a matching red-hot cheek. She needn't have worried. The diazepam had taken effect very quickly and Claire was now sleeping deeply, curled into the foetal position on her bed. Darren tapped Jessie's shoulder.

'Can I go in now?' he asked.

Jessie scrunched up her nose and shook her head, then allowed the door to close softly behind her. 'Let's you and I go and have a seat and a wee chat, yes?'

Jessie was relieved to see Darren nod, and he followed her into the living room without question before offering both detectives a seat. He blew out a huge breath and sat with his body tipped forward, his head in his hands.

'I can't believe this is happening,' he exclaimed, then sat bolt upright. 'I should have been here. I shouldn't have left him, them. But I've got to work.'

Darren's words tugged at Jessie's heart, but she couldn't afford to be swayed by emotion. She sat on an armchair opposite him. Dylan turned to face the door when he heard more vehicles arrive outside.

'That will be more uniforms arriving. I'll go.' Dylan said before heading out.

'What's happening?' Darren asked as he stood to peer out the window. There was a police van with its back doors open, and a flurry of uniformed activity. 'Where is he going?'

'Sit down, Darren. There are some more officers arriving to help with a door-to-door search, that's all.'

'My God, there's a dog.' Darren panicked and began to pace back and forth. 'Why is there a dog here?'

Jessie moved towards him and rested her hand on his arm. 'Come on, sit down. A dog is part of any search team. It's procedure.'

Darren's eyes searched Jessie's for answers as he sat back down. He tried to swallow back the terror that was rising in his chest. 'OK,' he murmured under his breath. His nerves were still fragile, and likely to spin out of control at the slightest provocation.

Jessie coughed to clear her throat and opened her notebook. 'You mentioned that Claire has been finding things tough since Finlay was born. What did you mean by that?'

Darren narrowed his eyes at her. There it was. 'Are you serious?'

Jessie hadn't anticipated that response. 'I beg your pardon?'

'Are you accusing Claire? Or me?' The volume of Darren's voice increased and he rocked the chair backwards as he jumped to his feet. 'What are you accusing us of? What do you think we've done to our own son?'

The atmosphere in this house was electric. Dylan would say Jessie's spidey senses were tingling. Darren's behaviour was totally in keeping with the fact that his son was missing, but his immediate defence of Claire before an accusation was made implied that he had already considered the possibility she was involved, and that concerned Jessie greatly.

'I haven't accused anyone of anything. I'm simply asking you to clarify what you meant. Please come and sit down.'

Jessie spoke softly. Diplomacy wasn't one of her strengths, but she did her best. And it worked.

'I'm sorry,' Darren said, and sat back down. 'My head is just…' He sighed. 'I'm sorry. I know you're here to help. My God, I actually feel sick.'

'Thank you.' Jessie acknowledged his anxiety. 'Let's start again, shall we?'

Darren nodded then slumped right back into the chair. 'As I said, Claire has post-natal depression. She's got pills for it. Health visitor does her best and Dianne next door, she's been great, but if you want the truth it's not been easy. Horrendous some days, in fact, but she's making progress, I think. I thought.' He slammed his hands to his face and shook his head. 'I just don't know anything any more.'

Jessie scribbled *PND* into her notebook with an exclamation mark next to it. 'I'm sorry,' she remarked, because she was genuinely sorry. Post-natal depression left women feeling terrible. Jessie knew that. And it wasn't easy on the families either, trying to support them while caring for the newborn.

'You can't possibly think Claire has done something to him. That's just ridiculous and' – he paused, his shoulders drooped – 'I don't know what else I can say.'

'Where were you this afternoon?' Jessie asked.

Darren hesitated before giving his answer. 'Work until three, then I… um…' He shuffled to the back of his chair, tapping his feet on the floor, then sniffed uncomfortably before scratching at his head.

Jessie's interest increased at his reluctance to continue. 'Then you what, Darren?'

Darren shuffled again in the chair and smoothed down his mop of thick hair. He closed his eyes and sighed. 'I was somewhere I shouldn't have been.' He muttered.

'Darren?' Claire's dishevelled outline in the doorway immediately interrupted their conversation, just when Jessie thought she was getting somewhere. 'What's happening?'

'Hello Claire, I'm Detective Inspector Jessie Blake. We met earlier.' The sight of Claire stood there made Jessie's cheek sting again.

Claire nodded and pointed to Jessie's face. 'I know, and I'm sorry about that.'

Jessie was relieved to hear it, because that memory meant Claire Lucas was lucid enough to be interviewed. A buzz from her phone distracted her. Jessie's eyes widened – no caller ID, again. She switched her phone to silent and stuffed it back into her pocket. Her ex-husband and his games would have to wait.

Something definitely wasn't right between these two, and she was determined to get to the bottom of it.

CHAPTER ELEVEN

Dylan knocked for a second time and waited. He watched the hall light switch on before Colin opened the back door. He held up his ID and smiled.

'Colin Davidson? I'm Detective Constable Dylan Logan. I know we met briefly earlier, but can I come in and speak to you and your wife, if that's OK? I know it's late, but the sooner we can talk to everyone the better.'

'Of course. Please come in.' Colin waved his hand to usher Dylan inside. 'We've been expecting you. Terrible business. How are Darren and Claire doing? Please, come through. We can talk in the living room.' He took hold of a gangly Labrador by the collar and pulled the dog away. 'Go on, Benson, go to your bed.'

Dianne Davidson was on the sofa. As Dylan walked in she tugged her long blue dressing gown tighter around her plump figure and ran her fingers through her brown, silver-peppered hair.

'Hello again, Detective.' She forced a smile. 'How's Claire?'

Interesting, Dylan pondered. Dianne only asked about Claire. That statement would definitely make the hairs on Jessie's neck stand up.

'They're doing as well as can be expected,' replied Dylan. Dianne didn't need to know about Dr Lambert's visit.

'Can I get you a cup of tea?' Dianne asked. 'Or coffee?'

Dylan shook his head at the offer. It was already late. Coffee now would mean a sleepless night for sure.

'No thanks, I'm fine. Did either of you see or hear anything out of the ordinary this afternoon, from three o'clock onwards?'

Dianne clasped her hands to her mouth. 'Is that when he was taken?'

'We're still trying to establish exactly what happened.'

Colin laid his arm around Dianne's shoulders. 'I was at work until five, then I got home just after. I'm renovating a property at the top end of Deich Burn, so I'm only five minutes away just now.'

'A nice spot.' Dylan pursed his lips with a nod. 'For yourselves?'

Colin scoffed. 'Not flipping likely. I'm a builder, not a millionaire.'

A ghost of a smile whispered across Dylan's lips. Shelly dreamed of owning one of the big houses along the top edge of the burn that flowed through the village. 'Millionaire's Row', people joked. The cottages that lined the bottom end had been built for the mill workers and weren't nearly as grand.

'I was here most of the day, although I did take Benson out for a walk, but I didn't hear anything,' Dianne chirped. 'This is so horrible. He must be so frightened. He's just an innocent little baby. Who would do something so awful?' Dianne had to choke back her tears. 'Is there anything we can do to help?'

Jessie was always telling Dylan to use his initiative. Now was the perfect opportunity. He turned to face Colin.

'I would appreciate it if you could give me your permission to search your property.'

Colin Davidson frowned. 'Why do you need to search here?'

'It's fine, of course you can search this house,' Dianne piped up. 'Anything, we'll do anything to help.'

Colin's eyes widened but he didn't say anything. Instead, he lifted up his hands in defeat, clearly a little unnerved by letting the detective wander through his home.

'Thank you,' Dylan said. 'This won't take long, don't worry.' He left Colin and Dianne to their discussion and pulled the door behind him, leaving it a little ajar. Dylan paused on the stairs to listen for any exchange between the couple. Sometimes even the smallest remark can be important.

'Don't look at me like that,' he heard Dianne say. 'Of course he was going to want to search here, but we've got nothing to hide, have we?'

Dylan put on a fresh pair of plastic gloves and opened the bathroom cabinet. He leafed through the variety of medicine packets on the top shelf. All in Dianne's name, except the high blood pressure tablets for Colin. Dylan recognised them because they were the ones his mother took. He also recognised the anti-depressant medication in Dianne's name. He closed the door and moved into the couple's bedroom, which was clean and tidy, if a little old-fashioned. A piece of paper, a printed-out email, caught his eye on one of the bedside units.

'Interesting,' he whispered under his breath. It was a booking confirmation for a family room for one night at a hotel in Aberdeen, close to the airport. *Why not Edinburgh or Glasgow?* thought Dylan. *Both are much closer*. The booking date was in two days. Dylan took out his phone and took a photo of the email, then placed it back down on the table. He opened the bedside drawer, hoping to find plane tickets, but there was only the usual bedside detritus: a pink glasses case; a John Grisham novel. He pulled out the book and leafed through the pages, then tucked it back inside and shut the drawer. On the unit top, next to an alarm clock and bedside lamp, was a small framed photo of a smiling baby girl dressed in a blue pinafore and white tights. She couldn't be more than five or six months old. Dylan lifted it and looked at it briefly, thinking how much the infant looked like Dianne and wondering how they were related. He replaced the photo frame and turned his attention to the couple's wardrobe.

In the bottom of their wardrobe, attracting his attention quickly, was a box with its lid askew. He crouched down and opened the lid completely. A lump filled his throat – it was filled with memories of a baby girl, the infant in the photo, who had evidently died several years ago. The framed picture of tiny footprints was heartbreaking. Dylan hated the thought of the agony they must have felt. Becoming a father was the most wonderful thing that had ever happened to him. To lose a child must be awful. He felt guilty for prying, but that was the job. He quickly shuffled through the papers and photographs, then replaced the lid and tucked it back away neatly, out of respect. Next, he pulled down a suitcase from the top of the wardrobe. Once he had unzipped the case and looked at the unexpected contents, he knew he had several more questions for Colin and Dianne. But first, he had to tell Jessie.

CHAPTER TWELVE

Darren's phone vibrated again on the bedside cabinet. He picked it up and saw three texts and a missed call from Maggie. He didn't have time to call her back. She was the least of his worries now. He clicked to return his dad's missed call instead.

'Hey Dad, you called?' Darren's voice quivered until it disappeared into a fog of foamy tears. 'Dad.'

Martin Lucas seemed alarmed by his son's call, and their exchange was brief.

Darren held the phone to his ear long after his dad had hung up.

'Darren,' Claire's soft voice tore into his pain and he closed his eyes before turning to face her. He wiped the mess from his face and inhaled deeply before exhaling slowly, pinching back the next barrage of tears. Claire moved forward and slammed her body close to his, and Darren held her tight while she gripped on and cried into his chest.

*

Jessie knocked on the Lucases' bedroom door, feeling guilty for intruding. 'I have to go out for a moment, but I've asked PC Wilde to stay with you until I get back.'

Darren nodded at PC Isla Wilde, who smiled gently from the doorway. The twenty-five-year-old had been with Police Scotland for three years, but this was her first family liaison role. She seemed stunned when Jessie had asked her to do it, but she'd been the first officer on the scene, which was Jessie's main motivation.

Jessie tugged the back door closed behind her and raised her eyes at Dylan, who had come outside to meet her.

'So, what have we got?' she asked.

Dylan scratched at the stubble on his chin. 'They gave me permission to search the house.' He clicked open the photo of the hotel booking.

'Very interesting,' Jessie muttered.

'Not just that. There's a suitcase in there filled with baby stuff and, to be honest, it looks ready to go. Really filled – nappies, wipes, onesies, hats, gloves and stuff. The kind of things me and Shelly would get ready for Jack if we were planning a trip.'

Jessie's eyes widened again. 'What are they saying about it?'

Dylan shook his head. 'I waited for you on that one.'

Jessie patted his arm. 'OK. Come on, let's see what they've got to say about it.'

*

Dianne dropped her coffee mug into the sink when she heard the back door open and close again. Colin met the two detectives as he exited the downstairs bathroom.

'Colin, I wonder if we could have a chat about the suitcase in your wardrobe?' Jessie didn't hang about. It was better for everyone if she came straight to the point.

'Colin doesn't know anything about it, Detective,' Dianne declared, and turned to face them. 'I'm sorry,' she ended in a whisper.

CHAPTER THIRTEEN

The look on Darren's face terrified Martin Lucas as he stepped into his son's house. He couldn't understand what was going on, and Darren hadn't seemed able to talk on the phone without breaking down. Once he'd hung up, he'd picked up his keys and headed out to his car. Now was not the time to tell his son he'd had another letter. The third in three weeks. He was concerned that something awful had happened. Darren wasn't the kind of man who openly showed his emotions, let alone burst into tears.

'Darren, what's happened?' Martin moved forward to pass PC Isla Wilde, who stood by the front door.

'I'm sorry, but I need to ask you to identify yourself, sir.'

'He's my dad,' Darren announced from behind her. 'Let him through.'

Isla nodded and stepped aside before closing the door after him.

Martin rushed forward as his son broke down in front of him.

The last time he'd seen his son cry was at his mother's funeral. That was twelve years ago, when Darren was just twelve years old. Losing his mum was hard, and having a father who couldn't cope must have been awful for him, but Martin was proud of the way his son had turned out. He would have liked Darren and Claire to wait a little longer to have kids, but becoming a grandad was great. Martin adored Finlay.

'Finlay's gone. He's been snatched,' Darren blurted out between sobs.

'What the hell do you mean, he's been snatched?' Martin couldn't compute the information. It didn't make any sense. 'How? When did this happen?' He glanced over Darren's shoulder at Claire, then back at his son, before turning to face the young police officer. 'Can you tell me what the hell is going on?'

'Can I make us all a cup of tea?' Isla had said it before she realised it, then blushed.

When neither of them answered, she wondered what to do next, but she needn't have worried. Circumstances quickly evolved in front of her. Claire clutched her forehead and announced that she felt a little dizzy, then leaned against the kitchen door frame before sliding down the wall onto the hall floor, her body writhing and twitching.

'Claire!' Darren fell to his knees and shoved the clutter of shoes and bags away from where she had fallen.

'Claire has epilepsy,' Martin explained to the startled-looking police officer. 'She hasn't had a seizure for years. Not even during her pregnancy. It must have been triggered by the stress of all this.'

'I'll call an ambulance.' Isla reached for her radio.

'No,' Darren said. 'She'll be fine in a minute. It's easing off now.'

Just as he said it, Claire's body stopped moving apart from the odd twitch, and within minutes she was sitting up, holding her head.

'What happened?' she paused, her eyes narrowed in confusion until the horrifying realisation hit her. 'No, no, please tell me I haven't?' She shook her head and hammered the carpet with her fist. 'I can't be having seizures. Not now.'

Darren scooped her into his arms and hugged her, whispering in her ear how much he loved her. Claire could only cling on as hard as she could and sob.

Martin covered his mouth with his hands and exhaled sharply through his chubby fingers, then turned to Isla.

'Maybe we will have that cuppa after all.'

CHAPTER FOURTEEN

'Where are you taking my wife?' Colin shouted. 'You can't do this. She's done nothing wrong. Dianne, honey, don't worry – I'll be right behind you.'

'Mr Davidson, come on back inside.' Jessie tried to de-escalate the situation as Dylan climbed into the car with Dianne. 'In the light of what we've found, you must understand we have a few questions for your wife.'

Dianne mouthed *I'm sorry* from behind the glass as the car was driven away.

'Dianne,' Colin muttered as he watched the police reverse out of his drive and disappear.

'Come on back inside, Mr Davidson.'

'It's Mr Davidson now, is it?' Colin shouted. 'Now that you've decided my wife is guilty. Guilty of what? Owning a suitcase of baby clothes?' Colin's anger boiled over and he vented his fury in Jessie's direction. 'Once my solicitor hears about this, you and your colleague are going to be the ones answering the questions.'

*

The sound of shouting outside attracted Darren's attention, and he rushed to the front door to see what was happening. He was stunned to see Dianne being driven away in the police car, and Colin arguing with one of the detectives. He was intercepted by Isla as he tried to make his way outside.

'Let me past!' he boomed, then shoved her aside with ease.

Isla only just managed to stop herself being toppled off her feet, throwing a palm against the door frame to catch herself.

'I'm so sorry. My son is not normally like this.' Martin Lucas reached out to help Isla, then followed his son. 'Darren!' he called after him 'Wait, son, wait.'

'What have you done?' Darren pushed Colin's shoulder, almost knocking the older man off his feet, which were already slipping on the frozen ground. 'Where's my son?'

A uniformed officer moved swiftly in between the two men, and Jessie was relieved he was a good two or three inches taller than both of them.

'Darren, come back inside,' Isla called out from behind Martin.

'Do what she says, son,' Martin added. 'Come on, this won't help them find Finlay.'

Hearing his son's name pushed Darren over the edge. The tension and fear burst out of him and he pulled back his fist and punched Colin, hard, almost breaking his nose.

'Argh! Jesus, are you just going to stand there and do nothing?' Colin yelled at them as he held his aching face. 'I want him arrested.'

'Darren Lucas, get back inside right now,' Jessie shouted, 'or I will arrest you.'

The tense atmosphere was threatening to get out of control. Thankfully, the volume of Jessie's voice appeared to startle Darren back to reality. He snarled one last time in Colin's direction then went back inside.

Jessie exhaled loudly, her heart racing, and shook her head. 'Take Colin back inside and get him cleaned up,' she told the uniformed officer. She undid her straggly black hair and then tidied it again abruptly into its scrunchie, then followed Darren into the Lucases' bungalow.

'I'm not going to apologise!' Darren blasted while he paced up and down the hall, his fingers clasped behind the back of his head. 'I'm not!'

'I know, I know. I was just on my way over to explain what's happened.' Jessie looked directly into his brown eyes, in the hope it would focus him and calm him down. 'OK?' She watched his rage wither slowly before continuing. 'On searching your neighbour's property, my colleague found something we want to ask Dianne a little more about, under caution, that's all.'

Darren crossed his arms over his chest, his shoulders hunched. 'Under caution? I know what that means. It can't be that little if you're taking her in.'

'Listen to me, Darren. Look at me.' Jessie demanded. 'If we don't do things right, by the book...' She sighed. 'Look, I don't have to spell it out for you, do I?'

'I know. I know!' Darren yelled then stormed off, slamming the bedroom door behind him.

'My son is just upset, Detective. I'm sorry.' Martin offered his hand. 'I'm Martin Lucas. Finlay's grandad. Like I said, this isn't him. He doesn't usually react like that.'

Jessie shook his hand. 'I'm Detective Inspector Jessie Blake. I'm leading the investigation into Finlay's disappearance, and I don't always shout like that either.'

A half-smile crept across Martin's lips just as Darren reappeared from his room, a sheepish expression pasted over his face.

'I'm sorry,' Darren whispered, then headed into the kitchen. 'I'll go and talk to Colin in the morning.'

'He's a good man, my son,' Martin choked back his tears. 'He doesn't deserve any of this. Neither of them do. This all seems so unreal. Like some kind of nightmare.'

'And I'm sorry you're all going through this, truly I am. I promise I'm doing everything in my power to find your grandson, Mr Lucas.'

Martin Lucas shifted uncomfortably before seeming to come to some kind of decision.

'We need to talk, Detective. I think I may know who took my grandson.'

CHAPTER FIFTEEN

After sitting in the living room with Martin Lucas and listening to his information, Jessie was still reeling. She hadn't fully processed what she'd been told when the front door burst open and a middle-aged man rushed towards her, followed closely by a woman of around the same age. 'Where's my daughter?' the man asked to the house at large, before he honed in on Jessie. 'Who are you?'

'Daddy,' Claire called out from behind Jessie, charging forward and throwing her body into her father's arms. 'It's Finlay. He's gone.'

Jessie was struck by the childlike behaviour Claire was displaying. The man held his distraught daughter close to his chest and turned his attention to Jessie.

'What does she mean? Where is he?' he asked, appearing visibly shaken by his daughter's state. 'Shh, it's OK, Dad's here. Shh, you know Dad can fix everything, don't worry. You know that. We'll get Finlay back.' He shot a look at the woman who'd arrived with him, who avoided his eyes, instead fixing a steely glare on Jessie.

Jessie felt momentarily unnerved as she watched the scene unfold around her, not least by the icy look of the woman whom she assumed to be Claire's mother.

'I'm Detective Inspector Jessie Blake,' she began. 'You are Claire's parents, then? Phil and Bridget Moran? We were called after your grandson was reported missing from his cot earlier this evening.'

'Missing from his cot?' Phil Moran pulled back from his daughter's embrace. 'Is this true? How can this have happened? How can he be missing?'

Jessie was about to reply but was interrupted before she'd even opened her mouth.

'Well then, why haven't you found my grandson yet? Surely you have the resources to find a six-month-old baby.' Bridget Moran spoke sternly.

Jessie was taken aback by this tiny, birdlike woman's abrupt question and, before she could answer, she was again beaten to it, this time by Darren.

'They've taken Dianne to the station. They want to ask her some questions.' He paused and stared at Jessie. 'Under caution.'

'Might have known. She takes far too much interest in Finlay, if you ask me.' Bridget scoffed and marched past everyone into the kitchen, ignoring PC Wilde's attempt to introduce herself.

*

Theresa Moran's eyes snapped open and she sat bolt upright in her hospital bed. She struggled to catch her breath. She swallowed hard and wiped her hand over her sweat-soaked face then rubbed the wetness on the hospital duvet cover.

'Stop it,' she slammed her hands over both ears and shook her head aggressively. 'I'm not listening any more. It's lies. All lies.'

She reached for her bottle of water and swallowed back most of what was left in it, then grimaced at its being lukewarm. That nightmare had been so real. They were inside her head and Theresa was desperate to push them out. Hadn't she done what they asked? Why couldn't they just leave her alone? She tossed back the duvet and pressed her feet into her slippers. She rummaged in her bag until she'd found what she was looking for and got right back into bed. The community nurse had told her about using an MP3 player and headphones to help her sleep. She chose a song that she knew would drown the voices out, and hoped sleep would come again soon, but she was scared to shut her eyes.

That was the worst dream she'd had for a long time. It was as if he was right there, his face staring up at her.

CHAPTER SIXTEEN

Jessie stared at her weary reflection in the station loos' mirror. It had been a hard few hours. Missing children were bad enough, but Finlay was just six months old. So vulnerable.

She hoped arresting Dianne on suspicion of the abduction of Finlay Lucas and letting her stew overnight would get results. She knew the suitcase and the hotel booking weren't the only evidence she would need, but it was a start. She'd chosen not to tell Darren Lucas the whole story because she feared how explosive his reaction would be.

Jessie's office had been her bedroom last night, and a couple of hours was the sum total of sleep she had managed to get. A quick text to her neighbour meant her cat, Smokey, hadn't gone without his dinner. Keeping a blanket in the bottom of her filing cabinet might be a cliché to some, but it was necessary. She'd seen an old guvnor when she worked in the Met do it and it stuck with her.

Jessie had been so absorbed in the case she had almost forgotten about the birthday card her ex-husband had sent. Almost. Pulling a stunt like that didn't come as a surprise, but she feared it wouldn't be long before Dan paid her a visit now that he clearly had her address. The fact that he hadn't turned up yet was another example of the control he craved. Making her wait and worry was part of his game. A game he'd spent years becoming very good at. It seemed to Jessie that prison meant nothing to Dan. Hadn't taught him anything. *Rehabilitation?* Jessie scoffed at the thought of Dan being capable of that.

Looking into Martin Lucas's background had kept her awake, too. His revelations were shocking and his theory that they could be connected to Finlay's disappearance was absolutely plausible, so Jessie had needed to dig further. What she had found was startling. He just didn't look the type. *But neither did Dan, did he? Appearances can indeed be deceptive.*

Jessie bumped into Dylan as she stepped out of the ladies'.

'Morning, Jess. Oh my God, did you sleep here?'

Jessie forced a smile. 'Bit cheeky, but yes, I did. I hope you enjoyed your kip.'

Dylan grinned. 'I did, thank you. Poor Shelly was up and down, though. She can't wait until this baby is born. She's getting restless.'

'That wee one will be here before you know it.' Jessie smiled then refocused her attention on the case. It was going to be another long day. 'Right, after you brought Dianne Davidson in last night, I had a very interesting chat with Martin Lucas, Darren's father, and then did some more digging of my own. It seems he's got a past he'd rather forget. Five years ago, Martin spent time in prison after hitting and killing a teenager, Laura McCabe, when he was drunk behind the wheel. Not just a wee bit drunk, but paralytic. Well over four times the limit. I'm surprised he could see at all. And it turns out Laura McCabe's big brothers – Peter and Tim – have been threatening some kind of revenge. They've been harassing him for months.'

'Well, that doesn't sound good,' Dylan chirped as they stepped into the staff kitchen. 'Do you think they're involved in little Finlay's disappearance?'

'Martin thinks so. He's been receiving threatening letters, anonymous of course, but it doesn't take a genius to figure out the source, promising all kinds of punishment for what he did to Laura. We won't know anything more until we've spoken to them later. They're next on my list, after Dianne. Her solicitor is coming in at half past eight for the interview.'

Dylan switched on the kettle. 'You want a coffee?'

'Aye, thanks, and make mine a strong one, will you?' Jessie yawned. 'Wake me up a bit.'

Dylan nodded. 'It's a tough case – a missing six-month-old. It doesn't look good, does it?'

Jessie couldn't disagree, but for now little Finlay was still just that – a missing person – and he would remain so until either Jessie found him or evidence proved him to be otherwise.

CHAPTER SEVENTEEN

When she woke up, Maggie McBride was disappointed not to see a reply from Darren waiting on her phone. She hadn't gone as far as to tell him she was pregnant, but she had made it clear there was something serious they needed to talk about. It wasn't right to give him news like that on the phone, and anyway, Maggie wanted to see the look on his face when she told him. Calum was so happy it was painful to watch. Maggie wasn't even sure until that moment whether she wanted to have the baby. She still couldn't believe she'd blurted it out like that. How could she be so stupid?

'I made you tea and toast.' Calum's smiling face burned into her. 'I'm going to pamper you now that you're carrying the most precious cargo in the world.' He laid the plate and mug of tea on the bedside table then leaned down to kiss Maggie's lips.

'Thank you,' she whispered as a small tear escaped and trickled down her face. 'I really don't deserve you.'

Calum kissed her again, his lips pressing harder. It wasn't that Maggie wasn't attracted to him, she just wanted Darren more. She couldn't explain it.

'I love you so much,' Calum murmured in her ear and gently rubbed his palm across her stomach. 'I'm going to take good care of you and our baby.'

Maggie's phone buzzing on the floor next to their bed interrupted Calum's plans for a romantic liaison.

'I better get that,' Maggie whispered.

'Leave it,' Calum suggested, and trailed his tongue across her neck with a deep sigh until Maggie gently nudged him away.

'I'm sorry, it might be a client. I have to get it.'

Calum laid one last lingering kiss on her lips then stood and walked towards their bathroom. When Maggie saw the caller ID, she pressed the answer button hard just as the caller hung up.

'Shit,' she muttered, and immediately called back.

*

Darren pressed his phone back into his jeans pocket. He hadn't slept much last night. Maggie's message sounded serious, and he didn't want her to keep calling. Not now. She had made her feelings pretty clear yesterday. Telling him she wanted more from their relationship than stolen, secret liaisons. The last thing he needed was more pressure, even before all this. Detective Inspector Blake said she would be back that morning, after she'd spoken to Dianne. He had been tempted to take one of the diazepam tablets Dr Lambert had given him for Claire, just to take some of the pain away. It seemed to work for her. She looked so peaceful, despite everything that was going on. He snatched the phone quickly when it buzzed almost immediately after he'd hung up.

Maggie's voice was so soft Darren could barely make out what she was trying to say, but there was no way he could go and meet her like she suggested. Not a hope in hell's chance of that, not now.

*

It wasn't right to tell him over the phone, so Maggie grabbed her running shoes, pulled on a warm fleece and headed out for a run. If Darren wouldn't come to her, she would have to go to him.

CHAPTER EIGHTEEN

Dianne Davidson hadn't slept a wink. How could she? Her secret had been exposed in the most humiliating way, and the look of hurt on Colin's face would never leave her. He had called out that he loved her, but how could he love her now? Dianne was so embarrassed. Being taken away like that was so humiliating. A suitcase full of baby clothes and a hotel booking surely wasn't evidence. She jumped when Jessie and Dylan entered the interview room. She had never had so much as a parking ticket before. She was terrified.

'Good morning.' Jessie sat down on the chair opposite Dianne, as Dylan offered her a soft half-smile of greeting. Dianne knew she looked dreadful, the dark circles under her eyes evidence of her rough night in the cell.

'Good morning,' she answered, her voice quivering before she coughed to compose herself.

Once the formal introductions for the interview were carried out, Jessie slid a photo of the open suitcase and one of the hotel booking details across the table. Dianne swallowed hard and averted her gaze. She sipped the water she'd been given. Her mouth was so dry.

'Can you explain to me why a suitcase packed with baby clothes and other items was hidden in your wardrobe? Were you planning a trip with an infant? Why did you have a family room booked so close to Aberdeen airport?' Jessie tapped the photos one after the other. 'Please look at the photos, Dianne. Whose baby are you planning to travel with? Because I know that you and your husband don't have any children.'

Jessie pursed her lips and waited. The last sentence was a cruel thing to say, she knew that. If someone said something like that to her it would hurt like hell, but she hoped the emotional trigger would reveal the truth, painful as that might be. Dianne turned her face back slowly, then lifted the photo of the suitcase and shook her head.

'I'm not planning a trip anywhere, with any child,' she said, without looking up from the photo. 'I've been buying this stuff for years. It started when I found out I was pregnant with our daughter. She died from cot death when she was six months old.' Dianne lifted the other photo, then swallowed back the tears and sighed. 'We had her after three rounds of IVF. She was beautiful. Everyone said she looked like me, and she was such a happy baby, always smiling.'

Dylan shot Jessie a concerned glance out of the corner of his eye, then frowned.

'I'm sorry for your loss – you and Colin,' Dylan said. 'That must have been very hard for both of you.'

Jessie was touched by Dylan's sensitivity, every time.

'You would think so, wouldn't you?' Dianne looked at Dylan, tears forming in her eyes. 'It didn't take Colin long to get back to normal. I mean, he said he had to work because we couldn't live on fresh air and assured me he was heartbroken, too, but it didn't seem to be the same for him, somehow. I couldn't and still can't get her out of my mind. Stacey. Our daughter's name is Stacey.'

'That's a beautiful name,' Dylan added.

'Thank you.' Dianne smiled then pushed the photos back across the table. 'I buy a cardigan here and there. Maybe some socks from time to time. Not so much since Finlay's been around for me to spoil.' The smile grew from a whisper to a wide grin when she mentioned Finlay's name. 'He's such a happy wee boy, too.'

'So, you're saying that you buy the baby clothes as keepsakes?' Jessie suggested.

Dianne nodded. 'Yes, you might call it therapy, of sorts. Being around the clothes, the bottles and toys – it just helps. I can't explain it.'

'And the hotel booking? For a family. How do you explain that?'

'It's the last room they had. I have an aunt who moved to Orkney many years ago. I've booked a surprise trip for Colin and me because she's going into hospital and wants me to house-sit for a few days. Feed the sheep, and generally keep the place ticking over for her while she's away. We fly from Aberdeen. I thought it would do us both good to get away too. It's two years since we lost Stacey.'

'I have to ask, Dianne, do you have any idea where Finlay Lucas is? Where were you yesterday afternoon?'

Dianne squeezed her eyes tight shut. 'If I knew where he was I would tell you, and I was at home most of the day yesterday. I've told you this already. Apart from when I walked Benson in Moncreiffe Wood. I visited Stacey's bench and took flowers. You can ask the girls in the Co-op – I bought a bunch of carnations on the way past.'

'Can anybody else confirm that?' Dylan asked.

'I was alone. The only other person I saw was Claire's sister Theresa, as she left Claire's house later in the afternoon. She seemed a bit frazzled, but that's her, really.'

CHAPTER NINETEEN

The noisy chatter outside the room woke Theresa from her dream. It took her a moment to remember but when she did, the sickness of the memory hit her stomach and rose in her throat. She was desperate to get up and run from it, but she struggled to keep her eyes open. Her body felt heavy from the sedation. She knew why that was. Every time they increased her medication it was the same. The knock on her door made her jump.

'Go away,' she stammered and ran her tongue over her lips. Her mouth was dry and her head seemed glued to the pillow.

'Come on, or you'll miss your breakfast,' the voice drifted under Theresa's duvet. 'I've kept you a roll and a wee box of cornflakes. Come on, sweetheart.'

Does she think you're stupid? the voice inside Theresa's head whispered.

'I know, don't worry, sshhh.' Theresa muttered her answer so the nurse didn't hear.

Theresa would not touch anything that nurse put aside. She hadn't eaten any of the food there since she arrived. It wasn't safe. She could smell it. The poison. Not just that – the voices let her know. Sometimes they were nice to her. Keeping her safe. The face that appeared close to hers startled her again, but the heaviness held her in place. Theresa hadn't invited her in.

'Go away,' she repeated. 'I didn't say you could come into my room.'

The young nurse, crouched at the side of the bed, smiled.

They know. The voice grew louder. *Hurry, they're coming for you.*

Theresa panicked and clumsily peeled back the duvet. 'Get out of the way.' She pushed the nurse over and made for the door, tripping as she tried to run, landing on her knees in the centre of the room.

'Don't touch me!' she screamed when the nurse reached out to help her up. 'I know what you're doing. I know what you're all doing.' She tapped her temple. 'Did you really think they wouldn't tell me?' She lashed out, and threw a slipper at the nurse.

'OK, it's fine, I'll leave you.' The nurse moved slowly past and left Theresa's room.

Good girl, but they're coming back. You know they won't let you get away with what you did.

'No,' Theresa slammed her hands over her ears. 'Help me, I have to get out of here.'

She pulled her shoes out of the wardrobe and quickly slipped them on. She grabbed her jumper from the end of the bed, then opened the door as quietly as she could. There was nobody in the corridor. She moved out and started to tiptoe past the nurses' office door, which was slightly ajar. Theresa didn't want to hang about to hear what they were saying once she heard her name being said, especially given the expression on their faces. She peered out the window of the patients' smoking room at the falling snow and tugged the jumper over her head, wishing she'd picked up her jacket. But it was too late now. She wasn't going back for it and risking being caught. She reached out for the ward door handle as a voice called her name.

'Theresa, where are you going?'

Theresa wasn't stopping for anyone, and pushed the handle down. It wouldn't budge. She shook it and tugged hard, then turned to see the nurse in charge walking towards her with his student behind him.

This is it. They're coming. Run, Theresa, run. The voice was urgent and Theresa couldn't ignore it.

'Stay back.' Theresa held up her hand. 'I'm warning you. I know what you're doing.' Her eyes darted between them, trying to decide which was the biggest threat.

'Come on, Theresa. Come on in and tell me what's up.'

The nurse's voice was gentle, but Theresa wasn't fooled by his smile. Not one ounce. She stared at the two other patients who had been attracted into the hall by her shouting. She frowned at them, whispering to each other.

Look, there's more of them.

'Stop it,' Theresa shook her head and glanced behind her. 'I can handle it.'

'Is she written up for anything else?' Theresa heard the student ask her colleague.

'What are you saying?' she called out. 'You can't touch me. I know my rights.'

The nurse in charge moved slowly back towards the treatment room, pulling his keys from his pocket.

'What's he doing?' Theresa boomed. 'Where is he going?'

Theresa spun round and reached for the locked door handle again. She tugged and pulled as hard as she could but it wouldn't move.

'Come on!' she screamed, much to the alarm of the other patients.

Oh dear, here they come. The voice intensified the warning.

Theresa glanced back to the other end of the hall to see two more smiling nurses walk towards her with their hands up.

'No! I said no! Open the door. I need to get out of here.' Theresa was frantic, yanking the handle furiously.

Within minutes she was back in her bed. The voices that had shouted all the warnings had been quietened, and the light in the room was dimming, until everything went black.

CHAPTER TWENTY

Jessie had no reason to detain Dianne after she'd established the sad reason for her suitcase and the hotel booking. She'd left a message for the aunt in Orkney, asking her to get back to her to confirm Dianne's story. The hotel were happy to clarify that Dianne had indeed only just managed to book their last room for that night. A family room.

Ultimately, Jessie couldn't see Dianne or Colin as a threat to Finlay. Quite the opposite, in fact. It was clear Dianne adored the infant, but Jessie still had a nagging doubt that Dianne knew more. After Martin Lucas's revelations and her own investigation, a meeting with Tim and Peter McCabe was much more pressing. A little bit of digging revealed the full tragedy the family faced after Martin drunkenly lost control of his Vauxhall Astra. His car skidded as it clipped the kerb, then mounted the pavement and collided with Laura McCabe, who had decided to walk home from school that particular summer's day. She wasn't killed instantly, spending six days in intensive care fighting for her life until she finally died. Martin Lucas was more than four times over the drink-drive limit at the time of the accident. He hadn't even stopped. Unaware that he'd hit her, he had carried on driving until his car came to an abrupt stop against a tree. He was lucky to walk away from the accident in one piece. Unlike Laura who, at fifteen, had had her whole life ahead of her. *What a tragic waste*, Jessie thought.

Losing their mother to a heart attack not long afterwards seemed to be the last straw for Laura's brothers, who felt it was brought on by the grief of her broken heart. They blamed Martin for their mother's death, and their father's continuing spiral into depression. Jessie wasn't surprised they were filled with anger and hate towards him, but what Martin did had nothing to do with Darren, and especially not with Finlay.

'Where are we headed?' Dylan asked, and shivered against the chill wind.

Jessie unlocked the doors on her Fiesta and got in without answering.

'So?' Dylan questioned. 'Are you going to tell me what you're thinking?'

'I think we need to pay Peter and Tim McCabe a visit, don't you? Time we found out more about these letters they've been sending. I've asked Martin Lucas to bring me them.'

Dylan's eyes widened. 'I totally get that they would be angry at Martin, and what better revenge than to hurt his family? But to do something to a six-month-old baby? That's extreme.'

'It's not just the letters – guess where the McCabe family garage is located.' Jessie watched Dylan frown and shrug at her question. 'Bridge of Earn. A mile away from Finlay Lucas's home.'

CHAPTER TWENTY-ONE

Martin lifted the top letter from the three in his sideboard drawer. The horrific notion that Laura's brothers would take Finlay to punish him was unbearable. He should have said something sooner. As soon as the first one arrived. If not to Darren, then maybe to the police – if he'd reported it straight away, maybe this wouldn't be happening. His probation officer would have known what to do. He would never forgive himself if anything terrible happened to Finlay. Darren and Claire would never forgive him either. The memory of what he did to Laura McCabe lived with Martin every day. He wished he could make her family see that.

He put on his glasses, then opened the envelope and peeled open the most recent short letter.

> *Martin Lucas,*
>
> *I hope you know that every minute you are free to live your life is a minute Laura has been robbed of. It would be better for everyone if you did the decent thing. Your son and his family wouldn't miss you. You let them down the day you killed her. Killing yourself is the only way. Surely you can see that. It won't bring her back, but it would be a start. Here's a photo to remind you whose life you stole. Look at her every day and hope that one day nobody steals someone precious from you.*

Martin sniffed and wiped the small tear that gathered in the corner of his eye. He pulled the photo of Laura McCabe's smiling face out of the envelope. His chest tightened, as it had done several times recently. More so since the letters started arriving. *Probably just the stress*, he reassured himself. Martin laid the three letters on the hall table to remind him to take them with him when he went to see that detective again. She wasn't sure if they had anything to do with Finlay's disappearance, but she said she was keeping every possibility open at this stage. She also guaranteed she was doing everything she could to find him. Martin believed her. He was confident in her ability to sort this out one way or another. She was tough. That was clear. Talking to her about his conviction hadn't been easy, but she listened patiently and intently.

The sound of post landing on the doormat made him turn. His heart raced dangerously fast as he approached the small pile. *Bills and statements. A couple of flyers.* His relief on not receiving another bit of hate mail flooded his system. He wasn't naive enough to believe this was over, though. Not one bit.

CHAPTER TWENTY-TWO

Maggie McBride stopped to catch her breath at the end of Darren and Claire's road. She leaned on her knees and exhaled sharply then guzzled from her water bottle. That police car looked like it was parked right outside their house, but it was a busy street. Perhaps that was the only space available. Maggie jogged closer and could see a policewoman standing in the living room window. She clasped her hand across her mouth and wondered what to do. What was going on? Maggie was torn, but if she didn't tell Darren soon she thought she was going to burst. She took a deep breath and walked down the drive and round to the back door. She knocked and let herself in, the way she always did.

'Jesus, Maggie, you scared the life out of me!' Darren exclaimed as he walked into the kitchen. 'What the hell are you doing here? This is not a good time.' He tried to guide her back out of the door before Claire could see her.

Maggie just blurted it out. 'Darren, I'm pregnant and the baby is yours.' That wasn't strictly a lie, Maggie told herself, because it could be true. She wanted it to be more than anything in the world. More than she'd ever wanted anything before.

'Shut up,' Darren covered her mouth with his hand. 'Are you stupid? You can't come here saying shit like that. What do you mean, it's mine? It can't be.'

Maggie's heart broke at Darren's obvious rejection. She hadn't expected this, and her hormones were already all over the place.

'Darren, how can you say that, after everything?' She started to reach out to touch his cheek with her fingers.

Neither of them had noticed Claire enter the room.

'Maggie, I'm so glad you're here.' Claire broke down at the sight of her best friend. 'Something terrible has happened,' she whimpered. 'Finlay's been taken.'

Maggie gasped and moved towards her friend immediately. She hugged her tight and held her close while she sobbed. Darren was angry with Maggie for being so careless, fearing Claire might have overheard them. Finding out like that was the last thing Claire needed right now.

'Shh, hey, it's OK. I'm sure the police are doing everything they can to find him,' Maggie told her. She couldn't leave now, could she?

Darren was reeling, and took a step away from the two women. He couldn't deal with Maggie and any pregnancy right now. Not until his son was safe. He heard a car pull up in Colin and Dianne's drive and peered out of the kitchen window to see them walking towards their back door. He ran outside to confront them.

'What did the police want to talk to you about, Dianne?' he called out. 'Where is my son? Did you tell the police what you did with my son?"

Colin ushered Dianne inside and closed the door after her before turning to face his neighbour.

'Look, we've got nothing to do with Finlay's disappearance. Now please, go back inside and leave us alone. Dianne has had a very difficult night and she needs to get some rest.'

Colin turned to walk away, but Darren grabbed his arm.

'Dianne needs to rest, does she?' he boomed. 'What about Claire? And me? How can we rest knowing Finlay is out there somewhere, probably scared and hungry? If you know something, please just tell me.'

Colin yanked his arm back and heard Benson barking and scratching to get outside.

'I'm sorry, Darren, I really am, but I have enough to cope with,' Colin muttered as he walked away with his head down. 'I hope they find your lad soon. I really do.'

CHAPTER TWENTY-THREE

'Aargh!'

The torque wrench had slipped from Tim McCabe's grip, sending it at speed onto his foot, clipping his ankle on the way past before landing on the workshop floor. He rubbed the bone and peeled back his sock to peer down the top of his boots. Tim sucked in air through his teeth when it started to sting. He was sure he'd torn the skin, and figured a nasty purple bruise would soon erupt. *Time for a brew.*

He reached for the rag in his pocket to wipe off the surface oil from his hands and moved into the little garage kitchen-cum-office, complete with traditional girly calendars plastered over the walls. He clicked on the kettle and snatched a mug from the draining board then rinsed away the residual washing-up bubbles. He called through to his dad when he heard him arriving on the forecourt.

'Kettle's on, Dad.'

Mike McCabe mumbled something in return. Tim rinsed the soap residue from the second mug in their grungy sink. The filth in the place was another consequence of the loss of his mum. Angie McCabe had kept the family garage spotless as well as doing all the accounts and invoices, but Martin Lucas had destroyed all that. His selfish, reckless behaviour hadn't just taken Laura's life. The thought of him living his life like nothing had happened sickened Tim.

'Where's your brother?' Mike asked. 'He better no' still be in his pit at this time.'

Tim placed his dad's mug on the table and glanced up at the clock on the office wall. 'He's up. He's just not in yet. He did mention something about being late. I don't know why.'

The sound of a car pulling onto the forecourt attracted Tim's attention. He dried his hands on a grubby, greying towel and headed outside.

'Good morning,' he smiled at the strangers and his eyes drifted over the bodywork of the Fiesta. 'What seems to be the trouble?'

Jessie pulled her ID from her pocket, as did Dylan. Tim's heart raced. He swallowed hard. A visit from the police was the last thing he wanted. Peter had assured him everything would be fine. Trust his brother to be late, today of all days.

It's fine, it's fine, keep calm, Tim told himself.

'What can I do for you, Officers?' Mike spoke from the garage doorway. 'I'm Mike McCabe. This is my garage. Tim, go and get the Morrison invoice sorted, son. Robbie is coming in later to square up.'

'Sure thing.' Tim smiled and nodded at Jessie and Dylan, then turned towards the garage door.

'So, what's the problem?' Mike repeated.

'It's actually your sons we need to speak to, Mr McCabe,' Jessie told him as she moved forward. 'Can we talk inside?'

Mike frowned. 'Yes, of course. Sorry, go straight in.'

Jessie shot a wide-eyed glance at Dylan, wondering why Mike was so quick to usher Tim inside. Tim turned round from the filing cabinet as they pushed open the office door.

'Tim, it's actually you and Peter we need to talk to you. Is your brother around?' Jessie asked. 'It would be better if you were together for this.'

Tim leaned his back on the cabinet and pushed the drawer shut with his weight. He swallowed hard, desperate not to show weakness. Peter always said he was a poor liar. Tim wondered if they could feel his heart thundering. It felt so loud and his head pounded. He was sure they could hear the blood surging round his head.

'Please, take a seat,' he muttered. 'What can I do for you? Peter won't be long.'

'Thanks,' Dylan answered, and pulled out a chair.

Jessie sat down on the opposite side of the table, and Tim felt trapped in the confines of the small room – it felt hot all of a sudden. He was relieved to hear the sound of Peter's Suzuki motorbike roar into the garage.

'That's him. Hang on, I'll go and get him.'

Jessie stood to obstruct his exit. 'Nah, it's OK. I'll go.'

She watched Tim blush and retake his seat with a forced smile plastered across his lips. Dylan allowed silence to fill the room. He knew Jessie would want the tension ramped up. Stressed people tell the truth faster than comfortable suspects. They are more likely to let information slip out accidentally. Dylan's phone buzzing made Tim jump.

'Sorry about that,' Dylan offered, and switched his phone to silent before raising his eyebrows in greeting to Peter when Jessie brought him in to fill the ever-decreasing space in the office.

'What's this all about?' Peter demanded without taking his eyes off his younger brother. 'We've got a busy book of jobs to deal with today.'

'Tell us about Martin Lucas.' Jessie didn't hang about.

'What about him?' Peter snarled. 'Son of a bitch pisshead killed oor wee sister.'

It was quickly becoming apparent to Jessie who the dominant partner in this team was.

'Tell me about the letters you've been sending him since his release from prison, Peter.'

Peter's bravado slipped.

'What letters?' He screwed up his face with a shrug and tried to lie. 'Don't know what you're on about.'

'Come on, Peter. Don't waste my time,' Jessie said. 'The colour burning in your brother's cheeks tells me you're lying, both of you.'

Tim shuffled uncomfortably in his chair and stared at his brother, searching his eyes for the right thing to do.

Peter looked away from Tim, shrugged again and stared Jessie down, his confidence returning. 'Don't know what you're on aboot, I told you.'

Jessie pursed her lips, eyes narrowed, and stared right back at him. He didn't intimidate her. It wasn't until Dylan spoke that she broke the glare.

'Look, it's not about writing a few letters. Martin's grandson has gone missing. Do you two know anything about that? Claire and Darren are desperate.'

Tim's chair scraped rapidly from the table as he stood. 'Finlay!'

Jessie and Dylan both turned, startled by his unexpected move.

'Do you know them?' Dylan asked.

Tim's hand had flown to his mouth in agitation, and he exhaled deeply through his fingertips. 'My ex-girlfriend, Theresa Moran, is Claire's sister. I saw Theresa just yesterday. She looked' – he hesitated, searching for the right word – 'strange. She looked strange. Kind of wide-eyed and staring, and she was in a hurry, running across the bridge. She didn't even seem to see me. She doesn't keep well.' He found himself rambling, unable to control himself. 'She has mental health problems. Has done for ages. She looked terrible when I saw her. Like she'd seen a ghost or something.'

Jessie didn't like the sound of that. Not one bit. Her blood turned cold at the thought that was growing inside her head.

'There you are,' Peter said. 'Go and speak to Claire's nutcase sister and stop harassing us about some letters.'

'Peter,' Tim blasted. 'Don't talk about Theresa like that.'

Finally, some backbone, Jessie thought.

'Where were you yesterday afternoon between three and five?' Jessie asked Peter without taking her eyes from his.

'I was on a job,' he replied, holding her gaze. 'Check the diary.'

Jessie was first to break the stare and turned to see Tim nod quietly in agreement, then look away.

'Martin Lucas is bringing the letters in for forensic analysis. You both realise that, don't you?' Dylan added, and split his gaze between the two brothers. 'If there's evidence to suggest either or both of you are involved we'll find out.'

Peter McCabe shrugged. 'Whatever.'

Jessie had nothing to bring them in on but wished Peter's arrogance could be used in evidence.

'You'll be seeing us again soon, I imagine.' Jessie's words seemed directly aimed at Peter, who scoffed and shook his head before walking out of the office.

She wanted to talk to Theresa Moran in the light of Tim's statement, but she meant what she said. Peter and Tim wouldn't be far from her mind. Jessie took one last look at Tim, who blushed and turned to avoid her gaze. She and Dylan followed Peter.

'Good day, detectives.' Peter lifted a hand and waved behind him as he moved away. 'Drive safe.'

Tim was relieved to see the back of the two detectives. He was angry with Peter. His attitude was going to land them in hot water sooner or later. He felt awful about sending those two detectives to Theresa. They seemed very interested in her behaviour all of a sudden. That was clearly the last thing she needed in her state. He looked across at Peter, who was unlocking the safe. Peter opened the door and pulled out a small metal box, then turned back to face Tim and smiled.

'Stop worrying. Everything will be fine.'

CHAPTER TWENTY-FOUR

Maggie hung the tiny socks back on the rail. But they were so cute, with their yellow trim at the ankle. She yanked them back and laid them in her trolley and moved on. She didn't get far, stopping at the pretty little dresses. She would love to have a daughter. Maggie wondered if she might jinx it by buying a dress so soon, and moved on. Her phone buzzed in her handbag, interrupting her daydreams. She sighed when she saw it was Calum. She pondered the idea of ignoring it but figured he would only call back in five minutes anyway, then ask her later where she had been. It wasn't worth the hassle.

'Hey, babe,' she answered, and listened to his dinner suggestion. 'No, it's fine. I'll get us one of the freshly made pizzas and a salad to go with it.'

That seemed to satisfy him enough to allow her to go back to her browsing. She was aware of how impatient she was becoming with Calum – and she did feel bad. As she moved out of the baby clothes aisle, a sudden tight cramping pain pulled on her belly, causing her to bend and clutch her abdomen. The warm trickle between her legs made her cry out.

'Help me, somebody help me.' Maggie tried to grab her phone from her bag but it slipped from her grasp and dropped to the floor. She fell to her knees, the pain terrifying her. She couldn't lose this baby.

*

Calum sat next to Maggie on the bed and held her close as she stirred from her nap.

'Hey you, sleepyhead.' He smiled and kissed the top of her head. 'You've been out for the count for well over an hour. Shows just how tired you were.'

Maggie stared at him without speaking, then burst into tears.

'What's this all about?' he squeezed her tight next to him. 'Doc says the baby's fine. He said you need to rest, that's all.'

'I know,' Maggie answered through her tears. 'I'm sorry, Calum. I'm sorry for worrying you, but I was so scared.'

'You silly woman,' he said affectionately. 'I said I was going to take care of you and this little one, didn't I?' He stroked Maggie's stomach, then lifted her hand to kiss her wrist. 'It's my job to worry now, isn't it?' He grinned and pulled her head into the warmth of his chest.

Maggie couldn't help feeling safe in his embrace. She always had. Calum had been the steadying influence that helped her grow up. He would do anything for her. This scare was a sign that Maggie had to start thinking about what she really wanted.

That's not true. She knew what she wanted. What it really meant was that she had to do something more to get it. It didn't matter who got in the way. If this scare had taught her anything, it was that she had to be determined enough to defeat any challenger.

CHAPTER TWENTY-FIVE

Jessie replaced the petrol cap and opened the driver's door.

'Pass me my bag, will you?'

'Sure,' Dylan reached down. 'Wow, what you got in here? A brick?'

'Very funny.' Jessie took it from him and waited until a builder's van passed before crossing the petrol station forecourt. She frowned at the smile the driver gave her and shook her head, then held the shop door open for the elderly woman who was coming back out.

'You're welcome,' Jessie muttered when a thank you wasn't offered. 'Hi there, pump three, thanks.' Jessie grabbed a couple of Mars bars and laid them down on the counter. 'I'll have these as well.'

Her phone rang on her way back across the forecourt. Caller ID unknown again. It irked her. She wished he would just stop.

'Hello,' she snapped on answering, and listened to the silent response. 'Dan, I know it's you.' Jessie thought she heard breathing on the other end. 'This is pointless. I got your card, OK?'

Before she could say more, the caller hung up. She shoved her phone deep inside her jacket pocket and climbed into her car.

'There, lunch is served. Don't say I'm not good to you.' Jessie tossed Dylan his chocolate before laying her bag back at his feet.

'Cheers. I'm a bit peckish, right enough,' Dylan said. 'Who was on the phone?'

'What?' Jessie asked as she ripped the wrapper from her own bar and took a large bite.

'Out there. I saw you on your phone. Has something happened? You looked serious,' Dylan stated.

'No, it's fine.' Jessie hated the thought of Dylan knowing. 'It was nothing. Don't worry about it.' The last thing she needed was questions. Even if Dylan did mean well. 'Right, let's see what Theresa has to say.'

Jessie hoped that was enough to curb Dylan's curiosity. She might tell him one day, she supposed. But today wasn't that day.

CHAPTER TWENTY-SIX

Claire curled her body into the foetal position and tried to get back to sleep. She ignored Darren – who she knew had popped his head round the bedroom door – grateful that he thought she was asleep. She couldn't believe she'd had a seizure. She had been seizure-free for more than ten years. She hoped this wasn't the start of regular seizures again. They had plagued her childhood and stalked her through her first year of secondary school. A change of medication when she was twelve stopped them. One of a new range at the time. Claire felt like it was a miracle. Being able to have a life and, soon after, a boyfriend. She met Darren when she was fifteen and had never been with anyone else.

It was no use – she wouldn't sleep now. She sat up on the edge of the bed and tucked her long, messy hair behind her ears. The silence was eerie. She couldn't stop thinking about the days she'd prayed for peace and quiet, but not like this. She really should shower, but the effort was too much. She spotted one of Finlay's socks on her dresser and leaned over to pick it up. She held it to her cheek.

'Where are you?' she whispered, and stared at his photo on the bedside cabinet.

'You're awake?' Claire turned at the sound of Darren's voice. 'I thought I heard movement. How are you feeling?'

Claire scoffed. 'How do you think I'm feeling?'

'I know, I'm sorry.' Darren moved closer and flopped down on the bed next to her. 'I don't know what I'm supposed to be doing.' His shoulders drooped. 'Are we meant to sit here and do nothing? Wait for them to tell us something?'

A strong gust of wind funnelled along the alley at the side of their house, catching on an empty plant pot which scraped along the chipped driveway. Claire pulled back the bedroom curtain to see what damage the wind had done. Not much, considering the gusts that had been blowing. She allowed the curtain to drop back into place and walked towards the bedroom door.

'Claire?' Darren called out to her, his voice full of pain.

Claire kept walking. She couldn't cope with Darren's suffering on top of her own.

CHAPTER TWENTY-SEVEN

'Colin,' a small voice drifted through from the bedroom.

Colin allowed his head to drop as he sighed. A selfish part of him had hoped to avoid her. Discovering Dianne's secret last night had come as a blow to the marriage he thought was built on honesty in every part of their lives. Dianne had cried and said how sorry she was so many times that Colin had lost count.

'I have to get going, honey, or I'll be late for the delivery at work,' he called out and glanced at his watch. 'I'll see you tonight. I'll bring home a fish supper if you like.'

Dianne closed her eyes when she heard the front door close behind him, and laid her head back down on the pillow. She'd dozed fitfully since being brought home from the station, but didn't feel rested in the slightest. She rubbed the tears away with the top of her white cotton nightgown. She was desperately sorry that Colin had found out like that. She hadn't deliberately tried to deceive him, not about any of it. She was surprised he'd never discovered the suitcase before last night, though. It wasn't like she tried to hide it. Heading into Dundee on the train and shopping for baby items made Dianne feel whole; like her daughter wasn't missing from her life. Like Stacey wasn't lost any more. It was as if Dianne was living her life the way it was meant to be, in some kind of alternative universe where she got to be the mum she should be. The last time Dianne had added to the suitcase was just before Finlay was born. Being able to focus on him seemed to help her, probably more than it helped Claire.

The knock on the back door stirred Dianne from her thoughts. She stared at her reflection in the mirror and wiped her wet face before opening the door. She was confused to see Claire standing there.

'Can I come in?' Claire whispered, her words barely audible.

Dianne opened her arms and nodded. 'Of course,' she murmured, as Claire fell into her chest and cried.

*

The woman held the baby close to her chest and stared down at him, sleeping soundly in his blanket. She checked the time on her watch. Their flight was delayed by half an hour, but shouldn't be much longer. The delay was less than usual, which pleased her. She was too old for the long ferry crossing now, she told herself. All the swaying made her feel sick these days, and she was keen to get back quickly. It had all been so sudden, so last-minute. But, as had been explained to her, sometimes things just happened that way. She should take the opportunity when it came. It had been inconvenient, but she'd managed to rearrange things to make it work. A voice came over the loudspeaker announcing her flight was ready to board. She rubbed her hip and winced as she stood to gather the one bag she had to take on with her. The infant stirred as she stood, until she rocked the little one gently back to sleep. It had been a long day, and she would be glad to get home and have a decent cup of tea.

CHAPTER TWENTY-EIGHT

Jessie hammered her fist on the door and rolled her eyes at Dylan while they waited. She could hear the sound of a radio playing and shook her head. She listened with her ear to the door while she hammered again. This time the music stopped abruptly, and footsteps were heard moving closer before the door opened. She offered Claire's father, Phil Moran, a smile as she held up her ID.

'Detective, come in, come in,' Phil held the door wide open for them. 'Has there been any news on my grandson?'

His words were urgent and searching, and Jessie genuinely wished she was going there to give him good news.

'Not yet, I'm afraid. It's Theresa we're here to talk to. Is she in?'

Phil's eyes dropped into a serious frown. 'Theresa isn't here. She was admitted to hospital yesterday.'

'I'm sorry to hear that.' Jessie contained her instinctive alarm, and acknowledged the information calmly. 'I hope it's not too serious.'

'My daughter suffers from bipolar disorder. My wife found her in rather a muddled state. Her mental health has deteriorated recently, Detective. We were very lucky to be able to have her seen and admitted as quickly as we did.'

Jessie's mind ticked over at speed. What might have triggered Theresa's deterioration?

There was a small piece of paper in Phil's hand, and when Dylan glanced towards it both detectives noticed how swiftly it was put away.

'Is your wife in?' Jessie asked, taking in the floral-carpeted hallway and stairs, her eyes coming to rest on the pine bookcase at the top, that bore a huge vase of pink and yellow carnations. Not unlike church flowers, she noticed. 'Did Theresa tell either of you if there was something specific that got her so muddled, as you put it?'

Phil shrugged and his eyes darted left and right. 'If she told Bridget then Bridget hasn't told me, but you have to understand, when my daughter relapses like this her mind is' – he tapped his temple with a finger – 'complicated. The way Theresa herself describes it is like all the buttons are done up wrong, so nothing fits or matches up properly. Different thoughts go with the wrong thoughts. If that makes sense. Everything turns foggy and she can't think. The voices come back, too.'

Jessie could see the years of worry etched on his face. It couldn't have been easy worrying about his daughter's mental health, and when Claire was diagnosed with post-natal depression, Phil and Bridget must have feared she was heading for the same future as her sister.

'Bridget isn't in either, I'm afraid. She was up and out before me this morning.' Phil shrugged again and abruptly rubbed at his left eye. 'She said she had to go out. She usually does the flowers in the chapel and there's a funeral today, so she probably went to help set up. She won't want to let Father McKinnon down.' He glanced sideways and ran a finger across the hall table. 'I'm heading over to Claire's, so that's where I'll be if you need me.'

Phil grabbed his car keys and slipped his feet into a pair of heavy boots, then tugged a winter fleece from a coat hook. *I guess we're done here*, thought Jessie.

'We'll be over to see Claire and Darren soon,' she informed him, before she and Dylan headed back to her car.

Dylan tightened his jacket around him. The sky loomed heavy above them, as if it might snow again at any moment.

'What do you make of the sudden hospital admission?' Jessie was curious to see if Dylan sensed the same unease about it that she did. 'Convenient?'

Dylan tugged at his seat belt, struggling to pull it across him.

'Hey, you have to treat her gently.' Jessie reached across and slowly encouraged the belt across Dylan's chest. 'She doesn't appreciate being manhandled like that.'

Dylan shook his head but said nothing.

Jessie figured there was no point trying to talk to Theresa today. They had been down this road before, and knew very well that mental illness makes interviewing people very difficult. So they'd focus on Bridget instead. Maybe Theresa told her mum what had distressed her so much. Did that have something to do with her frantic behaviour outside the McCabe's garage?

CHAPTER TWENTY-NINE

Father Paul McKinnon heard the heavy oak door of the chapel squeak open and shut just as he was finishing up the confession. Bridget Moran thanked him as she always did, and he was glad to help her. He'd known Bridget and her family since the girls were very small and had supported them throughout Theresa's illness. After learning of Claire's condition his heart hurt for all of them, and he included them in his prayers often.

'Please, come in. You're very welcome here.' Paul stepped forward to greet the strangers and frowned when they held up official identification. He pulled his glasses from his pocket and squinted at the IDs. 'Hello, Detectives. What can I do for you?'

'Hello again.' Bridget's face was stern. Even today there didn't appear to be any emotion in her eyes, Jessie noticed, and that bothered her. What was that all about? It made her feel quite uncomfortable, if she was honest.

Father McKinnon shot a glance at Bridget, then averted his eyes, his cheeks gaining a pink hue. 'Is there anything I can help you with? Please come through to the house. We can talk more comfortably in there. My housekeeper, Mrs Laing, might even make us a pot of tea and find some biscuits.'

Jessie shook her head. 'It's Mrs Moran I'm here to speak to, but thank you, Father. Her husband told us she would be here. Maybe next time.'

'OK, I'll be in the house if you need anything.' He lightly touched Bridget's back then left the three of them talk. 'Please tell Claire and Darren they will be included in my prayers.'

Bridget nodded while she watched him leave, avoiding Jessie's gaze – she could feel it burning into her cheek. Jessie waited for her to turn round, still unnerved by how aloof she was. How cold.

Bridget slowly sighed and split her icy stare between the two detectives. 'What can I do for you?'

Jessie glanced up at Jesus, hung painfully on the cross not far from where they stood. Bridget couldn't lie to her. Not standing under her Lord and Saviour.

'I was sorry to hear that Theresa has been taken ill,' Jessie began. 'Can you tell us what happened? Your husband mentioned she was upset about something that happened yesterday.'

Bridget sat down in the closest pew and pressed her khaki skirt tighter over her knees. She pulled a tissue from her shirtsleeve and wiped her nose. 'Not that it has anything to do with your investigation, but Theresa's mental health has been bad for a long time. I found out she has been skipping her medication and her mind was very mixed up, so I thought it would be better to have her be admitted so she can sort herself out. Before it got any worse. Maybe have her medication reviewed.'

'Does she know what's happened to Finlay? I imagine that would be a difficult thing to tell her. Probably best to leave that until she's feeling better.'

Bridget shot straight back up, startling Dylan, who stepped backwards involuntarily. 'Why would you ask such a thing?'

It didn't surprise Jessie. Of course Bridget would do that – become indignant and answer questions with questions. That way, she wasn't really lying in front of Him, was she?

'If there's nothing else other than your interest in Theresa's mental health then I have things I need to get on with.'

'So she didn't tell you what caused her such anxiety,' Jessie persisted. 'Did she tell you why she was at Claire's that day?'

'I don't know. Have you tried asking Claire?' Bridget suggested with a steely glare and tidied the collar of her jacket as she spoke.

Jessie watched the back of Bridget disappear out of the chapel's door. Their conversation was postponed, not over. Not over by a long shot. Bridget Moran knew far more than she was letting on, and Jessie intended to find out what.

CHAPTER THIRTY

Jessie hated public appeals with a passion, but they were something that went with the territory. She peeled her black scrunchie out and shook her hair, then traced her fingers through to remove as many tugs as she could find. She rummaged in her bag and pulled out a lipstick from the bottom of the chaos. She puckered her lips in the station bathroom mirror. It would have to do. Mocha was more professional than red, for sure. All the comb achieved was to make her stringy, thin hair look even worse. She tied it back from her face again, then pinched the skin on her cheeks. She exhaled loudly before making her way outside. These things always made her feel so self-conscious, and the sound of her own voice was weird to her own ears. Like someone else's voice had taken over. She wondered if everyone felt like that. Her throat was so dry, and her lips. She sipped from her water bottle before stepping out of the main door of the police station to stand in front of a small crowd of expectant faces; some she recognised, some she couldn't recall ever seeing before.

'My name is Detective Inspector Jessie Blake, and I am heading up the investigation into the disappearance of a vulnerable six-month-old baby boy. Thank you all for coming at such short notice, but it is imperative that we get this information out to the public as soon as possible.' Jessie held up a photo of a smiling, blond-haired infant. 'This is Finlay Lucas. Yesterday afternoon, between 3.30 and 5 p.m., he was taken from his cot and is now a missing person.'

Jessie's eyes scanned the crowd, silent apart from the odd click from a camera. Some held up digital recorders and phones to capture Jessie's words. It made Jessie feel self-conscious again, but she swallowed it down. Holding the press conference now meant they could make the evening's news bulletins and tomorrow's papers – that's what mattered, not her ratty hair and pallid skin.

'What I'm asking now is for anyone who was in the vicinity of Kintillo Road and Forgandenny Road in Bridge of Earn yesterday afternoon to please come forward. What you saw or heard might seem like nothing to you, but could be vital in establishing what has happened to Finlay. Did you see anyone in the area that you've never seen before? How did they seem? We also need any businesses and private residences with CCTV to contact us with any footage obtained yesterday afternoon. Even dashcam footage would be helpful to us. If anybody thinks they have seen a friend or relative with a baby they don't recognise, it is vital that you contact us immediately. Also, if a friend or relative who is acting out of character concerns you, please let us know as soon as possible, especially if they can be placed at the scene yesterday afternoon. I urge you in the strongest possible terms to contact us. All of this information and this photo of Finlay is on Police Scotland's website, Facebook and Twitter feed. Finlay's mum and dad are understandably anxious to find their son. Thank you.'

Jessie started to turn away, just as a barrage of questions came at her back.

'Detective Inspector,' one dominant male voice bellowed above the others, 'has he been kidnapped with a view to obtaining financial reward, do you think? Have his parents received a ransom demand yet?'

Jessie spun back round to address his point.

'At this time we are looking into every possible motive. Thank you. As you can probably understand, I'm not about to speculate. Thank you for your cooperation.'

Jessie shoved her shoulder into the station door and enjoyed hearing the crowd disperse behind her. She hadn't lied. Everything was a possibility right now.

CHAPTER THIRTY-ONE

The little one had kept her awake most of the night and she was exhausted, especially after the long day yesterday. But the infant had slept for a large part of the journey, so it wasn't surprising they were both wide awake most of the night. Right then, she regretted agreeing to help out. It was too much at her age and in her condition. With her hip so bad now. The little tyke was crying for breakfast, and she wondered where all that energy came from.

'Hey you, what's all this fuss about? I know I'm not as fast as Mummy, but it's coming, I promise.' She rocked the hungry child soothingly as she heated the bottle in a jug of warm water.

She checked the fridge. There were two left. She would have to get more made up if she was to babysit much longer. She was so out of practice with all this and she'd breastfed her sons anyway, and used real nappies, which hadn't done them any harm. They, on the other hand, had never fastened a terry nappy in their lives, choosing instead to use disposable ones on her grandchildren, which looked like paper to her. That couldn't possibly be comfortable, she'd told them, but their response was to laugh at their mother's old-fashioned ways.

'Here you go.' She offered the teat to the famished baby and the milk was guzzled with enthusiasm. 'My, you were hungry, weren't you?'

She lifted a tiny hand and watched it grip her finger.

'You're perfect, aren't you?' she whispered, and leaned her face close. She lifted the little hand and kissed it gently.

She watched those big round eyes struggle to stay open, and pulled away the bottle once her little house guest had had his fill. She lifted the boy up and held him over her shoulder to pat his back, then grinned at the loud rumble that started in his tummy and quickly erupted from his lips. She glanced across at the flashing red light on her answering machine. It would have to wait; she had meant to check it last night.

'I bet that feels better,' she laughed a little and laid him back into the travel cot, wondering just how long she would be caring for him now that the plan had changed.

CHAPTER THIRTY-TWO

Jessie was concerned that Dianne Davidson's aunt still hadn't called back to confirm what Dianne had told her. Jessie had left a message, but wondered whether it was worth asking for a local officer to pay her a visit. Dianne's story sounded legitimate enough to Jessie, but she needed to be sure. To lose a baby that way must be awful, and an anniversary can stir up so many memories. It was bad enough for Jessie to lose Ryan when she did – Dan's sentence could never be long enough for what he did. The death of her son had broken Jessie's heart. Jessie didn't think she would ever recover from the darkness that followed, or even if she wanted to. There were days it had been so bad she'd considered joining her son, but something always pulled her back from the edge. More accurately, someone. Jessie missed her friend Carol. She scribbled *Call Carol* on her notepad.

It would be good to catch up.

Jessie opened the file she'd been handed – details of the first few calls the station had received after her public appeal. She also opened her email on her phone to watch a video of dashcam footage that had been sent to the station's address overnight, with no note attached. It was blurry, but the child being pushed in the pram was clearly much older than Finlay. She laid her phone back down and focused on the file. The pile of paper inside was bigger than Jessie thought it would be at this stage, but clearly a missing baby stirs the emotions. As it rightly should.

'Davidson's builder's van, interesting,' she murmured and nibbled the end of her pen.

Why would someone call in about that? Colin lives right next door. Of course his van would be there. Maybe the caller didn't know that and was only trying to help. Jessie leafed through the pile and pulled out another one that caught her eye. A CCTV photo of another van parked on Kintillo Road, a little further along the street.

I wonder why they didn't mention that? She grabbed her car keys and yanked her jacket from the back of her chair. *Time to get some straight answers.*

CHAPTER THIRTY-THREE

Dianne poured a cup of tea from the pot then clicked the kettle on again. The young woman had barely spoken after coming round the day before; she seemed to be building up to something a couple of times but then retreated into silence before Darren had eventually come looking for her. Despite Claire's reticence, Dianne hadn't been surprised to find her at her back door again this morning.

'Here you go,' she said as she laid the mug in front of Claire on the kitchen table. She pushed the plate of biscuits closer to her. 'Come on, you have to eat. Take a biscuit at least. If you don't want a sandwich, at least have a Kit Kat or a Jaffa Cake.' Dianne tried to smile then quickly rubbed away a falling tear.

Claire's freezing-cold hand reached forward and lifted a Jaffa Cake from the plate. She held it close to her lips then pulled it away and dropped it on the table.

'Just one bite,' Dianne whispered. Claire looked at her with a fixed, glazed expression, like her eyes had misted over, and she emitted a slapping, grinding sound Dianne had never heard before. 'Oh, my goodness!' she screamed when Claire tumbled off the chair, writhing and jerking with white froth fizzing from the corner of her mouth. 'Oh, my goodness, what's happening? Don't worry. I'll get help.' Dianne left her back door hanging open as she ran as fast as her surgical pain would allow her and burst into next door. 'Darren, Darren!' she shouted into the house.

'What is it?' PC Isla Wilde intercepted Dianne in the hall, concerned by the commotion.

'It's Claire, I don't know what's wrong with her.' Dianne winced from the tugging pain low in her abdomen. 'She's having some kind of fit. I don't know what to do.'

The toilet flushed and Darren stepped into the hall. 'Dianne?' he called out.

'Come on, Claire is having another seizure,' PC Wilde told him as they followed Dianne, running, back to her kitchen.

Darren dropped to his knees and lifted Claire's motionless body into his arms then shook her. 'Claire, wake up.' He squeezed her cheeks and tapped them gently. 'Shit, she's not breathing.'

'I'll call an ambulance.' Dianne grabbed her phone and dialled 999. 'Come on, come on.' It felt like forever before her call was answered. 'Ambulance, please.' She pleaded with the operator and gave them the details before hanging up. Dianne gasped when she watched what was happening. Tears rolled down her cheeks now. She scrubbed her face with the palms of her hands to move the moisture out of her eyes and stop it obscuring her vision.

'Oh Claire, sweetheart,' she murmured, her voice trembling.

'We'll have to start CPR, Darren.' The young policewoman helped him lay Claire onto the kitchen floor and leaned her ear close to Claire's mouth.

'I already told you she's not breathing!' Darren shouted.

'Calm down,' PC Wilde replied. 'That doesn't help.' She began compressions, her own heart racing; she had to stay calm. 'One, two, three, four, five, six, seven, eight, nine, ten.' She listened again for breath sounds and repeated the compressions as Darren watched on, horrified.

Isla Wilde thought the ambulance would never get there. Her arms stung from continuous compressions. The sound of sirens had never been so welcome as Darren and Dianne clung to each other.

CHAPTER THIRTY-FOUR

Dylan sniffed and blew onto his hands, regretting losing his gloves, which he figured he must have left in Jessie's car. He stamped his feet against the winter chill, his every breath visible in the freezing air. He stood tall at the sound of the large wooden door being unlocked and pulled open.

'Can I help you?'

Dylan held up his ID to the greying older woman. She could only be five foot tall at most, and wore her hair in a neat, tight bun. She tugged her cardigan tighter against the cold air.

'I'm Detective Constable Logan. I wonder if I could have a chat with Father McKinnon, if he's there.'

Gertrude Laing looked him up and down then held the door wide open and ushered him inside.

'Go through. I'll go and get Father McKinnon for you.' Mrs Laing smiled before she marched towards the door at the end of the long hall.

Dylan's eyes wandered the length of the hall, coming to rest on the high ceiling. *No wonder it's cold in here*, he thought. He moved towards the reception room Mrs Laing had pointed him to. It was large, with tall windows. He was impressed with the antiques on display, especially those in a locked cabinet at the far end of the room. Father McKinnon's desk looked old, too. Mahogany most likely, although Dylan had no idea what period it was from. The chapel house dated back to the early 1800s, so he wouldn't be surprised if it was an original piece.

'Hello again, Detective.'

Dylan took hold of Father McKinnon's outstretched hand.

'I'm sorry for the intrusion again, Father,' Dylan said with a sombre smile. 'But as you know, time is against us. We are talking to everyone with a connection to Finlay's family.'

'Of course, and I'm happy to help in any way I can.' Father McKinnon flattened down his unruly silver hair then pointed towards the large mustard armchair by the window, before flopping down himself on a tall-backed leather office chair behind his desk. 'Please take a seat.'

'Thank you.' Dylan sat and retrieved his notebook from his pocket. He coughed once and clicked the end of his pen. 'How well do you know Claire and Darren Lucas?'

A gentle smile spread across Father McKinnon's lips. 'I've known Claire and her sister Theresa since they were no more than toddlers. Bridget and Phil are active members of our church community – always have been as long as I've been here, which is almost twenty years. Gosh, has it really been that long?' He shook his head with a long sigh. 'Where does the time go?'

Dylan smiled. 'So you would say you know them quite well, then?'

Father McKinnon's elbows rested on the edge of his desk and his eyebrows twitched. He exhaled another long breath.

'I would say so. Terrible business all this, with little Finlay.'

'Indeed it is.' Dylan tapped his pen on his cheek. 'Would you say they were a happy family, Father?'

Father McKinnon frowned. 'Yes, of course. They are good Christians, Detective.'

And that makes a difference how, exactly? Dylan thought, but he held his tongue. His own father was a good Catholic man to the outside world, but that didn't stop him punching Dylan's mum black and blue of a boozy Saturday night. Particularly when the result of the Old Firm derby didn't go his way.

'And Theresa. How much do you know about her illness?' Before an answer was forthcoming, the door creaked open and

Mrs Laing carried in a tray – a pot of tea and a plate of scones, which Dylan thought looked home-made.

'I'm sorry to interrupt, but I thought you two gentlemen would like some tea, and I've brought some of the scones left over from the bake sale. They're still fresh and tasty.'

Father McKinnon smiled and nodded gently towards her as she left after placing the tray on the coffee table at the centre of the room. He stood and began to pour them each a cup. A cup and not a mug. The crockery too looked old; antique. It had a delicate pattern of red rambling roses.

'Help yourself to milk and sugar, Detective.'

'Thank you.' Dylan tipped his three spoonfuls into the cup, forgetting that it wasn't his usual huge mug he was sipping from this time.

'What were we saying?' Father McKinnon frowned. 'Ah yes, Theresa.' He tutted before a wistful expression fell across his face. 'She's a poor soul, that girl. Her mind is troubled. So very troubled.'

Dylan sipped from his cup, regretting the volume of sugar. He placed it back down.

'So I've heard. Did Bridget tell you exactly what happened to her this time? What was so bad that caused her to be hospitalised?'

Father McKinnon rubbed the thin grey stubble on his chin and looked to Dylan as if he was choosing his next words very carefully. Dylan's eyes narrowed. Father McKinnon sipped from his cup then licked his lips.

'Bridget Moran came to me, Detective.' He hesitated while he sipped his tea again before wiping a drop that dribbled over his chin. 'She asked me to hear her confession, but as you know I can't divulge anything that was said in there.'

'So she didn't mention, just in passing, that her daughter was ill, or what might have triggered it?' Dylan kept his gaze steady. The priest shifted uncomfortably as he shook his head.

'The only conversation we had was during confession, I'm sorry.'

CHAPTER THIRTY-FIVE

Theresa slid her feet into her trainers and grabbed her hooded fleece from the wardrobe.

'Stop it, stop it,' she said to herself in the empty room, then stared into her reflection in the window. 'It's not true. You are lying. You're always lying. Lying is a sin.'

Instead of getting better, the voices had grown louder and more aggressive. They were shouting and telling her she would go to hell for what she'd done. Her mum had promised this was for the best, but Theresa didn't feel any better yet. All that had happened so far was that the nurse was giving her an extra pill she'd never had before. She overheard them talking about her. Whispering behind her back. They didn't know she'd heard them.

She tugged up the zip and pulled the gloves from the pocket. The knock startled her from her thoughts.

'You ready?' The staff nurse's smiling face peered round Theresa's door. 'Good idea with the gloves. It's chilly out there.'

Theresa nodded and followed him out of her room and through the door to the acute assessment ward. The pair walked in silence through the hospital grounds. 'Accompanied ground parole', it was called. Theresa hated that name, but she was happy to take whatever freedom they offered her. She felt suffocated in that place.

'Do you mind if I smoke?' the nurse asked, then offered Theresa a cigarette.

Theresa shook her head, then corrected herself. 'No, I don't mind and no thanks, I don't want one. I don't smoke. It's poison to the body, tobacco.'

'Aye, you're not wrong,' he agreed as he lit up.

'It's also a sin to deliberately poison your body.'

'Mm, you're probably right, Theresa, but I've been smoking for over twenty years.'

'Aren't you worried about going to hell, then? Does eternal damnation sound OK to you?'

Theresa fixed her stare on the nurse, who quickly smiled then looked away while he stubbed out his cigarette. He popped a stick of chewing gum in his mouth and offered one to Theresa while the silence returned. She shook her head politely at his offer.

He must really think you're stupid. You're not going to take anything he offers. That could be laced with anything.

They walked in silence for fifteen minutes. The cold air woke Theresa a little from the over-sedated fog she'd been in from the new medication. She couldn't see how that was supposed to help anyone. She muttered under her breath to ensure he couldn't hear. It was none of his business anyway. She felt the coins jingle at the bottom of her coat pocket.

'Can I go to the shop?' she asked.

'Sure thing, Theresa, no problem.'

When they arrived at the hospital shop he held out his hand to greet another nurse. It became clear to Theresa that they hadn't seen each other for some time.

'You go in, Theresa. I'll see you back here in five minutes.' He smiled and looked away from her and focused his attention on the tall, thin man with a neatly groomed goatee beard and small round glasses. 'Gosh, Tom, how long has it been, man?'

Theresa glanced around the empty shop and moved towards the chocolate bars. She knew exactly which one to buy.

'Is that everything, love?' The ruddy-cheeked, overweight woman who worked in the patients' shop grinned at her.

Theresa nodded as she reached for some change and handed it across the counter. 'Thank you.'

'You enjoy it, darling.'

Theresa nodded again without answering and turned to see a hospital maintenance man propping the fire exit open with a chair before walking through it and back towards his van. Theresa turned back to the woman behind the counter, who was breathing heavily while carrying a box of stock through the back. Then she peered out of the window in the shop door and saw the nurse who had escorted her puffing away on another cigarette and laughing with his friend. Her heart raced. She glanced back at the open fire exit. Bridget would be so cross with her, but she couldn't rest until she'd done the right thing.

CHAPTER THIRTY-SIX

Maggie McBride sat in her Mini and double-checked the documents she'd been asked to bring. Three months' bank statements. Evidence of her current address. The electricity bill should work. A reference from her boss. It had been easy to get hold of all of these things without Calum knowing. Too easy, perhaps. She shouldn't think about that. Not today. Maggie looked up to see a petite, well-dressed young woman lock up a smart, newish Nissan Micra and walk across the small car park in the apartment complex. Another new build. It would be perfect. Maggie knew that as soon as she'd found it online. A bit pricey, but they could make it work. Two bedrooms. Any further children would have to share to begin with, but it had done her and her sister no harm to share a room. If anything, it brought them closer together as kids.

'Mrs McBride? Hi, I'm Rachel. One of the letting assistants.' The pretty young woman held out her hand to Maggie and smiled. 'It's another cold one today.' She hunched her shoulders up against the chill and tucked her folder under her arm. 'Shall we head inside where it's a little warmer?'

Maggie reciprocated her warm smile. 'Hi, yes, call me Maggie, please.'

Maggie was impressed by the block's outside security immediately. A series of automatic security lights that tracked your movement as you made your way from the locked outside door, which required a pin number rather than a key to enter.

'The block is maintained by a company who are sent a code every time a bulb blows, so they can fix it straight away. They have a target of twelve hours in which to get the job done. The unique code tells them which bulb it is without having to test them all.' The girl grinned. 'It's genius.'

'It's certainly impressive,' Maggie answered as the pair waited for the lift. As soon as they stepped inside a voice asked them where they would like to go.

'Level three.' The assistant grinned again at Maggie, who noticed the only button in the lift was an alarm. Everything else was controlled by voice command.

'Wow,' Maggie exclaimed. 'Very high-tech.'

'Isn't it?' The girl agreed. 'I love it here.'

Her enthusiasm was definitely winning Maggie over. She hoped the flat lived up to expectations. Once she stepped inside, her emotions attempted to get the better of her. The property was bright and airy. Recently decorated in neutral colours throughout. Both bedrooms were a good size, with the master having a fantastic en suite shower room. Maggie could picture herself and Darren in the large cubicle, and feared she'd blushed at the thought.

'This is for you and your husband, is it?' the young woman asked, while she opened her folder on the kitchen table and rummaged in the bottom of her bag for a pen. 'Now, as I explained in my emails, the deposit is one thousand, payable up front, followed by a monthly rent of one thousand to be paid on the first day of the month, subject to successful references, of course. You both work, is that correct?'

Maggie barely heard what the woman was saying. Her imagination was running wild.

'Maggie?'

'What? I'm sorry, I was miles away. Yes, yes, we both work.'

'Why don't you go and have a wander round while I start on some paperwork?' The letting assistant smiled at her. 'Take your time. My next appointment is cancelled, so I've got as long as you need.'

Maggie moved from room to room, picturing Darren with her in each of them. It wouldn't be long now until those dreams were a reality.

CHAPTER THIRTY-SEVEN

'I came as soon as I heard,' Jessie jogged towards Darren Lucas just as Dylan rounded the corridor into accident and emergency. 'Have they said anything?'

Jessie thought she'd seen broken before, but it was nothing compared to the expression on Darren's face. He shook his head at her question before a young doctor walked towards them.

'Mr Lucas?' she asked.

'Yes, yes, that's me.' Darren surged forward. 'What's happening? Is she OK?'

'Claire is awake but she's a little groggy. She says she has no memory of what happened or of the seizure. She doesn't recall anything. I suggest her epilepsy has become unstable because of the stress. This must be difficult for both of you. I'm sorry to hear about your son – Claire told me.'

Darren scratched the back of his head and sniffed. 'Can I see her?'

'Of course. I've given her something for the headache and increased her anti-epileptic medication under the circumstances, which can be reviewed later. I would like her to stay for twenty-four hours for observation. Just to be on the safe side.' The doctor glanced from Darren to Jessie then back again with a sad smile. 'I hope you get good news soon.'

Darren nodded, then quickly shoved his shoulder into the double doors. Claire lay on her side, bundled up inside a blanket and curled into a foetal position, with a hand across her brow against the searing headache.

'Hey, you,' Darren kneeled by the bed and kissed her forehead before sliding her fringe out of her eyes.

Jessie felt all she and Dylan were achieving here was intruding on the couple's pain, further emphasised by the arrival of Bridget and Phil Moran.

'Come on, Claire's going nowhere,' she tapped Dylan's arm and whispered. 'Let's get a coffee. Then I need to ask the McCabes why they didn't mention their van was in the street the day Finlay was taken.'

'That's a bit suspicious, you're right. What are they hiding? And coffee, that sounds good. Hospital canteen does a good latte, actually.'

'I've also had a very interesting text from PC Wilde. Something she overheard about Mr Doting Husband.'

'Oh yes?' Dylan was curious.

Before Jessie could say more, the DC's phone rang. He held up the display to Jessie before answering. *Dianne Davidson*. A torrent of information came down the line as soon as Dylan answered.

'OK… so she knows Claire is here? … And how long ago was this? … OK, thanks for letting us know, Dianne.' He hung up and turned to Jessie. 'She says Theresa Moran turned up on the Lucases' doorstep, rambling and shouting for her sister. Dianne explained what had happened and offered to give the poor woman a lift, but she ran off. Do you think—' He broke off as a commotion from the ambulance entrance attracted their attention. 'Shit, Jess, look.' Dylan took hold of her arm. 'You want me to go?'

Jessie shook her head. 'It's fine. I'll handle it.'

CHAPTER THIRTY-EIGHT

The winters were getting harder on her ageing joints. Chopping her own logs for the wood burner would soon have to stop, especially now that neither of her sons had the time to help out as much as they used to. Taking proper care of the sheep was becoming harder, too, especially with her house guest staying longer than expected. But she didn't mind really. The little one was a tonic. Getting up at six on a biting cold morning was difficult at the best of times, but the baby had given her a renewed sense of purpose. The gales forecast for the coming few days filled her with dread, though. Maybe getting away from the farm, even if it was for an operation, would be good. That was assuming they got here in time to take the baby off her hands. She'd been firm with her on the phone about that.

She winced at the pain in her hip. That would have to do. She rubbed the joint and walked back into the shed to put away the axe. Cries from inside the cottage meant he was awake after his nap. She lifted a handful of the chopped wood and followed the sound.

'Hey now, little one.' Her eyes lit up when he stared up at her from his travel cot in the cosy living room. 'It's certainly warmer in here than out there, young man.' She reached down but struggled against the stinging pain from her hip. She held the infant close to her face and snuggled her mouth into his cheeks. He was lovely and warm. She didn't mind having him there. Not really. It's what family did for each other.

A car horn honked from the top of the long driveway up to the cottage. Sam, the grocery delivery man. Her border collie was barking and chasing the van to announce his arrival, too.

'Finally I'll have some fresh milk for my tea, wee one,' she cooed. 'Maybe even get a bit of toast and butter. Didn't fancy mouldy bread this morning.'

The baby giggled when she screwed up her face in mock disgust, as if he knew what she was talking about. He was such a content wee thing, despite his long day yesterday.

'Mrs—' Sam paused from calling out when he saw her coming towards him across the yard. 'Oh, you're there. I've got your delivery. Would you like me to bring it into the kitchen for you?'

'Thank you, Sam, would you? Finally, a decent cup of tea. When I got back last night my milk had turned. I'm gasping.'

The tall grocer smiled down at her, carrying three carrier bags in each hand. 'You've got company, I see. Who's this then?'

'Aye, and he's staying a bit longer than anticipated, too. This is… Och, excuse me a minute.' She moved towards the ringing telephone on the hall table, at the same time being reminded of the message she hadn't listened to yet.

'I'll leave the bags in the kitchen for you,' called Sam. 'Square up next time you're in town.' The grocer headed back to his van before she had a chance to thank him.

She answered the phone. 'Hello…? Thank goodness it's you. I've been getting worried.' She paused while listening to her caller as the infant gurgled in her arms. 'Yes, he's fine. When are you getting here? Because I'm not getting any younger, you know. It's all very well asking me to help, but it's a lot for me in my condition and I have to be back in Aberdeen in a couple of days.' She listened again and her shoulders drooped at what she heard. 'Just get here.'

She slammed the phone down, irritated by this very inconvenient development. They were really pushing what family meant to her to the limit. She pressed the button on her answering machine and frowned, then clasped a hand over her mouth as she listened. *That sounded serious.* She'd better call right back, and hope nobody would get in trouble because she'd left it this long to get back to them. When she couldn't get an answer, she hung up and decided to try again in a few minutes.

CHAPTER THIRTY-NINE

'Where is she? Why are you hiding my sister from me?' Theresa shrieked as she rampaged through accident and emergency, knocking trolleys and toppling equipment across the floor.

Jessie recognised Theresa's shock of wavy auburn hair immediately. She'd seen photos of her in both the Lucas and the Moran households. She lifted her hand to reassure the shocked receptionist, who was trying to calm the distressed, dishevelled young woman.

'Hello, Theresa,' Jessie called out. 'Come on with me, honey.'

Theresa turned to the sound of her name and narrowed her eyes at Jessie's outstretched hand.

Steady, this could be a trap. You don't know her, do you? How does she know your name?

'Who are you?' Theresa asked as she surged forward, ignoring the voice, unnerving Jessie with the speed of her approach. 'Can you take me to see Claire?' she spoke quickly, right in Jessie's face.

Jessie smiled, hoping that would soothe Theresa's obvious anxiety. 'I'm Jessie. Come on, you come with me.'

Theresa stopped and turned back to face the door. She glanced at the receptionist, who had replaced the telephone receiver – *no doubt she was about to call security.* Theresa felt her heart thud fast inside her chest. The voices were right. Who was this mysterious stranger who held her hand out for her to take? What if this really was a trap?

Jessie watched Theresa continue to frown at her gesture, and waited with her hand outstretched until the young woman cautiously edged forward.

'That's it, come on, we can chat in here,' Jessie told her while she opened the door to an empty side room. She would have preferred more distance between them and Bridget, but it would have to do. The light blinking on startled Theresa into withdrawing her hand until Jessie smiled. 'It's OK, everything's OK. Don't worry.'

I'm telling you. You shouldn't trust this woman.

Theresa's green eyes remained buried within a deep frown. She walked across the small room, past the unmade bed, towards the window on the far side. She peered through the partially opened blinds at the thick, falling snow outside, then stared down at her feet, as if realising for the first time that they were freezing.

Jessie wondered how Theresa had managed to get so far with no money or proper shoes – she only had some light trainers on her feet, which were soaked through. *How many people must have seen her yet stood by and done nothing?* At least Dianne had offered her a lift.

Theresa pulled the chair in the corner forward and sat down, saying nothing but staring intently in Jessie's direction. She still hadn't quite got the measure of this woman yet, but she seemed to know her name. Yet Theresa couldn't recall when or even if she'd ever met her before. Her mind had been so fuzzy recently.

'Where's my sister? Dianne said the ambulance brought her here.' Theresa tugged at her hair as she rambled quickly, twisting and twirling it around her fingers. 'When can I see Claire? Dianne said she had a seizure, but Claire doesn't have seizures any more. I tried to tell her that, but she called me a liar.' Theresa dropped her hair from her fingers and shot up at the sound of her mother's voice in the corridor.

'Shit,' Jessie muttered and followed Theresa out.

'Theresa! How— What on earth are you doing here?' Phil Moran moved forward but was swept aside by Bridget.

'You should be ashamed of yourself, Detective,' Bridget shot a glance of disgust at Jessie and wrapped her arm round Theresa's shoulders before removing her own jacket to swaddle her. 'Can't you see my daughter is unwell? Come on, I'll take you back, sweetheart.'

'But Mum, I need to see Claire,' Theresa tried to protest. 'I need to explain.'

'Nonsense,' Bridget interrupted. 'You need to come back to hospital with me. You're not well, darling, remember? Your mind has been all muddled up and the hospital is going to help you get it unmuddled again.'

Dylan joined Jessie, her disappointment morphing into frustration as they both watched the couple usher Theresa out of accident and emergency. Jessie shook out her hair again and roughly redid it into a messy bun.

'Shit,' she muttered again.

'Did she say anything at all to you?' Dylan asked.

'Nothing that made much sense.' Jessie shook her head. 'Bridget is keeping something from us. I know she is.'

'You think she knows something, don't you?'

'Damn right I do.' Jessie sighed. 'That family… I don't know, Dylan, there's something not right going on here.'

Dylan opened his mouth to answer but closed it when Darren stumbled out of Claire's side room, his ashen face staring straight ahead.

Jessie jogged closer and stood in front of him. 'Darren, what's happened?'

He continued to stare past her until she rested her hand on his arm. He opened his mouth to speak but could only mutter something inaudible at her.

'It's OK, you can tell me,' Jessie urged. 'Is Claire OK?'

Darren's mouth gaped open and he struggled to form the words. 'Sh-she…' he stammered. He turned to peer back in through the small pane of glass in the side room door then collapsed to his knees, his trembling legs giving way beneath him. Jessie shot a concerned look in Dylan's direction before crouching low next to Darren. She rested a hand on his shoulder.

'Tell me,' she whispered. 'It's OK to tell me.'

Darren pressed his temples in his hands. He shook his head, a look of horror growing on his face. Dylan peered into the room, and saw Claire curled up on the bed, sobbing and holding her head. He could hear her mutter what sounded like 'I'm so sorry' over and over into the pillow. His eyes widened at Jessie and he nodded to the room. Jessie shook her head. She didn't want anyone to move until Darren had told her what was going on. She rubbed her thumb back and forth on Darren's shoulder.

'It's OK,' she whispered again, this time offering him a smile and nod. 'You can tell me.'

Darren frowned. 'But it's not OK. Nothing will ever be OK again. She says she might have killed him.'

CHAPTER FORTY

When Darren had finished recounting his conversation with his wife, Jessie had to work hard to hide her shock. She knew Claire was troubled, but neither she nor Dylan had expected this.

'What's going to happen to my wife?' Darren asked, his thumb and forefinger pinching the inner corners of his eyes. Jessie helped him into one of the chairs outside the room.

'Are you sure that's what she said?' Jessie asked.

'Yes, I'm sure.'

Jessie peered through the side room window and exhaled loudly, her face serious. She turned to look at Darren before pulling out her phone without answering his desperate question.

'Excuse me just a minute, will you?' she nodded to Dylan to take care of him before walking out of earshot with her phone.

Dylan struggled for words. Claire's part confession was a shock to him, let alone Darren. She hadn't said she'd killed Finlay in so many words. More that she was scared because she couldn't remember whether she had. Darren stood and Dylan watched him stare in at Claire with tears in his eyes.

'How could she?' Darren stuttered, barely able to form a full sentence. 'My little boy.'

Dylan was relieved to see Jessie walk back towards them. She laid a hand on Darren's shoulder and he spun to face her. He rubbed at his wet face with the bottom of his polo shirt.

'I've arranged for a police officer to come and sit with Claire until she is given the all-clear to be discharged.'

Darren's brow fell into a frown. 'What happens after that?'

Jessie wished she could spare him any further pain, but that was impossible.

'Your wife has just confessed to you that she might have killed your son.' She kept her voice low and spoke close to Darren's ear. 'Claire will be taken to the station to be questioned. Do you understand what I'm saying?'

Darren glanced back into the room and shook his head. 'Yes, I understand,' he whispered. 'I understand completely.'

Before Jessie could add that he would also need to be questioned further, her phone buzzed in her pocket. She moved away from Darren to take the call in private.

'Hello, DI Blake speaking.' Jessie listened intently to what the woman was telling her. 'Yes, thank you for calling back. It's about your niece, Dianne Davidson.'

Jessie explained to the woman on the phone what had happened, and the woman sounded genuinely concerned about it. She asked if Dianne was OK, and said that if there was anything else she could help Jessie with she should call her without hesitation.

That's all well and good, Jessie thought. *But denying knowing anything about Finlay while a baby is clearly crying in the background? That's alarming.* She hung up without alerting the woman to her concerns. The last thing she wanted was to spook her into hiding the baby. She looked back down the corridor and saw that the PC had arrived to wait with the Lucases.

'Dylan,' Jessie called out, and waved for him to join her. She told him about what she'd heard in the background at Dianne's aunt's house.

'What's happening?' Darren called out to them and tried to follow as they headed towards the exit.

Jessie stopped and turned. 'Wait here, Darren. If there's any developments I'll let you know, OK?'

'But what's—' Darren stammered.

'Just trust us, Darren.' Jessie patted his arm.

All Darren could manage was a nod, despite the multitude of questions he must have had screaming inside him. Jessie hated leaving him like that, but she didn't want to tell him anything until she was sure herself.

She unlocked her Fiesta while talking to a colleague at the station. Getting a photo of Finlay to officers in Kirkwall as soon as possible was the priority right then. She tossed her phone into Dylan's hands as she reversed out of the hospital car park.

'If she's done this then she's a good liar, I'll give her that,' Dylan announced. 'Do you think Colin knows?'

'Aye, they're both up to their necks in it.'

CHAPTER FORTY-ONE

PC Naomi Carmichael put on her hat after getting out of the patrol car and pulled the photo of Finlay Lucas out of her pocket. She scratched the enthusiastic border collie's ear when it barked and leaped up to greet her, before pausing to peer through the window of the brand-new Mercedes parked outside the front door of the cottage. She spotted the baby seat straight away.

'Och, who's this now?' As her security light was activated, the woman peered out through the blinds and was surprised to see the young police officer being pursued by Meg the border collie all the way up to her door.

'Who is it, Mum?' A blond man in his early thirties looked up at the confusion on her face while he fed a bottle of milk to the baby in his arms.

'It's a policewoman. What is she wanting?' She turned to face her son, worried by the serious expression on the officer's face.

'Well, you won't know until you answer it, will you?' her son teased. 'You robbed a bank or something?' He laughed.

'Och, you're terrible.' She flicked a tea towel in his direction just as the loud knock sounded on the front door. 'Mebbe it's aboot Dianne.' She answered the door.

'Hello, Mrs Sutherland? I'm PC Carmichael. Would you mind if I come in?'

Betty Sutherland held the door wide open for the officer. 'Of course. Whit's all this aboot?'

PC Carmichael glanced at Finlay's photo as she moved closer to the baby, now sat up giggling on the man's knee.

'Police on the mainland, in Perth, are very concerned with the whereabouts of a baby linked to your niece, Dianne Davidson.'

'I know, I've spoken to a detective about this already. I told her I didn't know anything about a missing baby.'

PC Carmichael shifted her eyes from Betty to the baby. The man quickly grasped what was going on and turned the child to face the officer.

'This is Archie Sutherland. My son. My mum has been babysitting while my wife and I have had to travel for work. It was all a bit last-minute.'

'Aye, and I had to take him to Aberdeen Royal for my anaesthetic assessment, didn't I?' Betty directed that statement towards her son.

'I know, and I've said I'm sorry. It won't happen again.'

The officer held the photo close to the baby's face, but his brown eyes and mass of dark brown curls had already given away the fact that he was not Finlay Lucas.

CHAPTER FORTY-TWO

Dianne Davidson laid her iron down and lifted Colin's shirt off the board before carefully draping it across one of the dining chairs. She heard a car pull up outside and looked out to see DI Blake and DC Logan approaching the front door. She switched the iron off at the wall, closed her eyes and sighed before opening the front door.

'Hello, Detectives. Come in.'

'Thank you, Dianne,' Jessie greeted her as she followed Dylan inside.

Dianne smiled, despite the horrible darkness that was building inside her stomach.

'Go straight through to the kitchen. Don't mind Benson. He's always just pleased to see people.' Dianne nibbled on her thumbnail as she joined the two detectives. 'What can I do for you?'

'I've spoken to your aunt,' Jessie stated.

'That's good, then, she told you—'

Before Dianne could finish, Jessie's phone buzzed in her jacket pocket. She was pleased to see the Kirkwall station number. Hopefully with good news.

'Just a second, will you please excuse me? I have to take this.'

Dylan and Dianne sat in silence while Jessie took the call in the hall, Benson rubbing his face into Dylan's trouser leg for attention. Dianne smiled awkwardly and scratched the back of her head.

Jessie re-entered the kitchen. 'OK, thanks then, bye. Thanks for letting me know.'

'What's happened? Is it Finlay?' Dianne was scared by the deflated expression on Jessie's face. 'Tell me.'

Jessie stared from Dianne to Dylan and stuffed her phone back down into her pocket.

'It's not him,' she whispered.

The Davidsons' door closed behind Jessie and Dylan as they walked across the gravel drive back to Jessie's car. She really had hoped they'd made a breakthrough. At least if Finlay was on Orkney he was most likely being cared for, especially as the woman suspected of having him was Dianne's family. Dianne clearly adored Finlay, and appeared as concerned as his own parents about his disappearance. Jessie unlocked her car but stood outside the driver's door and stared back at Dianne's shadow, watching from behind the curtain. It was now over forty-eight hours since Finlay had last been seen. The critical period between finding a missing person and the unthinkable. The presence of the McCabes' garage van on Kintillo Road, near the Lucases' bungalow, needed further investigation as a matter of urgency.

'What now, Jess?' Dylan asked when she finally got in the car.

'The McCabes' van. They didn't mention that, did they?'

'Do you reckon they're hiding something?' Dylan asked.

'What do you make of them? The letters to Martin and stuff?' Jessie remarked.

'Aye, they're capable of the letters for sure. But they've lost a sister, grieved for their mum.' He shook his head. 'If they're involved in this, they haven't hurt him. Tim looked genuinely shocked, too. You'd have to be a pretty good actor to fake that.'

'Stranger things have happened, Dylan.'

Jessie started the engine, but before she was even in gear her phone buzzed again.

'DI Blake,' she answered. Her stomach lurched at the words she was hearing. Nausea rose in her stomach and she wanted to be sick right there.

Dylan stared across at her, alarmed by the expression on her face. She saw him staring at her, anticipating the response she didn't want to give. She shook her head slowly. This was the call they had been dreading.

CHAPTER FORTY-THREE

Jessie tugged up the hood on her forensic suit and moved slowly towards the taped-off area. Street lighting from the outskirts of the village barely reached the scene. An eerily silent crime scene. Her hopes for a positive outcome had been smashed in an instant. One phone call had changed the entire investigation. A shocked dog walker had called the emergency services after finding a tiny body tucked into a bag and hidden neatly under a pile of large twigs. She wouldn't have found him had it not been for the persistent barking from her Great Dane.

This never got easier. Jessie pressed the mask hard against her face as she approached the floodlit clearing on the dense, tree-lined path. She asked Dylan to join the fingertip search with the other officers, which would stretch along the entire length of the woodland path once daylight returned. An area of four miles between Bridge of Earn and the edge of Perth. She didn't think her DC should see this if he didn't have to.

Considering the amount of people at the scene, the atmosphere was thick with silence. She approached the entrance to the tent which had been erected around his little body. Jessie inhaled a last huge breath and steeled herself. She peeled back the tent door and was greeted by the sombre face of pathologist David Lyndhurst, crouched low over an open rucksack. His assistant, Benito Capello, stopped snapping the crime scene photos and turned when he heard Jessie approach. He nodded without speaking as she walked closer. Jessie's heart thudded. She could feel every molecule of blood rushing around her body, ending in a deafening pulse in her head. The civilian part of the woman she was cried out that she should turn back, but Jessie wasn't only that woman. She was the lead investigator into the disappearance of a vulnerable baby boy. He needed her; now more than ever.

'Hello, Jessie,' David spoke quietly as he looked up.

'David.' Jessie's voice quivered and she coughed once to clear the tightness that was choking her throat.

She edged closer and crouched next to him, staring at the back of the tent for a moment before allowing her eyes to drift down to the bag. It was a fairly standard rucksack – Jessie had a similar one for the rare occasions she went to the gym. There was nothing on the outside of the bag to suggest the horrifying contents. Several people had passed by it, assuming it had been dumped but unaware that it hid a terrible truth. She peered inside.

He looked like a doll that had been broken and discarded by a spoilt child. His little denim dungarees were unfastened from one shoulder and hung down loosely towards his stomach. His blond hair was filthy, and looked like it was painted onto his misshapen head. Jessie was relieved Finlay's eyes were closed. Looking into his eyes would have finished her.

'You OK, Jess?' David whispered.

Jessie couldn't answer him. She didn't know if she was OK. This was a scene nobody could ever unsee. Ryan's face rushed into her mind with such force she had to stand and take a step back to compose herself. She would never forget that sight for as long as she lived. She inhaled a large breath and blew it back out slowly. She had to focus.

'When will you have a time of death for me?' she asked without taking her eyes off the broken, twisted little body that lay partway out of the bag.

'He's been dead at least forty-eight hours. I'll have more for you once I get him back to the lab.'

Jessie nodded then took another step away. Her legs trembled, and she felt hot tears sting the backs of her eyes. She squeezed them tight shut in a bid to halt their escape. Memories of losing her own son hit hard. She couldn't break down now. Not in front of everyone. It wasn't until she felt Benito's arm around her shoulders that Jessie realised her pain was obvious to them.

'I have a flask of coffee in my car,' he whispered close to her ear as he guided her outside.

'It's fine, I'm OK.' Jessie wasn't fooling anyone. Nothing about her was fine.

'Well, you can keep me company for a few moments then, and you can watch me drink mine.' Benito gave a gentle smile, his large brown eyes soothing her aching heart a little.

'Thank you,' she whispered.

Her legs continued to tremble the entire way back down the woodland track to Benito's car. She was relieved to see it parked at the entrance to the wood, because she wasn't sure how much longer they would support her. Once inside, Jessie sipped the hot sweet coffee, surprised by how comforting the warmth trickling down her throat felt. Benito's Italian roots certainly came out in his coffee-brewing skills. She swallowed down one last sip and handed him the cup.

'Thank you. That was incredibly kind of you, Ben.'

'You remembered.'

Jessie allowed the ghost of a smile to spread across her lips when she recalled him telling her his friends call him Ben, the day they met. 'I remembered, and I owe you one.'

She got out and walked towards the team planning the fingertip search. She heard Ben call gently after her: 'I'll hold you to that.'

Jessie glanced back down the short path towards him, and saw a private ambulance arrive at the small car park. She watched the driver move to the back of the vehicle, remove a trolley and begin to wheel it along the snow-covered woodland path. Jessie nodded at him as he passed her.

When the driver returned, the body bag that Finlay lay in was too big. No child should ever be inside one of those. Now it was Jessie's job to find out why Finlay Lucas had ended up there, and she would stop at nothing to find out. There was no doubt about that. Claire's apparent confession. Theresa's mental health breakdown. Bridget's reluctance to talk. The McCabes' van seen close to the house. She had lots of pieces, but how did they fit? That was the question.

CHAPTER FORTY-FOUR

Darren couldn't think straight. He told the officer watching Claire that he was going to the gents' but instead continued past it and outside into the hospital car park. He needed air. There had been a few police officers stationed at the hospital, but most had left suddenly a little while ago. *Why had they raced off like that?* He walked towards a young woman who had just lit a cigarette.

'Any chance I could have one of those?' he asked. His head spun with so many different scenarios. He couldn't focus on what the truth might be. Claire didn't know what she was saying. The seizure must have caused her mind to get into a muddle, giving her memories that weren't real. He desperately hoped that was the case.

The woman turned, surprised by Darren's question, then tucked her hand into her pocket.

'Yes, sure, here.'

'Thanks.' Darren's head buzzed with his first draw. It had been a long time. Smoking was just another memory of his misspent youth.

*

Jessie and Dylan drove in silence from the site where Finlay's body had been found to the hospital, each of them locked in their own thoughts. Part of Dylan had been clinging to the hope that Dianne really had kidnapped the boy, and had hidden him with the help of an accomplice. He had wondered, too, if perhaps Colin was in on it.

They spotted Darren at the entrance to accident and emergency. It irked Jessie that he had been allowed to leave the building, but that was something she would deal with later.

'Detectives,' Darren squashed the cigarette under his trainer and stood up from the bench to greet them. His eyes narrowed then widened as he searched their faces. 'W-what?' he stuttered. 'Tell me.'

'Darren, let's go inside so we can talk.' Jessie moved closer and reached out for Darren's arm but it was snatched away.

'No, no, God, no,' he mumbled. His legs became weak under him and he flopped back down on the bench, next to the woman who had given him a cigarette. He dropped his head in his hands. 'No, no, no.'

Jessie asked the young woman to leave and took a seat next to him.

'I'm sorry to have to tell you that the body of a baby boy has been found.'

Jessie heard the words coming out of her mouth and hated saying every single one of them.

'God no, no, no, this isn't happening.' Darren squeezed his head. 'There has to be some kind of mistake. Not Finlay.'

'I'm so sorry,' Jessie responded, and watched a broken man crack a little more.

'Where is he?' Darren asked through his tears. 'I want to see him. I need to see my son.'

Dylan kneeled in front of Darren. 'Finlay is with the pathologist. He will let us know when you can see him. We will take good care of him, I promise, and I'll take you to him when it's time.'

Dylan's compassion almost broke Jessie's composure. Darren's face twitched in confusion, seeking out answers before digesting Dylan's words. He acknowledged him with a nod.

Jessie left Dylan sitting in silence, close to Darren, and made her way to Claire's hospital room. She looked in at the person who may have left her six-month-old son battered and broken, in a rucksack in Moncreiffe Wood. But when, and how? It didn't make any sense.

'DI Blake,' the uniformed officer stood as Jessie walked into the room.

Claire turned and sat bolt upright at the sound of his voice. 'Detective? Have you found him? Have you found my baby?'

'We have. I'm sorry to have to inform you that the body of a baby boy was found earlier this evening in Moncreiffe Wood.' Jessie paused, and steeled herself for what she had to say next. 'Claire Lucas, I am arresting you on suspicion of the murder of Finlay Lucas. You are not obliged to say anything, but anything you do say will be noted and may be used in evidence… Do you understand?'

'What are you talking about?' Claire shouted. 'I don't understand.'

'As you have not been discharged yet, an officer will stay with you until such time as we can transfer you to Perth Police Station for further questioning. Do you understand?'

'Darren? Where's Darren? He will tell you I didn't do this. Where's Finlay? I want to see my son!' Claire screamed, before crashing back down onto her pillow, thrashing and twisting with white foam frothing at the edges of her lips.

'I'll get help.' The uniformed officer rushed out of the room, leaving Jessie with more questions than answers as she looked on helplessly at her murder suspect having another massive seizure. A mass of bodies gathered round the bed and Jessie watched doctors administer diazepam to help bring an end to the thrashing and twitching. This was awful. Claire was clearly unwell, but Finlay was dead and Claire said she couldn't be sure, but that she might have done something to him. Jessie shivered. Having a suspect would normally help, but not this time.

The drugs took effect, and a few minutes later Claire came round. 'Where am I?' she asked, cradling her head in her hands. She glanced at Jessie. 'Who are you? Where's Darren?'

'I'm going to have to ask you to leave,' the doctor told her. 'Claire needs to rest.'

Jessie knew he was right, but there was no way her suspect was being left alone.

'That's fine, but my officer stays.' Jessie took the doctor aside. 'This woman is in custody, and does not leave this room without this man.'

'I'm not sure I can agree to that, Detective.'

'Would you rather we handcuffed her?' Jessie's gaze was firmly fixed, and the doctor blinked first. 'Not only that, but Darren Lucas does not enter this room. Is that clear?'

CHAPTER FORTY-FIVE

Jessie was so glad to kick off her boots – they'd been pinching her little toes all day. She was also relieved to feel the blast of heat from the hall radiator. Her boiler had evidently lived to fight another day. She grabbed the pile of post that had gathered on her doormat and flicked through it quickly before tossing it onto the hall table. Nothing that couldn't wait. No more unsolicited post from Dan, at least. The more she thought about that birthday card the angrier it made her. She dropped her bag onto the floor nearby and wandered barefoot into the kitchen, Smokey's body curling around her ankles as she moved. It was a miracle Jessie didn't trip over him more often, the way he weaved and clung close to her legs. His purring vibrated up her calf, soothing away the ache.

She wished he could calm the sick feeling in the pit of her stomach when she thought of Finlay's broken body. The team at the scene – Benito Capello and David Lyndhurst in particular – had been so tender, despite the unpleasant task they had to do. Respectful. The pathologist had already called her to confirm the time of the post-mortem the following morning.

Jessie needed a drink. She poured the last of a bottle of Chardonnay from the fridge into her wine glass, which never moved further than her draining board. She opened the drawer next to the fridge and pulled out two white envelopes, taking a large swig of her wine before putting the glass down and opening one of them. Slowly, she slid out the small square photo and laid it next to her glass. The tear that she'd allowed to build escaped and trickled down her cheek onto her jaw, before dripping onto her chest. She rubbed her thumb over her wet face, then sipped from her glass again. She kissed the tips of two fingers and pressed them against the image of an infant who looked like he was sleeping. The hospital had dressed him in a tiny white robe and taken this photo for Jessie to keep. She tidied the photo away and thought again of the scene.

Why had Finlay been dumped there? What had happened to him? Jessie just couldn't get her head around it. She would have to wait until the post-mortem results before forming too many theories. She also still had to figure out what Bridget Moran was hiding, because she was definitely hiding something. And what about Claire's pseudo-confession?

Smokey's cries for his supper briefly interrupted Jessie's train of thought. Swallowing down a large gulp of wine, she picked him up so that she could nuzzle his soft fur close to her cheek. His gentle purr made her cheekbone vibrate, and he drooled a little as he moved. Jessie could smell that he had been to her next-door neighbour's flat recently. Dave's flat smelled very feminine, even floral, for a man close to fifty years old who lived alone. She pulled a pouch of cat food from the cupboard above her microwave and bent down so that Smokey could jump out of her arms before she squeezed the contents into his dish.

'Here you go, greedy guts,' she said, placing his bowl on the floor, Smokey's face already in it before she could lift her hand away. She pressed the empty packet down into the already full bin, then tugged the bag out and tied it tight. 'Back in a minute, wee man.'

She stepped into her pumps and headed outside to her wheelie bin. She tutted at the blinking street light at the end of her drive. As she turned to go back inside, a sound made her stop and spin round. Not quite a crunch or a rustle. Just a sound that shouldn't be there, in the empty street. Her eyes scanned up and down the deserted road. Traffic in the distance briefly broke the silence, followed by the horn of a train crossing the bridge at the other end of town, echoing in the stillness of the late hour. The noise was closer. There it was again. She scurried quickly back up the stairs and into her flat, locking the door and snatching the chain across. *Probably just your imagination*, she tried to tell herself. *Dan wouldn't, would he? Not really?*

*

Dan's calves ached from crouching. He'd dared not breathe as he'd watched Jessie move so close to the conifer hedge he was hiding behind. Now wasn't the right time, but it was so good to see her again. She hadn't changed. She was so close he could almost touch her, but he didn't dare; not yet.

He peered up at Jessie's living room window, unable to decide what his overriding feeling really was. He still missed her, and he knew he'd done wrong. There was no doubt about that fact. But Dan had been punished. Surely everybody deserves a second chance, although it looked like it was going to take more decisive action to get her to listen. A cruel necessity, perhaps. She had ignored the birthday card, but he tried not to get too upset about that. Perhaps she wasn't ready. This was going to take time. Little steps start a great journey. One day he would win her back again.

What they had in the beginning was so good. They had passion. They shared a closeness Dan had never experienced until Jessie Blake crashed into his life. The beautiful Scots lass had brought light into his dark world when she'd joined the Met. He'd been so nervous about asking her out. Before Jessie, he'd had a reputation as a bit of a lady's man, flirting and leaving a string of one-night stands in his wake, but she was different. Their impulsive wedding in Las Vegas was the happiest day of Dan's life. Jessie had looked so beautiful, standing there next to him. He'd felt like the luckiest man alive. He had promised to take care of her, but he'd let her down.

Now, he planned to give it everything he had to make it up to her and win her back. If that meant playing a little dirty, then so be it. It would hopefully only take one firm nudge in the right direction to make Jessie listen, but Dan was sure that once they had opened up a dialogue she would finally understand. Finally appreciate how much he was hurting.

The echo of screeching laughter drifted towards him as he made his way down the street to the bike. He started up the engine and grabbed his helmet from the back. He smiled at two barely dressed teenage girls, who giggled at him as they passed. Dan watched them for a moment then became angry with himself for it. If he was going to show Jessie he had changed, then eyeing other women, fantasising about what he wanted to do to them, would have to stop. But that was going to prove difficult if young women made themselves so available to him like that. Didn't they realise what men like him were capable of? Didn't they care, or was it an invitation to play?

CHAPTER FORTY-SIX

Jessie edged closer to the mortuary door, wishing that something would happen to pull her back. Anything at all. She would be happy to believe in miracles right now. Perhaps some kind of natural disaster, maybe? She had appreciated David's call all the same. They had spoken after she'd left the hospital the night before, and the pathologist had sounded tired as he'd arranged for her to attend the post-mortem. The sooner she found out what had happened to Finlay would clearly be the best thing; for everyone. She took a deep breath and nudged the double doors open with her shoulder, but was surprised to see Benito waiting to greet her.

'Hello, is David around?'

Benito frowned. 'You haven't heard?'

'Heard what?' Jessie glanced around the room, thick with the smell of disinfectant and other assorted chemicals.

'David was admitted to hospital late last night with chest pains. I have been carrying out Finlay's post-mortem this morning. He didn't want it to wait, so he asked me to do it. He knew how important it was.' Benito was a qualified medical examiner, working with David for more experience.

Jessie clasped her hand to her mouth. 'Oh my God, is he OK? Has he had a heart attack? What ward have they admitted him to?'

Benito shrugged. 'I'm not sure right now, but he's OK, yes. He called me about half an hour ago to tell me to tell you not to worry.'

A soft smile crept across Jessie's lips. 'Typical David. Worrying about other people first. I'll give his wife a call after.' Jessie hesitated, thinking again of the task at hand.

Benito read her thoughts. 'I know.' He reassured her with a nod. 'Shall we get started?'

Jessie blew out the large breath that had stalked her throat. 'Yes.'

Benito handed her a suit and mask, then pinched a pair of gloves from the box before backing through the inner double doors. 'I'll see you in there.'

*

Jessie stared at Finlay's twisted body, illuminated by the harsh bright lights above the cold steel table. Again, Ryan's face flashed into her mind. His life had been stolen, too. By someone who was supposed to protect him. Jessie realised long ago that the pain of losing a child never leaves you. You just adapt and survive until moments like these remind you what you've lost. Then the agony threatens to overwhelm you again. She listened to Benito speak into his tape recorder, describing what she saw in front of her. The only things he couldn't capture were the emotion of it and the smell or, more accurately, the lack of that distinctive baby smell that all infants have. That was long gone. His physical description of broken, twisted limbs was painfully accurate. The first cut had been horrific, and it took everything Jessie had to control her urge to run from it. She couldn't let Finlay down. She had to put her own feelings to one side. He needed her to be strong. She had to endure. She swallowed back every urge to run out of there and never go back.

Benito raised Finlay's right leg slightly. 'You see the edge of this bone? Where it's fracture is brittle and crumbly, you could say, rather than a clean cut.'

Jessie glanced down at it and nodded. 'Yes.' She barely managed the whisper before coughing to clear her throat.

'The fact that the bone looks crumbly indicates this fracture occurred after death.'

Jessie's head snapped up. '*After* death?'

Benito nodded. 'The bones become brittle post-mortem, so yes, all these breaks happened after his death.'

Jessie was perplexed. 'Have you ever seen anything like this before? So many fractures, I mean, caused after death?' Jessie couldn't take her eyes off the tiny body. So many thoughts were spinning in her mind.

Benito nodded again. 'Once before. Many years ago.'

'How, and why?'

'It was a baby who'd passed away from sudden infant death syndrome, or cot death, as it's more commonly known. The father shook his daughter so hard, trying to rouse her in his panic, that the little bones broke under the pressure.' His sombre face held hers. 'She looked a lot like Finlay.'

'So is that what's happened here?'

'I can't be certain how the post-mortem injuries occurred, and I'll have to wait for some test results, but yes – I think Finlay died as a result of sudden infant death syndrome.'

'But,' Jessie tried to find the words, 'why the hell does a cot death victim end up in a rucksack hidden in Moncreiffe Wood?'

CHAPTER FORTY-SEVEN

Gertrude Laing swept around the dining table in the chapel house kitchen, wondering how such a well-dressed, tidy man could make such a mess when he ate. She glanced out of the window to see Bridget Moran moving quickly from the bus stop across the road towards the chapel. She lifted her hand to wave, but her gesture was abruptly ignored, which was unusual. Bridget had a reputation for being aloof, but she and Gertrude were good friends. Well, as good and close as Bridget allowed people to get, that was. She'd made Bridget many a cup of hot sweet tea while they chatted about their lives. She figured Bridget must have been distracted, and thought nothing more of it as she returned to her chores. She swept the collected crumbs and flicked them into the small compost bucket that sat on the kitchen window ledge, then brushed the mess on the worktop into her hand and flicked it in beside them, wiping the excess on her apron. She tugged the bin bag and tied it tightly before heading outside with it. Raised voices caught her attention, and she stopped to listen before Bridget charged past her on the pavement, her face red.

'Bridget, is everything OK?' she called out, startled, but Bridget surged past without so much as a glance in her direction. 'Bridget?' she tried again. 'What's happened?'

Gertrude was worried. She'd never seen Bridget look so scared, but was helpless to do anything as she watched her friend retreat down the road. Gertrude was left scratching her head in confusion, and returned to the hall only to overhear Father McKinnon on the phone. She quickly realised it was Bishop Menzies on the other end of the line. It took her a moment to process what she was hearing, but when she did, she listened on. She covered her mouth, fearing Father McKinnon would hear the rapid breaths she was trying to stifle.

What did he mean, he couldn't handle this alone?

CHAPTER FORTY-EIGHT

'Morning, Jess,' Dylan said as he walked into the office, relieved to get inside. The weather was showing no sign of abating.

'Get yourself a coffee and come into my office as soon as, will you?'

'Sure thing,' Dylan unzipped his jacket and tossed it across the back of his chair then followed Jessie into her office. The coffee could wait, judging by her expression.

'Close the door,' she told him without looking up.

'What's the latest?' Dylan probed.

'I attended Finlay's PM first thing this morning. The indications are that his fractures were inflicted after death. Benito says he is still trying to establish definitive cause of death for us—'

'After death?' Dylan cut in, scratching his cheek. 'I didn't expect that.'

'Yes, I know, you and me both. Benito has a theory. I'm just waiting on him to confirm it.'

'What about Claire? Is she part of his theory? What do we make of the confession?'

What *did* Jessie make of it? She had no idea.

'She's been arrested pending further investigation. I've got someone with her at the hospital until she's fit to be discharged. The mother and sister are hiding something, though, aren't they? What do you make of them, Dylan?'

Dylan shrugged. 'It's weird. I get an odd vibe off Bridget Moran. I don't like it.'

'I'm glad to hear you say that, because I do too.'

Jessie's phone buzzed against the desk. She answered straight away.

'Benito, hey, how are you?'

Jessie's head drooped forward while she listened and sighed. *Perhaps it was better for Finlay that it happened this way*, she thought. That was a blessing at least. It was unlikely he had suffered. Not that she supposed that would be much comfort to his family. Finlay was and would always be gone from their lives. She thought of Darren's broken expression when he'd told her what Claire confessed to him. But Claire's confession just couldn't be possible now, could it?

'Results of the post-mortem?' Dylan suggested, his eyebrows raised as Jessie put the phone down.

Jessie nodded. 'Benito has confirmed his theory and initial findings. Cause of death is sudden infant death syndrome.'

Dylan listened in disbelief. 'Cot death? But then why was he dumped?'

CHAPTER FORTY-NINE

Maggie stood under the hot water, her face directly beneath the steaming spray. She ran her fingers over her stomach and wondered when the pregnancy would start to show. She couldn't wait to show it off. She turned and allowed the water to flatten down her long blonde hair, then cascade over her shoulders and roll off her breasts. She was tired but she was happy. Happier than she'd felt for a long time, despite little Finlay being missing. Surely they'd find him soon, though? Then, once Claire was feeling a bit better, she and Darren could talk to her.

She grabbed her towel from the back of the shower cubicle and tied it around herself. She flopped down onto the edge of her bed and scrolled through her phone. Her heart leaped to see a text from the letting agent, but it sank again when Calum opened and shut the front door. She would have to read it later.

'I'm in the bedroom,' Maggie called out, rubbing the towel over her head.

She heard Calum shout something back to her but she wasn't really listening. Something about getting some shopping in? She wasn't sure. He was a good man, and Maggie knew she should feel guilty about all the plans she was making. Plans that didn't include him. His voice echoed along the hall once again. This time he said he was putting the kettle on and did she want anything. Maggie sighed.

'Yes, go on then. I'll be through in a minute, thanks.'

She stared at her reflection in her dresser mirror. She looked as tired as she felt, but the midwife assured her it would pass. As would the nausea. As long as she was getting plenty of rest and eating properly, both she and the baby would be just fine. Calum's voice interrupted her thoughts again, this time insisting she should have a sandwich. He was making one. What did she fancy. Maggie closed her eyes and sighed.

'Anything, really. Surprise me,' she shouted back. 'Make it cheese and pickle, actually. I quite fancy cheese, thanks.'

'What did you say?'

Maggie jumped when Calum's face peered round the bedroom door. She hadn't heard his footsteps.

'Jeez! You scared me half to death. Don't creep up on folk like that.'

Calum flopped down next to her and began kissing her neck. 'You smell good,' he murmured.

Maggie pulled away. She could see exactly what direction Calum wanted this to go in and that was the last thing she wanted.

'Not now, babe,' she whispered.

'Are you sure?' Calum tested, and continued to place soft, nibbling kisses on Maggie's shoulder until she rose from the edge of the bed.

'I said not now,' she snapped, and moved away. 'I have to get dressed. I have to be somewhere. I'm going to check on Claire.'

'You want me to come?' Calum asked. 'I don't have a client until twelve.'

Maggie smiled and shook her head. That was definitely not what she wanted.

CHAPTER FIFTY

Darren's eyes blinked open and for a wonderful few seconds his life hadn't changed irreversibly. Claire would be lying next to him, her messy blonde hair strung across her face as she slept with her mouth open, a hint of a snort escaping when she inhaled. Finlay would be sleeping in his cot in the room next door. His blanket would be crumpled at the bottom after he'd kicked it off in the night. But none of that would ever happen again.

If he hadn't been screwing Maggie, if he had been there at home with Claire and Finlay, this wouldn't be happening. His life would still be good. Yes, it had been hard, but it was good. Darren tossed back the duvet and sat up at the edge of the bed, rubbing warmth into his goose-pimpled arms. It was already lunchtime. He couldn't believe he'd slept so long, but after getting home from the hospital at such a late hour he shouldn't have been surprised. Even after being told of Claire's arrest, he hadn't wanted to leave the hospital. He'd sat outside her room until the nurse on duty suggested it might be a good idea for him to get some rest. He was so deep in shock that he'd only thought to contact his dad, and Claire's parents, once he'd got home. He couldn't remember what he'd said to any of them other than that he needed to be alone. A gentle tap on his bedroom door startled him, and he watched it swing slowly open.

'Maggie, for Christ's sake, you scared the life out of me. When did you… I mean, *how* did you get in?'

'I still have your spare key, remember?'

Darren had forgotten that, and they had Maggie and Calum's key. It's what best friends do, isn't it? Maggie tossed her jacket onto the end of the bed, then sat close to Darren without speaking. She reached for his hand and gripped it. Darren lifted his head and turned to face her. He heard every beat of his heart in the silence between them.

'Finlay's dead. They found his body yesterday evening. And Claire's been arrested.' He said the words almost without emotion, as if he was describing the plot of a film. He felt so numb.

Maggie was quiet for a while, seemingly trying to process the news. 'I'm so sorry,' she eventually whispered, and gripped his hand a little tighter.

Darren snatched his hand out of hers and took hold of her cheeks. He pressed his lips firmly on hers. His heart ached. He didn't break away until he became aware of a persistent knocking on the front door. He moved quickly to answer it.

'Come in, come in.' He held the door wide open for Jessie and Isla Wilde. 'When can I see him? DC Logan promised he would take me to him.'

'I know,' Jessie agreed. 'PC Wilde and I will take you to see Finlay this morning.' She thought it was a good idea if Isla came too. She glanced over Darren's shoulder to see a young woman walk out of the bedroom. Jessie did her best to hide her repulsion. *How could he?* she wondered.

Darren caught her glance. 'Er, this is Maggie. McBride. She's a close friend of Claire's… of ours. She came to see how I was. Anyway, I'll go and put some clothes on.' Darren turned, but Jessie interrupted him.

'Can we talk first, Darren?'

'Yes, come through.' He grabbed a sweater from the back of the sofa and slouched down. He scratched at his face and sniffed, clearly dreading what was to come.

It was clear to Jessie that Maggie felt awkward, but that didn't bother her. She deserved to feel that discomfort.

'I have the results of the post-mortem.' Jessie took a seat close to Darren on the sofa.

Darren surged to the edge of his seat. 'What happened to him?'

Jessie's eyes drifted briefly from Darren to Maggie, then right back at him. 'Finlay passed away from cot death, Darren. Our pathologist was able to come to this conclusion after ruling out everything else.'

Jessie wished Darren would say something. Instead he just stared at her, a look of utter confusion on his face. Maggie clasped both hands across her mouth. When he did start to talk, it was a jumble of words in search of a sentence.

'But… that's not… I mean… why… how can that be? How is that even possible?'

'I know this must be confusing for you.'

Darren stood, then stared at Maggie, now searching her face for answers. Finding none, he left the room.

'Darren,' Maggie murmured, then tried to follow him. 'Where are you going?'

'Leave him,' Jessie urged. 'Just give him a minute.'

Maggie sat on the empty armchair by the door and lifted one of Finlay's little vests from the arm. She ran her fingers across the garment, then held it to her cheek.

'I can't believe this is happening.' She spoke through her tears.

Before Jessie could respond, Darren's voice called out to her.

'OK, I'm ready.' He reappeared in the doorway. 'I want to see my son.'

CHAPTER FIFTY-ONE

Jessie was reluctant to allow Maggie to join them, but didn't want to seem cruel by telling her no. Darren needed all the support he could get, and Claire wasn't able to come. Whether Jessie condoned their relationship or not wasn't important. She lifted her hand to acknowledge Benito, waving to them from David's office. He made his way down to let the group inside.

'Hello, Mr Lucas, I'm Dr Capello. I'm so sorry for your loss.'

Darren didn't answer. He clutched Maggie's hand in his and concentrated on putting one foot in front of the other. His legs trembled so much and his heart fluttered in such a disorganised pattern he wondered if he might be having a heart attack. He squeezed Maggie's hand as they got closer to a large window set into the wall of the hallway. *Finlay is in there.* A pair of navy-blue curtains were pulled across on the inside. He stopped suddenly. His chest felt like it was trapped in a vice.

'Hang on, please.' His lips were so dry. He ran his tongue over them but that too was dry. 'Can I just have a minute?'

'Of course,' Benito stopped next to him. 'We will go at your pace. We don't have to hurry.'

Benito opened the door to a room next to them and switched on a lamp in the corner. 'We can sit in here for a while.'

Jessie knew right away what this room was, with its low lighting and comfortable sofa and chairs. It had a kettle and even a mini-fridge, where she assumed they kept the fresh milk. The temperature was different, too. It was warmer, much warmer than the hall. It was designed for comfort. The kind of comfort grieving relatives crave. Darren allowed Maggie's hand to fall from his as PC Wilde placed a cup of water into his trembling hand. She laid her own hand over his to support him.

'Thank you,' he murmured, before walking across to the window and peering out at the rest of the world, carrying on as usual. There was even a bin lorry in the distance, overtaking a bus by a set of traffic lights where people waited on either side to cross. It was amazing, the detail he picked out in that moment. The teenagers in school uniform, who he assumed should actually be in school. The elderly man who narrowly avoided colliding with them on his motorised scooter. Darren sipped the last of the water. It had done nothing to moisten his dry mouth, but he appreciated the officer's gesture. He set the cup on the worktop next to the kettle and took a deep breath. Part of him wanted to put this off for ever, but another part of him wanted to discover they were wrong. That it wasn't Finlay at all. He turned to face the door.

'I'm ready.'

'Do you want me to come in with you?' Maggie stepped forward.

Darren shook his head at her offer. This was something he wanted to do alone. The trembling in his legs remained with every step he took behind Benito, who stopped just outside a white door.

Jessie watched them walk down the hall. Benito's compassion was beautiful. Isla Wilde laid her arm around Maggie's shoulders when it became clear she too was struggling. She was human, after all.

'Is he in there?' Darren whispered, and rested first his fingers then his head on the door. 'Is that where Finlay is?'

CHAPTER FIFTY-TWO

Jessie's mind drifted back over the day. Darren Lucas. Benito Capello. Maggie McBride. Every one of them invaded her mind. As well as Ryan. She'd thought about him so much these past few days. Part of Jessie knew how Darren felt, and Dianne, but her circumstances were very different. She'd needed that glass of wine last night. It was strange that Smokey hadn't come in for breakfast this morning. She'd stuck a note through Dave's door, asking him to feed him if she was late getting home. Dave was a lifesaver in that respect.

'Good afternoon, ladies,' Dylan said as he entered the incident room, smiling when he spotted PC Isla Wilde sitting across from Jessie as he let the door swing out of his grip. 'How are we all?'

'Fine, fine, come on in, join the party,' Jessie teased, also trying to break the dark mood.

'Hello again, Isla. Good to see you.'

'Hi Dylan. Good to see you too,' Isla responded.

'I've asked Isla to join us on this. We now have a specialist family liaison officer in place, and she's been closer to the Lucases than we have. I thought having her on board might help.'

'Good idea,' Dylan agreed with a smile. 'Welcome to the dream team.'

Isla couldn't stifle the little chuckle that pushed its way out of her mouth, then blushed, fearing Jessie would think her behaviour inappropriate. She needn't have worried. Jessie continued as if it hadn't happened.

'As you already know, the PM shows Finlay Lucas died from cot death.'

Dylan raised his hands in exasperation. 'I'm struggling to get my head around this, I have to be honest with you.'

'The mystery has deepened, I'll give you that.' Jessie shrugged and stared at Finlay's smiling baby photo on the board. 'There's something about Theresa, and the Moran family in general, that irks me. Claire, too. What the hell is that partial confession about? We now know she didn't kill him. We're going back to the McCabes', too. Why was their van in the street? It might be a perfectly plausible reason, but until we talk to them again we won't know. We've left that thread hanging long enough – Isla, I want you over there today.'

Isla nodded. 'Sure thing.' She took a deep breath and tentatively added her thoughts, despite her growing anxiety. She was keen to impress Jessie. 'Claire isn't very well – mentally, I mean – is she? Is her confession even admissible? I mean, she confessed to Darren, allegedly.'

Jessie spun to face her. 'Allegedly?'

'Allegedly,' Isla repeated with a shrug. 'We only have Darren's say-so. She hasn't been interviewed yet.'

Before Jessie could comment further, her phone buzzed in her pocket. 'Hold that thought,' she told them while she answered it.

'Well spotted,' Dylan whispered to Isla. 'I'd better be careful. You'll be after my job next.'

Isla smiled. *Not your job, but CID for sure*, she thought. Isla had wanted the transfer for a while, and this opportunity was too important to mess up. This was her chance to shine, and she was going to grab it with both hands. She swallowed down her nerves.

'Right, guys,' Jessie began. 'Claire Lucas is downstairs. She's been discharged and transferred over, and we have extra time to question her.'

'Brilliant,' Dylan exclaimed. 'Time to hear it from the horse's mouth.'

'Or not,' Isla added.

'Indeed, or not,' Dylan smiled. 'You're absolutely right.'

Jessie felt a little guilty that she could only take one of them in with her to the interview room. Isla was so enthusiastic, and had a detective's instinct; she reminded Jessie a little of herself. But she wasn't officially part of the team yet. *Your time will come*, Jessie thought.

'Isla, before you head out to the garage, could you do a bit of digging on the McCabes? Anything and everything. Thanks.'

'No problem.' Isla pulled her chair closer to the desk and logged into the laptop in front of her.

'Dylan, you're with me. Let's see what Claire has to say.'

CHAPTER FIFTY-THREE

Darren's legs burned from running. His cheeks stung in the freezing temperatures. His skin was pitted purplish-red from the icy wind that had increased in speed and ferocity in the past couple of hours. Those four walls had been killing him. Squeezing him tight until he was suffocating. A flurry of white flakes peppered his hair. This was a living nightmare. He stared into the window of McCabe's Garage, unable to make out who the figures were that were obscured by the condensation on the front window, before making his way across the bridge towards Moncreiffe Wood. His chest felt tight against the bitter cold as he sucked in as much air as he could. He couldn't stop.

Until he came to a tree. *That* tree. It was identical to countless others in the wood except for one heartbreaking truth. A small piece of police tape fluttered in the gusting wind, left behind accidentally by forensics officers when they were finished. Darren stood completely still, listening to the wind blow through the trees that surrounded him. He felt so small. So exhausted. So numb. What the hell had he done? How could he have been so stupid? But it was done now. He would just have to live with the consequences. They all would.

Tim McCabe was still reeling from what he'd been asked to do when he saw Darren Lucas run past the garage. An image of Theresa's frantic gait shot into his head. At least Darren was dressed for the weather, and had on his running shoes. Tim felt bad for the man, he really did. He thought about Theresa, too. He should have gone after her the other day. It was the least he should have done, considering their history.

The sound of a car pulling onto the forecourt brought him out of himself. His eyes widened when he saw the young female police officer getting out of a patrol car and walking towards the garage door.

'What the hell?' he muttered under his breath, then cursed Peter's absence once again.

*

PC Isla Wilde pushed open the door. She was more nervous about visiting the garage after her little bit of digging into the family back at the station. They'd been loosely linked to a few previous investigations, and some social media trawling had thrown up more questions. Blake and Logan were also still pretty sure the McCabe brothers had been threatening Martin Lucas. All that would have to wait, though. *Just get some answers about this van*, she told herself.

'Hello, anyone in?' she called out as she moved through the workshop. She knocked on the door that led to the back of the garage, then waited. She listened, then hammered again. This time louder, and longer. There was definitely movement inside, but nobody was coming to answer her. She banged one last time with the palm of her hand, gaining a much better response.

'Hang on, I'm coming. There's no need to break my door down.' Mike McCabe seemed taken aback by the sight of the officer standing in the doorway and quickly halted the nervous grin that was growing on his lips. 'Hello, Officer. I didn't realise it was the police. I'm sorry. You'd better come in. I'm Mike, the owner.'

'Thank you, I'm PC Isla Wilde.' She followed him into the small garage office. 'Your company van was spotted in the vicinity of

Kintillo Road around the time Finlay Lucas went missing. Were you driving it, Mr McCabe?'

'No, that would have been one of my boys. You'll be wanting to know if they saw anything suspicious?'

'Of course,' Isla replied. 'Are either of them here?' She glanced pointedly at two mobile phones lying on the desk.

Mike frowned. 'No, sorry. Peter's ill today, and Tim's out on a job.' He nodded at the phones on the desk. 'Look – I can't even call him. Stupid boy has left his phone here. Do you want me to pass on a message, or something?'

Isla was disappointed. She had hoped to be able to bring something more concrete back to DI Blake. The two mobile phones had been explained away, but that didn't account for the two mugs waiting next to the kettle. She wasn't sure what the McCabes were hiding, but she wanted to do some more digging before telling Jessie.

'Nah, it's fine. I'll come back later. Don't worry about telling them I was here. I'm sure I'll catch up with them.'

Mike watched her get back into her patrol car and drive off.

'You can come out now. She's gone,' he called out in the direction of the toilet.

CHAPTER FIFTY-FOUR

Jessie didn't think Claire Lucas looked well enough to be discharged from hospital, but she was prepared to trust the doctors on it. This couldn't wait. Claire's father had arranged for his solicitor, Michael Rogers, to go to the station as soon as he'd heard. Michael was a friend of the family's from church, too, apparently. Jessie knew Rogers' firm – they didn't come cheap. Clearly Phil Moran wanted the best for daddy's wee girl. Rogers shuffled papers on the table as Jessie and Dylan took their seats opposite Claire, who kept her head down. She didn't even lift it to confirm her name and that she understood why she was there.

'I'd like to start by asking you, Claire, did you tell Darren that you'd done something to Finlay?' Jessie waited for an answer.

Michael Rogers whispered into Claire's ear.

'Claire,' Jessie repeated. 'Did you tell him that you'd done something to Finlay?'

Claire lifted her head, then shook it. 'I don't remember.'

Rogers whispered in her ear again, much to Jessie's irritation. Was that part of their training? The art of the perfect whisper?

'Do you know what happened to your son, Claire?'

'He died,' Claire said, without looking at her.

'How did he die?'

This time Claire looked Jessie in the eye. 'I don't know.'

'Would you like me to tell you?' Jessie continued, but Michael Rogers interrupted.

'Where are you going with this, Detective? This seems highly irregular to me. I insist on a break, so I can consult with my client.'

Claire shook her head, her eyes wide and searching. She grabbed for Jessie's hand. 'No, I don't want a break. Tell me, please, what happened? Nobody has told me anything. Not even Darren.'

Jessie shot a glance at Rogers, then allowed her eyes to drift back to Claire. She patted the back of Claire's hand. 'Post-mortem results indicate that Finlay passed away from sudden infant death syndrome. Do you know what that is?'

Michael Rogers was furious. 'Detective Inspector Blake, I really don't think—'

'Shut up!' Claire stood up and screamed in his face, then spun back to Jessie. 'What do you mean? Of course I know what that is. Cot death. How is that even possible? Who took him?'

'I'm sorry, Claire,' Jessie probed. 'That's what we need to find out. How did Finlay's body end up in Moncreiffe Wood?'

'I don't know.' Claire fell back into the chair and sobbed, then wiped her face with the sleeve of her cardigan before clutching her head in her hands. She started swaying from side to side. 'I can't remember.' She balled her hand into a fist and started hitting her forehead. 'Why can't I remember?'

'I think it's time my client had a break,' Rogers insisted.

Reluctantly, Jessie had to agree with him.

CHAPTER FIFTY-FIVE

Jessie swallowed down a couple of paracetamol in the hope of relieving the headache that was beginning to grow.

'What did you make of that, then?' Dylan asked, setting a mug of strong coffee down in front of his boss. 'Strange answer, "I can't remember", don't you think?' He sipped from his mug and looked between Jessie and Isla, who'd filled them in on her fruitless trip to the garage. She'd also told them she planned to keep looking into the McCabes.

Jessie rubbed at her temples, cursing the pain in her head. She prayed it wouldn't take the pills long to kick in.

'What's your take on all this, Dylan?' Jessie was curious. 'What do you make of Claire?'

'I've been thinking about the epilepsy,' he announced.

'Yes, and?' Sometimes her DC would benefit from getting to the point. Maybe that was the headache talking, though.

'Seizures and blackouts. Memory loss, even. Perhaps she genuinely doesn't remember and *fears* she has done something.'

Isla Wilde remembered something a childhood friend once told her, and jumped in with it. 'When I was a bairn, I had a pal who had a big brother with epilepsy.'

'Go on,' Jessie invited.

'Katie's brother used to have blackouts. Periods when he just couldn't remember what he'd done. She said they thought his epilepsy caused it. He had memory loss and a really bad headache after a seizure, too. Temporal lobe epilepsy could explain what's happened.'

Jessie felt like she was getting a clearer picture of Claire Lucas. She'd lived with epilepsy most of her life, which, if Darren was to be believed, was under control. But that was the key question. Could Darren be believed? Could Claire? Had any of that family been telling the truth? The one thing that can't lie is physical evidence, which showed Finlay's death to have been a sad, unpreventable tragedy. But what happened to his body afterwards was very much preventable. Someone removed him from his cot, broke his bones and dumped his body like it was a piece of rubbish. Jessie needed to find out who that person was. Or, indeed, people.

Without enough evidence to hold her, Claire had been bailed pending further investigation. It served no purpose to hold her in a cold police cell. She had no recollection of confessing to Darren, and there was no evidence against her. The young woman might be fit enough to leave hospital, but she was still weak. Jessie wasn't an ogre. She wasn't going to keep her there just for the sake of it, no matter how much the sight of Finlay's broken body distressed her.

'Wilde, you're with me. We're going to have another chat with Bridget Moran. See if she's ready to shed any light on Theresa's illness, and whether what Tim McCabe saw has anything to do with what happened to Finlay.'

PC Wilde grabbed her jacket. She wanted to punch the air in victory, delighted that Jessie was taking her and not Dylan this time, but she resisted.

'Dylan, I'd like you to go back to Father McKinnon. See if you can shake some information loose. Hopefully he's had time to think about what withholding information might mean for him.'

If Father McKinnon was willing to tell them what Bridget Moran had spoken to him about, his information could fill in the missing pieces. Before she could leave, the phone on her desk rang.

'DI Blake,' she answered, while trying to push her arm into her jacket sleeve. She waved at Dylan to wait a minute as she took in the information from the call. She frowned and dropped back into her chair. 'OK, thank you.' Jessie put down the phone. 'Curiouser and curiouser.'

'What's happened?' Dylan asked.

'Dianne Davidson has been rushed to hospital after a suspected overdose. Colin just rang from A and E. He says he needs to talk to me. He said it was urgent.'

CHAPTER FIFTY-SIX

Gertrude Laing dusted the top shelf of the pine Welsh dresser in the kitchen, taking extra care around Father McKinnon's display of antique toby jugs. His set from the First World War were his favourite. His Henry VIII was the most recent addition; he had been so proud of himself when he'd haggled the price down, leaving the antiques dealer in Abernyte scratching his head over how he'd let it go so easily. Something about the dog collar influenced his decision, most likely. The doorbell chime echoed through the hall. Gertrude wiped her hand on her apron and walked towards the front door, knowing Father McKinnon was taking confession this evening. She wondered if Bridget Moran would be there again. She seemed to have been there permanently recently.

'Hello,' Gertrude held the door wide for Dylan. 'Come on in, Detective. I'll call Father McKinnon for you, but I can't say when he will get the message –he doesn't take his phone into confession.'

'That's fine, I'll wait for him,' Dylan answered. 'If that's OK?'

'Of course, go through.'

Dylan pushed open Paul McKinnon's office door and moved towards the bookcase. Some of the volumes on its shelves must be over a century old, he decided. He peered closely at a copy of the Bible that looked even older than that. He lifted his head when he heard Father McKinnon's shoes on the wood floor of the hall.

'Detective, hello again. What can I help you with?' he held out his hand, then sat down behind his desk. 'Please take a seat.'

'Thank you,' Dylan answered with a smile.

'Terrible business.' Father McKinnon shook his head. 'I've told Bridget and Phil the church doors are always open to them, and Claire and Darren too, of course.'

'Yes, it's a very difficult time for them all.'

Father McKinnon scratched at the two-day growth on his chin. 'What is it you think I can help you with?'

Dylan noticed that the priest looked nervous. The pink flush on his cheeks increased and he seemed unable to sit still. He crossed and uncrossed his legs several times, on top of shuffling his feet more than once or twice under the desk.

'I believe you've heard Bridget Moran's confession since Finlay went missing. Is that right? I wondered if you'd seen her again today, or yesterday perhaps.'

He shook his head and looked away. 'I'm sorry, no. I haven't seen Bridget since we both saw you and your colleague at the chapel. Not since little Finlay was found.'

That had to be true, but Dylan sensed he was holding something back. A bit of appropriately placed pressure might release his burden.

'Can you tell me what she discussed with you during confession that day?'

Father McKinnon's focus returned and he looked shocked. 'You know I can't disclose what's said in confession.'

Dylan's fingers rubbed across his cheek while he considered his next move. He wished he'd had time to shave that morning – he was beginning to look like a hobo.

'What if I told you that any information you gave me could help shed light on what happened to little Finlay Lucas? Wouldn't you like to help?'

Father McKinnon sat right back in the tall-backed leather chair and pinched his fingers together before tapping them on his lips. On this he could be adamant. He was unwavering on the importance of confession to his faith. He had to protect his congregation. There was so much at stake, after all, and God had given him the responsibility when he took his vows thirty years ago. His career in banking in the mid-1980s had shown Paul what his true path was. He was sure he'd seen the devil himself in that world.

'I'm sorry, but you don't seem to understand how important the sanctity of the confessional is. It's something I cannot break. Under any circumstances.' He glanced towards the Bible on his desk. 'Even these.'

Jessie was not going to be pleased, and Dylan hoped they wouldn't have to take the matter further with Father McKinnon. He seemed like a genuinely nice bloke. Committed to his faith and to his congregation. Dylan wished he would remember that Finlay was also one of his flock.

CHAPTER FIFTY-SEVEN

The hospital wanted Dianne to stay in for observation, especially after finding so many of her antidepressants in the vomit she'd produced. They told her how lucky she was that Colin had arrived home when he did. Lucky was not the overriding feeling she'd had when she woke in the back of that ambulance. First Stacey. Now Finlay. *How many more babies were they going to rip from her arms.*

Colin paced up and down outside the cubicle curtain. The on-call psychiatrist had told him he would refer her for an emergency mental health assessment, but even that could take more than a week. Would there be enough support for her at home until then? Colin knew what that meant. It meant they didn't want to admit her to the mental health unit unless they absolutely had to, because resources were so limited. He didn't think she really wanted to die. Dianne was hurting, and it was her way of crying out for help, of stopping the pain. That was how she explained it the last time. She didn't want to leave him. She just wanted the pain to stop. The grief was physical as well as emotional. Every part of his wife's body had ached for Stacey. Now it was aching for Finlay, too.

*

Jessie hadn't long entered A&E when Colin Davidson spotted her and approached. The look on his face said it all. The strain of the past few days was evident in the dark circles under his eyes. It was like their own child had died, not Claire and Darren's.

'Colin, how is she?' Jessie asked.

He shrugged, then led Jessie away from Dianne's cubicle. 'Not good. Can I talk to you?'

Jessie pursed her lips and nodded. 'Of course, yes – that's why we're here.' She turned to Isla and handed her some change. 'Get a couple of coffees, will you?'

Colin moved towards the row of chairs by the entrance and sat down.

'What's up, Colin?'

He slid forward in his seat and tucked his head in his hands, then lifted it up to face her.

'Look, it might be nothing at all, but I think you need to know about the arguments.'

'Arguments?' Jessie's eyes widened.

'Claire and Darren, they've been having terrible rows. I've heard Claire screaming, really screaming.'

Jessie was alarmed. 'Do you think Darren ever got physical?'

Colin shook his head firmly. 'No, no, quite the opposite, Detective. She seems to have such a temper on her, Claire. I wouldn't like to be on the wrong side of it. I hate to think she's…'

Jessie knew what he wanted to say but couldn't. It was unthinkable to her, too, but if Benito was right, Claire wasn't responsible for cot death, no matter how bad a temper she had. The violent battering of his dead body, perhaps, but not his death.

'Could you ever hear what they were arguing about?'

A small voice, barely audible over the clattering and chaos of the department, called Colin's name.

'I have to go.' Colin stood and left Jessie scratching her head. Still no clearer. If anything, her confusion deepened.

'Here you go,' Wilde smiled and handed over a plastic cup of coffee. 'Watch yourself, it's hot.'

'Shit, you're not wrong.' Jessie put the cup down on an empty seat and sucked her burned thumb.

'What did Davidson want?'

'He says Darren and Claire argue, I mean really argue, proper screaming fights, and he suggested that Claire possibly gets violent with Darren.'

Jessie struggled to see Claire's small frame being able to cause Darren much damage, but she knew domestic violence wasn't about that. It was about control. She shrugged. So many questions. She glanced at Isla as they carefully sipped their scalding coffees. She inwardly applauded PC Wilde's enthusiasm, and knew she'd make a good detective one day. Before she could start planning the PC's potential place on her team, she received a text. A number she didn't recognise. That made Jessie feel uneasy.

'Everything OK?' PC Wilde asked, seeing the DI frown.

'Yes, it's fine, don't worry,' Jessie told her. 'You get off. See you tomorrow.' Jessie's eyes dropped straight back to her phone. She had to open the message, didn't she?

I'm sorry it had to come to this.

Had to come to what? What the hell did that mean? Jessie knew instinctively that the message was from Dan. She feared what her ex-husband meant. After suffering years of abuse at his hands, she knew he was capable of almost anything.

CHAPTER FIFTY-EIGHT

Jessie felt like she was no closer to learning the truth about Finlay's death, or more accurately, what had happened to him after he died. It was more the *why* that bothered Jessie. If he'd died in his cot, who'd moved his body, and why do that? Why had he suffered so many post-mortem injuries? Why compound the already awful tragedy? Jessie increasingly saw Theresa Moran as the key to this whole mess – she'd been seen at the house on the day Finlay disappeared, and near the woodland where his body was found – but she was unfit to be spoken to. Bridget Moran must know more about what Theresa had seen and done that day than she'd let on.

Rather than drive home straight away, she decided to have one last try with Father McKinnon, alone. Dylan had texted to let her know that the priest had played his questions with a straight bat, but she refused to give up, and would seek legal advice on the subject if she had to. She wanted to avoid that, though. She also wanted to avoid her flat for a little while longer, and any potential follow-ups to Dan's text awaiting her there.

St Mark's Chapel had a handy location, just on the edge of the centre of Perth and on a bus route that had services every fifteen minutes. No excuse to miss Mass. She turned into Melville Street, and cursed the fact that she couldn't find a space outside the building. Instead she found herself halfway along Balhousie Avenue before she could find a place to park up. It was dark now, but the snow that lay thick on the North Inch, reflecting the large moon that was already up. She walked past the derelict St Mark's school building, pondering how sad it was that such a sturdy structure had been left abandoned for so long.

As she walked up to the church, she was surprised to see the lights on in the chapel – she'd thought to catch McKinnon at home rather than in the church itself. She tried the door, but it was locked. She thought that strange, if the priest was inside. She hammered her palm on the door and listened for movement, but when she got no response she moved down the drive towards the chapel house door. She rang the doorbell and listened to the chime echo through the listed building. When she got no answer, she walked around to the back door and knocked again. This time she heard a loud crash, like a glass or cup smashing on the hard floor. She tried the door handle and it gave immediately. She called out as she cautiously entered the property, which was in darkness.

'Father McKinnon, it's Detective Inspector Blake.'

She switched on the hall light, realising that what she thought was a back door actually led into a small utility room that had been added to the building sometime in the 1980s. She pushed open the door between it and the main house, which led into a large oval kitchen. In the darkness she heard gurgling. *Water draining slowly down a blocked sink?* She switched on the kitchen light and gasped.

'Father McKinnon!' She pulled out her phone to call an ambulance.

She watched him try to speak as she gave details of their location to the emergency services. Blood was seeping from several stab wounds to his chest, trickles of blood also dribbling from the sides of his mouth. That had been the source of the gurgling sound. Jessie dropped to her knees and grabbed a tea towel from the back of a chair, narrowly avoiding the smashed glass scattered around them. She pressed hard on the largest of the wounds, which oozed onto her hand, quickly covering it completely.

'Hang in there, help is on its way.'

She was torn between telling him to relax and keep his strength and begging him to tell her what the hell had happened. He struggled to talk through the blood travelling up his throat, coughing to clear his airway. She watched the remaining colour drain from his face while his blood poured onto the hard wood floor of the kitchen. His attacker couldn't be all that far away. The speed with which the blood was leaving his body suggested the attack couldn't have happened that long ago, otherwise he would have died long before help arrived. As it was, Jessie feared he wouldn't make it. He gave one long, horrific gurgle before his eyes rolled back until all Jessie could see was the white. He fell silent. His chest stopped moving up and down.

'Father McKinnon, can you hear me?' Jessie shouted, shaking his shoulders to get a response. 'Shit! Don't you dare die on me, you hear me?'

She laid him completely flat and began compressions. She could hear sirens blast in the distance and literally prayed they were for them.

'Come on, come on, don't you dare die on me,' she repeated. She could hear running footsteps on the stone-chipped driveway. 'In here, side door!' she heard herself scream at the top of her lungs.

'What's the casualty's name?' The paramedic – who looked about twelve to Jessie – asked as he prepared his equipment. 'I'm one of the first responders. Keep going with the compressions. You're doing a fantastic job.'

Jessie didn't feel as confident as he was suggesting she should. She was covered in Father McKinnon's blood, which had even sprayed into her hair. She could feel it hardening by the minute. She had never been so relieved to see anyone than when two more paramedics ran into the kitchen. Jessie did as she was told and moved back so they could do their job.

'He's in VF!' one of the paramedics shouted. The woman yanked a mobile defibrillator out of a large red bag and had it ready to use in seconds, as a third paramedic grabbed a ready-prepared syringe from his bag.

Jessie was in awe of their teamwork. All three of them knew exactly what to do and when to do it.

'Clear,' the woman called, before she shocked Father McKinnon's motionless chest, causing him to rise and fall with a jolt. The younger man felt for a pulse before stepping back so she could shock him again, but not before turning up the dial on the defibrillator.

It was like a beautifully choreographed dance – all three of them had done these moves many times before. She watched them load him into the back of the ambulance while one of them continued with the compressions.

'I'll follow you in my car,' Jessie called out, and ran down the street.

CHAPTER FIFTY-NINE

Jessie flashed her ID at the A&E receptionist, but imagined she knew her pretty well by now, given the amount of times she'd visited this week.

'I'm with Father McKinnon. Can you tell me where they've taken him?'

'He's been taken straight to Resus. You can wait outside, and the doctor will come and talk to you soon.' She turned away to answer the phone.

Jessie nodded her thanks and jogged towards the uncomfortable, flimsy-looking chairs outside the double doors to the resus area. She peered through the small window in the door to see a flurry of bodies working on Father McKinnon. An older man in blue scrubs lifted his head to look at the clock above the bed. The curtain was pulled around the cubicle and Jessie's heart sank.

Her legs became uncertain beneath her and she bumped down onto one of the plastic chairs. She stared down at her hands. There wasn't an inch of skin that wasn't covered in his blood. Adrenaline had pushed her through the trauma, but now it was over. She hadn't noticed the doctor walk out until the double doors almost hit her knee on their backswing.

'Hi, I'm the A and E consultant. You're the police officer here with Father McKinnon? I'm sorry to tell you that he passed away from his injuries a few minutes ago. We did everything we could, but his injuries were just too severe. The knife ruptured his liver, spleen and penetrated a major artery.' He dropped a hand onto Jessie's shoulder. 'I believe you did your bit, too, in trying to save him.'

Jessie could only nod.

'Again, I'm sorry.'

First Finlay. Now the murder of a priest. Not to mention the fact that Jessie had to decide whether they were linked – but it didn't take a genius to figure that one out.

St Mark's Chapel and chapel house were now active crime scenes.

CHAPTER SIXTY

Dylan was shocked to see a bloodstained Jessie when he and PC Wilde arrived back at the hospital. They'd both rushed there when Jessie had texted them about Father McKinnon's murder. She looked terrible, and was now dressed in a set of blue scrubs. She held up the bag that contained her clothes.

'Evidence.' She tried to smile, her face white as a sheet. 'We need to get this to Forensics.'

'We can deal with this.' Dylan took the bag out of her hand. 'Go home, boss. We'll be fine until morning. You can give your statement then, too.'

Jessie couldn't disagree with him. She was now desperate to get home. She felt like Paul McKinnon's blood clung to every part of her. The smell was sickening and she wanted to claw at her hair to remove the blood that had sprayed her. She was looking forward to a long, hot shower, that was for sure. The sight and sound of him gurgling and gasping for breath haunted her. She wondered if there was more that she could have done, but what?

'You're right. First thing tomorrow morning, you two. I don't want to hang around on this. Isla – plain clothes, please. You're with CID for the duration of this case.'

'Thanks, boss,' Wilde chirped. 'See you in the morning.'

Jessie was heartened by the way Isla had blossomed, and was glad that she had pushed for her to help out on this case.

*

Jessie closed the front door of her flat, glad to shut out the rest of the world, but was confused by the silence – Smokey didn't come running to meet her. Then she spotted the scrap of paper on the floor. She picked it up and stepped out of the clogs the hospital had given her. They were not the easiest of footwear to drive in, but she was home in one piece at least.

'Smokey,' she called out with a frown, as she lifted the glass from the draining board and poured herself a small glass of wine, sinking a good portion of it immediately. Just what the doctor ordered. 'Smokey, where are you hiding, you silly wee man?'

It was unusual for him to stay away this long. As she walked she unfolded the note that had been stuffed through her letter box and her blood ran cold. First the birthday card, now this.

CHAPTER SIXTY-ONE

Phil Moran put down the phone. He was in complete shock at the news. Who would do something like that to such a lovely man? A man of God. Bridget would be devastated when she got back from visiting Theresa. He'd have to tell her when he got back from Claire and Darren's. *What a mess.*

*

'Claire, you have to eat something.' Darren pushed the plate of toast and jam closer to her.

When she didn't respond, he walked away. There was no point getting into an argument over toast. If she didn't want to eat, then fine. His phone buzzed on the kitchen table.

'Hey,' he answered as he closed the door. Her call couldn't have come at a better time. 'Yes, I can talk.'

By the time Darren hung up, he felt better. He felt like someone was listening to him. Maggie cared how he felt. How he was grieving. It was just her and him. He wondered if he was selfish to lean on Maggie like that, but living through this nightmare was hell for him.

'Only me,' Phil called out as he shut the back door. 'Claire, sweetheart, are you up?'

Darren met his father-in-law in the hallway. 'Hey, Phil. Kettle's just boiled if you're wanting one. Help yourself.'

'Aye, I will, thanks.' Phil flattened down his thick brown hair. 'Is she up?'

'Aye, she's in the living room.' Darren told him, before heading into his bedroom with his cup of tea.

Phil pressed open the living room door with one finger to find Claire slumped on the sofa, a plate of uneaten toast on the coffee table in front of her. It was a pitiful sight. He wasn't surprised to see her in her pyjamas because it was still early, but he could smell that she needed a shower and her hair was thick with grease. The living room was a mess. The floor looked like it hadn't seen a hoover for months, and a thick layer of dust covered every available surface. There were piles of rubbish all over. He opened the living room curtains. The flood of morning sunlight reflecting off the snow-laden ground stirred Claire from her stupor. Phil opened the window a little. Just enough to allow some fresh air to penetrate the stale odour.

'Daddy,' she whispered.

'Hey, I'm here, sweetheart.' He sat down on the sofa and pulled her close to him, her head coming to rest on his shoulder while he stroked her hair. 'I'm here.'

*

It was no good. Darren had to get out of these four walls. He felt like they were closing in on him. He grabbed his car keys and headed out the back door without saying goodbye to Claire. She had her dad; she didn't need him. Darren switched on the radio in the car as he started up the engine. He pushed in the CD that was jutting out of the machine. A bit of metal sounded like a good idea. It was Calum that had got him into Metallica. The memory caused a flash of guilt, but without Maggie, Darren could not have coped. If anything he needed her more, now his life was a living nightmare. Was Maggie really pregnant? Could it be his?

He didn't know where to turn. Thinking about a new life felt like a betrayal of his boy, his Finlay. Perhaps Finlay's death was his punishment for his weakness. Darren accelerated, testing his old Ford Focus to its limits while 'Enter Sandman' blasted so loud, it drowned out the ongoing dialogue in his mind almost immediately.

CHAPTER SIXTY-TWO

Jessie pulled on the handbrake and switched off her car's engine in the garden centre car park. They had reached a compromise, at least. It was a public place. He said all he wanted to do was talk, and that he was sorry it had to come to this. *Sorry?* Jessie scoffed. She didn't think Dan Holland was capable of feeling sorry for anyone but himself, because if he was, then he wouldn't have made Jessie live through his reign of terror. She feared he had harmed Smokey during the night. His note had made it clear Jessie had no choice but to meet him if she wanted her cat back. She questioned how he'd found out her address, but he said he didn't want to get anybody in trouble. Or had he just been following her, she wondered?

She edged closer to the front door of the garden centre. Every step was like pushing through thick mud, fear making her legs heavier with every step. Her throat was tight and her lips dry, but she couldn't forget the reason she was here. She had to dig deep and find every ounce of strength that was hiding from her. Then she saw him. Her heart quickened briefly and she stopped dead. Every part of her wanted to run. She glanced round the busy coffee shop. At least they weren't alone. She'd promised herself a long time ago she would never allow Dan the opportunity to corner her again.

'Jessie,' Dan murmured and stood when he caught sight of her, the shock in his eyes obvious. It was clear to Jessie immediately that he could see the physical changes in her.

She approached his table and sat opposite, but avoided making eye contact.

'What can I get you?' the pretty blonde waitress startled her by appearing from behind.

Jessie feared she had lost the power of speech. But she reminded herself why she was there, and how far she'd come since ending her marriage to this monster.

'Can I have a latte, please?' she asked, her voice trembling until she coughed and regained her composure. Dan Holland wasn't going to win. He had no hold on her now.

'I'll have the same, thanks love,' Dan told the girl, his eyes following her momentarily as she moved away. 'It's good to see you, Jessie. It's been a long time.'

Not long enough, Jessie thought.

'You look well, Dan,' Jessie knew she had to pull herself together. He didn't have the upper hand today. Dan Holland would never have the upper hand again.

'I'm sorry about all this, but you didn't respond to my card. All I wanted was to talk. To explain a few things.'

'What's to explain?' Jessie's anger grew inside her. Her fear was morphing into fury.

'Things have changed. I've changed. I'm trying to put the past behind me. Behind us. I've had a long time to think about what happened. To us, and to—'

'Stop right there. Don't you even say his name.'

'What? I lost a son too,' Dan pleaded, but Jessie was having none of it.

'Don't even go there.'

'Look, I just want a chance to explain.'

'I've changed, too, as it happens. I've put the past behind me. Ryan will always be part of me but I've put *you* behind me.' She pointed her finger at him for emphasis. 'Where is Smokey?'

Dan seemed smaller and thinner than Jessie remembered. He'd lost weight all over, particularly in his face, which had narrowed considerably, causing his chin to jut out more than she remembered. Even his eyes looked smaller, but Jessie supposed that was because they weren't wide with rage today. Instead, he was pathetic.

'He's in the car. I managed to borrow a motor from one of the guys in the hostel. I explained the situation and he agreed to lend it to me. He's a good guy.'

'You're in Greyfriars hostel, then?'

A ten-minute bus ride from her flat. *How convenient*, Jessie thought, fear rushing back into her system for a moment.

'Yes, just until I can find a job and get on my feet again. One of the support workers there says there's some labouring work coming up on one of the new developments at Charlotte Gate. She'll put in a good word for me. I don't know, but I'll sort something. I want to make things right.'

With Greyfriars being full of ex-cons and addicts, Jessie felt Dan fitted in very well. A silence fell over their table. Jessie watched some of the other customers' breakfasts arriving. Jessie's nerves meant she'd skipped breakfast, so her stomach grumbled at the sights and smells that drifted towards her. The waitress returned with the two coffees, Dan's eyes following her again for a moment as she walked away. *You've not changed*, Jessie said to herself.

'Are you planning to stay in Perth, Dan?' Jessie asked. 'Because I can't see that there's anything for you here. Your mum will be missing you, I'm sure.'

'For now. I was hoping we could sort some things out.'

Jessie shot him a look of disbelief. 'Are you serious, or just seriously deluded? You really must be kidding, right?'

'What's that supposed to mean?'

'Come on. You're an intelligent guy. Work it out.' Jessie sipped her coffee and wiped the milky froth from her top lip with a napkin.

Dan stirred his drink and stared into it before sighing.

'I don't expect you to believe me, but I've changed. I know it will take time to prove it to you.'

Jessie leaned across the table, her finger outstretched, almost connecting with his grubby black sweater. 'I don't give a damn. I just want my cat. And then I want you out of my life.'

As Jessie drove away from the café, listening to the sound of Smokey snoring in his basket in the back of the car, her mind moved back to Father McKinnon. She needed to forget about Dan and concentrate on the case. What was there to be gained from killing him? Apart from his guaranteed silence, that is. But why kill a man to silence him when he was bound by his faith to keep your secrets?

CHAPTER SIXTY-THREE

Lisa McKinnon had hopped on the first available flight. She was based in Durban, but had been visiting friends in London when she'd heard the news. Her resemblance to her uncle Paul was staggering. Apart from the blonde colour, her hair was strikingly similar – just as unruly and thick as his, although she wore the mussed-up look with rather more panache. Her eyes were chocolate brown, too. She even had his nose. She had turned up at the station late morning, and explained to Dylan that she was his last surviving relative. She had then insisted on waiting for Jessie to arrive before explaining why she was there.

'Please have a seat, Miss McKinnon. I am so sorry for your loss.' Jessie's hand stretched out to shake hers.

'Thank you. I was told you were with my uncle when he…' Lisa's eyes filled up. 'When he died.'

'Not exactly – your uncle was pronounced dead at the hospital, but it was me who found him.'

Lisa pulled a tissue from her cardigan pocket. Jessie recalled having a cardigan just like it, until it was torn to shreds by a certain mischievous kitten. Smokey was now safely ensconced at home, with Dave once again ready to look in on him.

'I can't believe someone would do that to Uncle Paul. Stab him in his home. The chapel house of a church, too. Were they after money for drugs? My uncle was far too generous. They must have known about all his money.'

'A search of his home didn't suggest that as a motive. Neither Paul's laptop nor any of the antiques had been touched. Gertrude Laing confirmed to us that nothing was missing, so I think we can rule out robbery.'

'Poor Gertrude. She must be terribly shocked. She and my uncle were very close. Where was she when it happened?'

Gertrude Laing was due in very soon to give her statement, but on initial questioning she had been with a local sewing club she attended once a week, in the home of another of Father McKinnon's parishioners.

'Mrs Laing wasn't there. She had left by that time.'

Lisa pinched a button on her cardigan between her thumb and forefinger and frowned. 'Why were you there, Detective, if you don't mind me asking?'

'I was hoping that your uncle could help me with an ongoing inquiry.' Jessie didn't want to explain any further than that. This wasn't the time.

'Was my uncle in trouble?' Lisa gasped, visibly shocked by the suggestion.

Jessie shook her head at Lisa's comment, then pursed her lips. 'I was hoping he would be willing to share some information, that's all. But your uncle wasn't keen.'

'That doesn't sound like him. I can't believe for one minute he would withhold information from the police. That would go against everything he believed in and held dear.' Lisa shook her head. 'No, you must be mistaken.'

What Lisa said was true. Jessie knew that. Paul McKinnon would love to have helped, but his faith was holding him back. Jessie wondered just how torn he must have been. Alternatively, perhaps there was nothing to tell. Perhaps Jessie had this whole thing wrong, but she doubted it.

'The information I wanted came from the confessional,' Jessie explained.

'Ah, I see.' Lisa smiled. 'He would never betray the sanctity of the confessional. He would rather—' She broke off when she realised what she had been about to say. 'It's something he could not do. He would be risking so much by telling you anything he heard there. His work in the church was his life, and if that was snatched away from him, well, he couldn't have coped with that. His life would have been over in any case.'

Lisa sniffed and blew her nose.

'I'm sorry. I know this might seem hard for you to understand, but I'm investigating a case that involves the death of a six-month-old baby. I had to try and persuade him to talk to me. I feel strongly he knew something about it. It must have been playing on his mind, too. Not being able to share the information with us. I do understand he was in a very difficult situation.'

'He was a good man.' Lisa reached into her brown leather satchel and took out a photo from the inside pocket. 'That was us on North Beach in Durban the last time Paul visited, three years ago.'

Jessie found herself grinning back at the happy, smiling face of Paul McKinnon, who had just stepped out of the waves, a surfboard tucked under his arm. She was surprised by how attractive he was.

'That's a really good picture, and a fantastic-looking beach.' Jessie handed it back.

'Yes, it was one of his favourites. He said he loved the sun, and understood why Grandpa had loved it there. My father and Uncle Paul spent their childhoods there. Grandpa was a farmer out there until poor health brought him back to the UK.'

It was hard to picture the Paul McKinnon Jessie had met as a surfer. He seemed so serious. So pious.

'You said earlier that Paul had money, and that any potential burglar might have known about it.'

'Yes, my father and Uncle Paul inherited everything after my grandma passed away. The entire two-million-pound estate was split equally between the brothers. Paul lived very frugally, too.

He preferred instead to give generously to a variety of charities. I can check which ones, and let you know.'

Jessie nodded while processing this news. *Paul McKinnon inherited a million quid?* One question burst to the front of her mind.

'Paul didn't have any children, did he?' Jessie probed. 'Who would be in line to inherit on Paul's death? We know he was called to the priesthood a little later than some, after having initially worked in the financial sector.'

Lisa dropped her head and rubbed at her nose. 'I'm the last remaining member of the family, Detective. I'm an only child, and as Paul was childless, it would fall to me, I expect.'

The grieving young woman in front of Jessie didn't look like she needed the money. The leather satchel looked like a designer brand, although she didn't recognise the name on the front pocket. Jessie wasn't particularly interested in designer gear. Lisa's boots, though, were unmistakably Christian Louboutin. *What would they have set her back – a grand?* Jessie knew that. She was worth checking out, just to be sure. It was important not to rule anything or anyone out at this stage, and Lisa McKinnon did seem to get here very quickly, despite not being asked to come. As far as Jessie knew, nobody at the station had actually told her that her uncle was dead.

CHAPTER SIXTY-FOUR

Jessie hadn't slept well the night before, and was feeling it as the day wore on. She'd woken in a cold sweat after seeing images of a thick black oozing sludge seep through the edge of every window and door in her flat, and no matter how hard she tried to seal them and stop the flow, the liquid kept coming until it was about to suffocate her. After that, every noise had sounded like Dan trying to get into her flat. Meeting Dan before heading into work had seemed like a good idea at the time, but now she hoped her third coffee of the day would help.

Her superiors would want a separate investigative team to hunt for Paul McKinnon's killer, but Jessie didn't want to separate the two cases just yet. She sat and stared up at the whiteboard and glanced from Paul's photo to the sweet smiling face of Finlay Lucas and back. She grabbed a marker pen and wrote Lisa McKinnon's name in the corner in small letters with a question mark and a circle around it. She didn't know why she did the circle thing. It was a habit that had developed unnoticed, until Dylan pointed it out to her. It was a way for her to imprint the information into her mind, perhaps. Like the circle was there for emphasis.

'Hi boss,' PC Wilde chirped from the doorway.

Jessie turned to her and smiled. 'Get yourself a strong coffee, PC Wilde, because I have a job for you. Lisa McKinnon is Paul McKinnon's niece. I want you to find out everything you can about her: financials, the lot.'

'Sure thing. I'm on it,' she grinned. 'After I've made my coffee of course, boss.'

Dylan walked in, lunch in hand, and started to hang up his parka.

'Don't bother hanging that up. We've got somewhere we need to be – you can eat on the way.'

Jessie and Dylan parked a little way back from the Morans' drive and walked the rest of the way. Jessie rang the doorbell and waited. She heard the tapping of high heels on the wood floor and stood tall to face Bridget. This time she was going to answer Jessie's questions whether she liked it or not. The door opened.

'Mrs Moran, can we come in and ask you some questions, please?' Jessie did her best to use her seven extra inches in height.

'Am I under arrest for something?' Bridget responded, her face stern.

'No,' Jessie shook her head. 'But refusing to talk to the police can be viewed as obstruction, which my colleague and I may have to review at some stage.'

The two women stared each other down while Jessie waited for Bridget's response.

'Who's that at the door?' Jessie glanced over Bridget's shoulder and saw an older woman calling from the kitchen doorway, leaning into her Zimmer frame to support herself. 'Don't leave them standing out in the cold. Come in, I'll put the kettle on.'

It was obvious that Bridget was seething at this invitation. She shot Jessie a look of disdain as she passed. Jessie smiled at Dylan's grinning face.

'You didn't say we were having company,' Phil's mother Margaret said to Bridget in a fluster. 'Bridget, you go and make us all a nice pot of tea. Use the leaves, mind, not the bag rubbish. That stuff leaves a rim round my mouth something chronic.' She ushered the detectives into the living room. 'I'm Margaret. Well, Peggy to my pals.' She chuckled. 'I don't think we've met, have we?' She narrowed her eyes at Dylan. 'I think I would remember your handsome face, lad.'

Jessie had to stifle the giggle that tried to escape.

'Mind you, I have trouble remembering a lot these days.' She tapped her forehead. 'Alzheimer's. But I'm not dead yet, as I've told them. They're no' getting their hands on my fortune yet.' Margaret Moran laughed aloud.

Jessie and Dylan introduced themselves, and Peggy Moran got right back to her friendly blethering. As Jessie heard the kettle coming to the boil in the kitchen, she decided she could make the most of the old lady's lack of reticence. Bridget Moran might be happy to stonewall her, but her mother-in-law seemed more than willing to talk…

'I was sorry to hear Theresa was poorly again,' Jessie said.

Margaret shifted awkwardly in her armchair by the window.

'Aye, she was ranting and raving like she does when she doesn't take her pills.' She tutted as she shook her head. 'Her and Bridget were whispering to each other here before they took her back to hospital the other day. They were thick as thieves, muttering about goodness knows what. Poor girl looked traumatised. So sad. Such a young, pretty girl. She should be married and giving me a couple of great-grandbairns by now.'

Dylan glanced at the door and raised his eyebrows at Jessie fleetingly. She gave the briefest of nods; an agreement that he should go and intercept Bridget.

'I'm sorry to hear that. Do you have any idea what they were whispering about?' Jessie asked casually.

Jessie heard voices approaching the house, and a moment later the front door opened and closed.

'Och, I don't know.' Margaret had been distracted by all the noise, too. 'Who's that now?'

'Shit,' Jessie muttered under her breath as Claire Lucas joined them, followed by Phil Moran.

'You go and sit, darlin'.' Phil stopped when he noticed Jessie. 'Hello, Detective.'

The tip-tapping of Bridget's heels marched towards them, but this was too important to leave.

'Mr Moran, your mum says Bridget and Theresa were whispering about something, and that Theresa was distressed. This would have been just before she was admitted to hospital, the day Finlay went missing. Were you here at that time?'

'Detective, I'm going to have to ask you to leave,' Bridget spat. 'I did not invite you into my home. How dare you come in here and question a frail, elderly woman.'

Jessie watched everyone fall silent while Bridget spoke. It was clear who ruled this house.

'I'm sorry if I've upset you, Peggy. It wasn't my intention.' She nodded towards the door for Dylan to leave with her. 'We'll see ourselves out.'

'She called me Peggy,' Margaret said to her son, a look of confusion crossing her face. 'Who was she?'

'It's fine, Mum, don't worry,' he reassured her, then followed Jessie and Dylan to the door. 'Look, my mum has dementia. She makes stuff up, stories. Stuff she even believes herself at times. Doctor says it's common, like a coping mechanism to compensate for the loss of memories. Her concept of reality is a bit off, you could say.'

'I'm sorry to have troubled you, but we will be in touch again.' Jessie assured him. She caught sight of Claire staring at them from the window. She turned away as soon as she was spotted. They would be back with a warrant next time.

As Phil Moran closed his front door, Jessie's phone rang in her pocket.

'Tell me you have some good news for me, Isla.'

Wilde told her she didn't know if the revelations about Lisa McKinnon's finances could be seen as good news, but it was certainly a development Jessie hadn't expected.

*

The boy lined up his shot as his friend waited, shivering between the goalposts on the North Inch. He began his run-up, but leaned back a fraction too far as he struck the ball, sending it flying high above the bar and into a cluster of cherry trees that had long since shed their leaves.

'Bad luck,' the keeper laughed while the boy kicked his heels into the frozen ground in disgust. 'But I'm no' getting that back.'

The boy picked his way through the trees towards the ball, rubbing his bare arms against the cold – his jacket was too thick to play football in. He scooped up the ball, but a little way past it caught sight of something shimmering against the snowy ground. He moved closer, and when he got a good view of what it was, he let out a blood-curdling scream.

'Don't touch it!' his friend exclaimed after rushing in after him. He snatched out his phone. 'I'm calling my dad. Come on, let's get out of here. They might come back.'

CHAPTER SIXTY-FIVE

'Answer that, will you?' Jessie asked Dylan when her phone rang in her bag.

'DI Blake's phone.' Dylan frowned while he listened before his eyes popped open at something he'd been told.

Jessie stopped at the traffic lights on the Edinburgh road as Dylan hung up.

'They think they've found the knife that killed Paul McKinnon. Well, they've found *a* knife, I mean. A couple of lads playing football found a large kitchen knife, and it's got blood on it.'

Jessie doubled back at a roundabout and headed back towards the station.

'Where was the knife found?' she asked.

'Seems like it was tossed into a clump of trees on the Inch. Close enough to the chapel house to be our murder weapon. Chucked by a panicked assailant?'

'They got any fingerprints off it?'

'They're working on it now. It's literally just come in.'

'Did the examination of McKinnon's home give us anything?'

Dylan shook his head. 'Forensics are still gathering trace evidence, but nothing yet – apart from the blood, obviously. No sign of forced entry. It looks like Father McKinnon either knew his killer or felt safe enough to let them in.'

Jessie indicated onto the Dunkeld road and then into the station car park.

'He was a priest. You don't get much more trusting than that, do you? But if it was a junkie there would have been plenty for them to nick, but nothing was taken.'

'True,' Jessie acknowledged as she reversed into the space closest to the front door. 'So, we're back to him letting in someone he knew, aren't we?'

PC Wilde smiled to greet them as they arrived back at the incident room.

'Forensics have got their samples from the knife. They managed to pick up a fingerprint on the handle. A good one, too. They're looking for an owner now. And they've got a blood match – it's Paul McKinnon's.'

'That was flipping quick. Good on them.' To say Jessie was pleased was an understatement. DNA and fingerprints never lie. They can't keep secrets. She picked up a photo of the knife from Isla's desk. Dylan whistled theatrically when he saw it.

'You know who has knives like this?'

Jessie's eyes widened.

'The Morans have a block of this kind on their worktop, next to the cooker. I saw them when I followed Bridget into the kitchen earlier.'

Jessie playfully punched the top of his arm. 'Yes! I knew you'd be useful one day.'

'Very funny. She's one scary woman.'

'Seriously, though, you definitely recognise it?'

Dylan narrowed his eyes at the picture. 'Yes, I'm sure. Viner. My mum has them, too. The Morans' block wasn't full – that doesn't mean much yet, but I bet if we search the kitchen we'll find a very large knife missing.'

Jessie uncurled her thick wool scarf, draped her jacket over the chair and picked up her desk phone. Bridget wasn't going to let them in again without a warrant.

CHAPTER SIXTY-SIX

Maggie McBride was nervous, and wished Calum would stop rambling in her ear. They were twenty minutes early for the ultrasound scan. The nausea and sickness were really starting to bite, and her appetite was terrible. The only thing she was managing to keep down for now was chicken soup. The tiredness was becoming a problem, but she was lucky to have a sympathetic employer who was happy to let her have a few days off. Maggie was desperate to pee, but she had been told to ensure she kept a full bladder for this scan. She struggled to get Darren out of her mind. He had asked both the McBrides to give them space. Maggie understood his reasons, but that didn't make staying away from him any easier. Darren and Claire knew she and Calum were only a phone call away.

'Maggie McBride?' the small, shrill voice of the radiographer called out.

Calum was first to his feet, enthusiastically grinning back at her. 'That's us, Maggie.'

'I know, I heard her,' Maggie told him. 'I'm pregnant, not deaf.'

'Hop onto the bed and lift your top and slide your trousers down just a little,' said the radiographer once they were in the consultation room. She smeared the probe with jelly, which exited the tube in a crude splodge, then was forced to shake the tube hard to empty it completely. 'Sorry, this is a little cold.'

She isn't kidding, Maggie thought to herself. She saw Calum's eyes searching the screen, trying to make out a shape amid the blob of moving pictures.

The radiographer brought the screen further round and turned the volume up. She pointed out a moving oval blob and drew her finger along the edge. 'OK, we have a very healthy heartbeat, and this line is your baby's spine, which from what I can see looks normal.' She screwed up her eyes for a closer look and typed something into the keyboard in front of her. 'Good, yes, everything looks good. Do you have any idea how far along you are?'

Maggie couldn't remember when her last period was. 'No, I don't.'

'I would say you're about nine weeks along, giving you an early summer baby. Congratulations.'

Calum covered his mouth with one hand and squeezed Maggie's with the other. He couldn't take his eyes off the screen. Maggie could see a tear forming in the corner of his eye. He wouldn't admit it in front of this stranger, but he wanted to cry with joy. He had always told her he wanted children.

'Would you like a picture? It doesn't cost anything.' The radiographer ripped a pile of paper from a huge roll and handed it to Maggie, before pulling the screen back to face her. 'You can give yourself a wipe clean with that.'

'Yes, a picture would be great,' Maggie told her, trying to soak up the jelly as best she could. 'Nine weeks, you think? How accurate could that be?'

The radiographer smiled. 'At least ninety-nine per cent, although babies sometimes are a law unto themselves. They come when they're good and ready. My son was two weeks early and my daughter was three weeks late, so it's not an exact science. Be sure to make your first antenatal check-up appointment on your way out.'

'Thank you,' Calum said while he wiped the tears away with his thumb.

Maggie reached for him and hugged him once they were back in the waiting room. 'You big softy, come here.' Calum clung on and then leaned down to press his lips to hers.

'I love you so much, Maggie. You've made me the happiest man in the world.'

'You go on. I'll catch you up. I'm going to give my mum a quick call.' Maggie smiled to hide her lie.

She should feel guilty, but seeing her baby on the screen had already filled Maggie with pure love, no matter what was about to happen. Whether this baby was Calum's or Darren's didn't matter. This was Maggie's baby. She would decide its future. She sighed and hung up without leaving a message when Darren's phone went to voicemail.

CHAPTER SIXTY-SEVEN

The smug sneer disappearing from Bridget Moran's face as she read the search warrant was the best thing Jessie had seen in a very long time. She could sense the anger pulsing through Bridget's veins. Jessie sent PC Wilde into the living room and Dylan upstairs. She wanted him in Theresa's room before Bridget could obstruct him.

'Phil, call your solicitor.' Bridget glared at Jessie while she spoke. 'You have no grounds for this. I hope you realise what you're doing, Detective, because you have just made the biggest mistake of your career, I can assure you.'

'Excuse me, please. I would like to get past.' Jessie was enjoying every minute of this, but in particular the moment Bridget stepped aside so she could walk towards the kitchen.

'Hello there,' Margaret Moran greeted Jessie with a cheerful grin as she sat at the kitchen table sipping a cup of tea.

'Hello again, Peggy. How nice to see you,' Jessie replied. She moved closer to Bridget's knife rack and glanced into the empty space – it certainly looked like it would hold the size of knife used in Paul McKinnon's murder.

*

Dylan pulled on his gloves and opened the top drawer in Theresa's bedside cabinet. The drawer was disorganised and chaotic. Loose sheets of paper with lists written and then scribbled over, then repeated on the same page. He lifted up a diary, which had a pink glittery unicorn on the cover. A bit immature for a woman in her twenties, maybe? But maybe he only thought that because Shelly had never been a fan of pink or glitter in all the time he'd known her. Every page of Theresa's diary was written and scribbled on, with the margins full of sketches of flowers, principally daisies. He pushed the diary into the back of the drawer and lifted out a small wooden box with a daisy painted on the lid. He opened it and took out a locket, then dropped the box onto the bed. After struggling to open the locket, he was shocked to see the smiling face of Finlay staring back at him. She clearly loved her nephew. Dylan unfolded the slip of paper that had been in the box with the locket.

'*Thank you for being the best Auntie in the world,*' he read, then exhaled slowly.

*

PC Wilde couldn't help but think she'd been given the raw end of the deal, as Bridget stared at her every move. She carefully replaced the cushions she had lifted, out of fear more than respect, but was nevertheless followed by Bridget plumping and moving them back into the positions of her choosing. The mahogany television unit in the corner had a drawer on either side, with a shelf in the middle. The unit was dwarfed by the widescreen television on top of it, which Isla figured to be at least fifty inches. She could feel Bridget's eyes bore into the back of her neck while she opened the first drawer. The contents were much as she expected – neatly lined-up telephone directories and takeaway menus.

'What did he say?' Bridget boomed at Phil when he returned from calling for legal advice. 'Surely they can't do this,' she insisted.

'He said we have to let them do their job, and to let him know of any developments.'

'Developments?' Bridget blasted. 'What's that supposed to mean?'

'It means if we find anything of interest,' Jessie told her as she walked into the living room to join them, with the knife rack in a clear plastic evidence bag.

'Why do you have that in a bag?' Bridget roared, barely able to control her fury. 'I need them.'

Jessie held the bag up to allow Bridget to look more closely. 'Can you tell me where this one is?' She pointed to the only empty space, and watched Phil frown then move towards his wife without saying a word.

'What? Why are you asking me such a damn stupid question?'

Phil's eyes widened. His wife had never uttered a swear word since he had met her over twenty-five years ago.

'Look, what's this about, Detective?' Phil intervened. 'I don't understand what's going on here. Could you just explain what you're doing?'

'Certainly,' Jessie nodded. 'The knife that was used to stab Father McKinnon matches the knife that is missing from here.'

Bridget released an immediate snort of indignation at Jessie's inference. 'Are you serious? Are you really trying to tell me that you think I killed Paul?' She shook her head and ran her fingers over her neatly pinned grey hair. 'I am speechless. First you accuse us of having something to do with Finlay's death, and now we've apparently murdered Father McKinnon.'

Jessie allowed Bridget to finish, then added, 'I'm not saying you were all involved.'

'Ah, I see, just me then?'

'Where were you yesterday between three o'clock and four thirty in the afternoon?'

'I was here at home, alone.'

'Can anyone verify that?'

Bridget laughed with derision. 'I said I was alone, so unless the invisible man was here to give me an alibi—'

'I think, then, that perhaps I have more questions for you, Mrs Moran. This time under caution.'

'Are you arresting me for something?'

The two women eyeballed each other, neither one willing to budge.

'Not yet,' Jessie began. 'But I would appreciate it if you could come in to the station to clarify a couple of things for me.'

The tension in the room was electric. Jessie became aware of goosebumps on her arms, and not because she was cold. She bristled with anticipation. She became aware of everyone's eyes on her while she pushed Bridget to the brink. She could arrest Bridget for obstructing an investigation, but she needed more than that. What was it about the woman? Jessie struggled to understand her opposition to every aspect of her investigation. She was shocked to see Bridget turn away first, then stunned by what she said next.

'I will come to the station this evening once I have made arrangements with my solicitor.'

Dylan's voice shouting from upstairs drew Jessie's attention.

'Excuse me a moment.'

Jessie's heart rate returned to normal now that she was removed from her verbal duel with Bridget. She headed upstairs, taking them two at a time, and joined Dylan in Theresa's room.

The filthy, bloodstained baby socks in the evidence bag he held in his hands left a nasty taste in her mouth.

'Where were they?'

'Under the bed.'

Finding those socks didn't give Jessie the satisfaction that it should. Nothing would bring Finlay back to his mum and dad. But why did Theresa have his socks under her bed? Hidden away, as if they were a guilty secret? They needed to bring Theresa in. Having a mental illness does not mean you can hide from justice.

CHAPTER SIXTY-EIGHT

'What's up with you?' Peter McCabe asked his brother. 'You've had a face like fizz since I got in.'

'What's that supposed to mean?' Tim snapped back, angered that his big brother was so calm about everything. 'Does none of this bother you at all?'

Peter threw back his head and laughed. 'My little brother. The voice of my conscience every time.'

Tim shoved past his brother, shooting him a look of disgust.

'Hey, there's nae need for that, Tim. It's just business, you know that.'

That last bit was too much for Tim. He spun round and surged back towards Peter.

'Business? Is that all this is to you?' he roared, fearing he would lose control. He pushed Peter hard, once, with the palm of his hand. 'Oor van was parked in that bairn's street, for God's sake.'

'You think I don't know that?' Peter yelled back, and squared right up to his brother. Both men stood at over six foot. 'You don't think that's been on my mind too?'

Tim didn't respond. Instead, they just stared each other down, breathing heavily to control the anger. Tim blinked first and stepped back.

'Look, I'm just saying—' Tim began.

'I know what you're saying. I'm no' as hard-hearted as you've got me pegged,' Peter shouted to interrupt him. 'I know we were there.'

'*You* were there,' Tim boomed. 'With oor van. I was here. With that.' He pointed to the safe in the far corner of the room.

Peter scoffed and shook his head. 'Don't tell me the money hasn't come in handy.'

'How long is it going to be here?'

'Just until it cools down. You know the drill,' Peter explained. 'But the longer it's here, the richer we become, little brother.'

'Whatever.' Tim knew when he was defeated and walked away. 'I've got work to do.'

He couldn't yet tell his brother that someone else knew their secret. Not just that – they'd tried using it as leverage to get him to do something unspeakable.

CHAPTER SIXTY-NINE

The weather outside the station reflected Phil Moran's mood. Bleak and icy-cold. The snow had been falling steadily since lunchtime and there was now a thick carpet covering the police station car park. The roofs and bonnets of the cars of the early shift wore a heavy layer, too. The garage next to the station had put up a SOLD OUT sign on the diesel, which didn't help his mood – he was hoping to refuel after attending the station with Bridget. He couldn't get his head around it. It was ridiculous to think Bridget could do something like that, and especially to Father McKinnon. If he was inclined to think that way, Phil might have been concerned that Bridget and Paul's relationship was more than it should be.

'Detective, how long is this going to take?' Phil Moran shot up from his seat in the waiting area, but froze when he saw who was walking behind Jessie. 'Theresa! What on earth is going on?' He raced forward to hug his daughter, who was sobbing over and over that she was sorry.

'Mr Moran, please take a seat. I'll be back out shortly to talk to you. Your wife and daughter will be fine. I just need to ask them some questions.' Jessie dropped a hand onto his arm. 'Please.'

Jessie turned to walk away, but was halted by Phil's grip on her shoulder.

'I need to make a statement,' he insisted. 'Now.'

*

'So let me get this straight. You're saying Bridget was with you yesterday?' Jessie couldn't find the words to describe her feelings. 'You do know it's a criminal offence to lie to the police?'

Phil Moran looked at his feet and avoided eye contact. 'Yes, I do. I'm not lying. I just forgot – got confused with my times, that's all. Bridget must have been the same – that's why she said she was alone. Everything has been so chaotic since Finlay. Bridget can't have anything to do with Father McKinnon's murder. She was with me.'

'So where is the knife? It wasn't in the kitchen.'

He shrugged. 'I don't know. We must have lost it.'

A loud knock on the door interrupted them. PC Wilde popped her heard round and asked Jessie if she had a minute.

'What's up?' Jessie asked, after following her out and closing the door.

'We finally have a witness who can give a definitive description of someone recognisable and connected to Finlay Lucas.'

Jessie's eyes widened at the best news she'd had for a long time.

CHAPTER SEVENTY

Dylan handed Theresa a cup of water then took his seat opposite her. Her eyes were red from crying. He thought it strange that what she seemed to be most upset about was letting her mum down. Not the fact that her dead nephew's socks were under her bed. He slid the bag containing the socks towards her and tapped his finger on it.

'I'm showing the suspect exhibit B6. Theresa, could you tell me what these are?'

Her solicitor whispered into Theresa's ear, then scribbled something down on his pad. Theresa tugged on her hair, twisting it between her fingers.

'No comment.'

'You can't even tell me what these things are?' Dylan shrugged.

'No comment,' she repeated, this time in a whisper.

'I need you to speak louder for the tape.'

Theresa sipped from her cup then coughed to clear her throat. 'No comment.'

'I'll tell you then, shall I?' Dylan lifted the bag up and held it closer to her. 'This is a pair of baby's socks. Light blue ones, with a white trim across the top. Can you see that trim there?' He pointed to it with a sweeping motion of his finger. 'Most likely to fit, say, a six-month-old.'

'Detective, I object to your question. Is it even a question?' the solicitor interjected, then whispered to Theresa again.

'Can you see the dirt the socks are caked in, and the little bloodstains peppered around the heel?'

Theresa glanced up at him. 'No comment.'

'I'm glad to see you looking so composed now. You seemed very upset on your way in here,' Dylan continued. 'What was it you were so sorry about? Was it to do with these socks?'

'Please stick to the facts. That is merely conjecture.'

Her solicitor was damn good at his job. Dylan had to admit that.

'I apologise, Theresa.' He laid the bag with the socks back down and moved them closer to her.

'Do you have any idea how the socks came to get so dirty?' He paused to allow her time to process his question. 'Why did you have such dirty baby socks under your bed? A bit of a strange thing to have, don't you think?'

'No comment,' she repeated.

'Don't you want to know why Finlay's body was found in Moncreiffe Wood? Because I would, if he was my nephew. Did you put him there?'

Dylan could see Theresa was getting rattled. Until then it had been about socks. But this was bigger than just a pair of filthy socks. She was about to say something other than 'no comment' until her solicitor put his hand on hers. He whispered into her ear once again. Dylan watched her expression change in an instant.

'No comment,' she murmured and wiped away a tear, avoiding eye contact with Dylan.

'Theresa, come on. You'll feel better if you tell me. Isn't confession good for the soul?' Her solicitor was not pleased with that one. He removed his half-moon spectacles and waved them towards Dylan to show his disapproval.

'That was uncalled for, Detective. You should know better. In fact, I'm very surprised at you.'

Dylan glanced from the solicitor to Theresa, who was trembling in her chair. She covered her ears with her hands then screamed out loud.

'I didn't mean to do it! It was an accident! Tell Claire I'm sorry.'

'Tell Claire you're sorry for what, exactly?' Dylan's pulse quickened as he pushed her to say more. He wanted to shout out, *Just tell me!* His knees were bouncing with the growing anticipation.

Her solicitor got to his feet, gesticulating his disapproval with his finger.

'Enough, Detective. My client needs a break.'

Dylan wanted to scream at him, *What if Finlay was* your *son?*

Instead, he tapped the table with his thumb. He had to bite his tongue. Sadly, the solicitor was right. Confession under duress was inadmissible.

'Interview suspended.' His eyes drifted to his watch and he gave the time for the tape.

Dylan gathered up his papers and reached for the bag of socks, but Theresa grabbed them and held them to her chest.

'I'm so sorry,' she whispered. 'I'm so very sorry. I didn't mean to.'

'What are you sorry for, Theresa?'

'Detective, this interview is over for the time being.' The lawyer dropped a hand on Theresa's arm. 'Come on, it's time we got you home.'

Theresa smiled, attempting to hide the guilt that Dylan could see gripping her. He was so damn close to an answer. He hoped Jessie was having more luck.

CHAPTER SEVENTY-ONE

Jessie's mind was reeling. A witness. They finally had an impartial witness, and what he'd told them was like finding the missing pieces to the jigsaw puzzle. A Royal Mail delivery driver had seen the appeal on Facebook, then heard the news that a body had been found in Moncreiffe Wood. It was only then he'd put what he'd seen together with the case. He'd seen a woman with long red hair acting erratically, about halfway up the woodland track to where Finlay's body was found. He didn't get a close look at her face, but she was pacing back and forth, and she might have been wearing a rucksack or sports-type bag. He said he wished he'd gone and asked if she was OK, but he was already late – he was only in the car park because he was taking a break there, looking out over the River Earn, after delivering to Moncreiffe Estate House. He'd also seen a small, slim jogger and a plump woman in her late forties with a dog, but she'd been at the Estate House end of the wood. Perhaps most importantly of all, he'd almost run over Bridget Moran as she'd hurried across the road at the entrance to the woodland car park. He'd been on the receiving end of her steely glare many times as the village postman – being late with her mail had been his crime. Jessie would now have to see where each of these pieces fit.

She took her seat opposite Bridget and a solicitor she hadn't seen for a very long time. Jessie had done battle with Lacey Montgomery in the past; Michael Rogers' partner was nicknamed 'the shark' at the station because she stalked and devoured her prey without mercy, gnashing and tearing strips off an unprepared detective. Her attitude did not reflect her physical appearance at all. A slim woman, standing just shy of five feet, Lacey still had the ability to terrify even the most hardened detectives. It takes a bulldog to defend a bulldog.

'Hello, DI Blake.' Lacey smiled.

Jessie admired how great Lacey Montgomery looked for her age; she must be sixty but could easily pass for forty. The only hint at her real age were the few strands of silver that were peppered through her neatly coiffed wavy brown hair, held fast with layers of spray, giving it an almost helmet-like appearance.

'Ms Montgomery,' Jessie answered boldly.

Once the formal introductions were over, Jessie didn't want to allow Bridget any time to get comfortable.

'Can you tell me, Mrs Moran, what you were doing in Moncreiffe Wood the day your grandson disappeared?'

The postie had admitted he couldn't tell exactly where Bridget was going, but she was close enough to the wood for Jessie to view the sighting as positive. He also couldn't confirm the girl he saw on the path was anyone he knew, but the fiery red hair was good enough for Jessie at the moment.

Lacey Montgomery slipped her glasses on and read from her notepad.

'My client is here to talk to you about a missing knife and Father Paul McKinnon's death. Please stick to the topic.'

'I'm sorry, but a witness has come forward who places your client in a location close to where Finlay Lucas's body was discovered.' She paused. 'Your client's grandson.'

Lacey whispered in Bridget's ear and Jessie clenched her fist under the table in anticipation of the answer she knew was coming.

'No comment.'

Jessie knew she'd rattled her. She just had to get her to crack.

*

Phil Moran sat with his head in his hands, considering his options. It was his job to take care of his family and he was failing. He hoped it wasn't too late to change that. It was the right thing to do. He watched Dylan chat with the sergeant at the desk and tried to get his breathing under control. He inhaled, listening to the thudding of his heart. He stood and wiped his sweaty palms on his trousers, feeling every drop of blood rushing through his aching head, and the pounding only got louder with every step.

'Everything OK, Mr Moran?' Dylan was disturbed by the look on Phil's face as he approached.

'I need to talk to you, Detective. I need to revise my statement.'

*

The ghost of a smile grew on Bridget's face.

'You're absolutely right. I apologise,' Jessie conceded.

'Thank you. I would appreciate it if you would stick to the matter in hand.' Lacey Montgomery wrote on her pad while she spoke.

'What happened to the knife that is missing from the block you have in your kitchen?' Jessie continued.

She smiled as Bridget began to open her mouth to answer, until Lacey whispered in her ear again.

'No comment,' Bridget repeated, failing to hide the smile growing on her lips.

Jessie shook her head, gave a long, sharp sigh, then sniffed. She would have to dig deep for this one. Staying within the law. Bending rather than breaking protocol. Jessie was a damn good detective. She'd never met anyone who could beat her; not for a long time, anyway.

'Bridget, and I hope you don't mind me calling you Bridget?' Jessie dropped her pen and sat back in her chair. 'You're a mother, right, and a grandmother, of course?' Jessie waited and watched Bridget frown. 'What, you can't answer that question either?'

Bridget shrugged.

Yes, come on, that's it, Jessie coaxed inwardly.

'Stick to the point, Detective Inspector,' Lacey Montgomery challenged her.

'You must miss him' – Jessie wasn't finished; not by a long shot – 'his cute, smiling face.' She scrunched up her nose. 'Those gorgeous, blue eyes. I bet he was always giggling, wasn't he? Bridget? I bet Finlay was a happy little baby, was he?'

The small interview room buzzed with tension.

'I am going to have to ask you again, DI Blake, to consider your words very carefully or I will be terminating this interview and removing my client.' Lacey's stern gaze was an attempt to intimidate her, Jessie knew that, but she wasn't budging. Bridget's resolve was about to break – she was sure of it. It was to her great irritation, then, that Dylan chose that moment to knock on the door.

She answered the door. 'This better be good, Dylan.'

'You need to come, now.'

CHAPTER SEVENTY-TWO

'Right then, Mr Moran, in your own time, when you're ready.' Jessie leaned her elbows on the table, briefly wondering just how much this family would be billed by Rogers and Montgomery solicitors.

Phil Moran pushed away his cup of water with a trembling hand. He closed his eyes and took a deep breath, reminding himself over and over in his head that this was the right thing to do. It was the only thing to do.

'You have to understand one thing before I tell you. My wife is not a bad woman. She loves her family with everything she has, heart and soul. She loves her girls more than anything in this world. She would do anything to protect them. I will tell you everything, and I'm sorry you haven't been told before today. When Claire came to us and said she was pregnant, Bridget was so disappointed. We both were. We wanted more for Claire, and wanted her to wait, you know? Wait. Don't get me wrong – Darren is a decent, solid young man and a hard worker. He stood by our daughter. He didn't have the best of starts in life, but despite that he is a good, strong man. I couldn't ask for a better son-in-law. He works hard to provide for my daughter.'

Jessie was beginning to think Phil had forgotten what they were here to talk about until he continued.

'Theresa doesn't keep well, mentally. You already know she has bipolar disorder, which makes her thoughts confused and chaotic. Sometimes she suffers from hallucinations and even delusions. How much do you know about it?'

'A fair bit,' Jessie informed him.

'Well, then you know how deeply rooted delusions can get. Theresa visited Claire that day because she believed Finlay had a message for her. A voice told her to go to him and that the message was vital for her survival.' He laughed uncomfortably. 'I know it sounds silly to us, but to Theresa that is real.'

'So you're admitting she was there that day.'

Phil nodded. 'Yes, she was. The voices were so loud, screaming at her that she had killed him, Detective.' For the first time his composure slipped, and he rubbed his eyes with his palms and sniffed. 'Theresa panicked and shook him, she said, but he didn't wake up.'

Jessie slid his cup of water closer and lowered her voice. 'Take your time.'

Phil grabbed the cup, his hands continuing to tremble, and sipped. 'Thanks. She took him and ran,' he added.

Jessie was stunned by what she was hearing.

'Where was Claire when this was happening?'

'Taking a nap, I think. Theresa wasn't very clear about that, but I assume she was in bed or napping on the sofa.'

'So Theresa was able to let herself in?' Jessie asked.

Phil nodded and took another sip of water. 'Yes. She must have gone straight to Finlay's room to get this message, or whatever it was.'

'What happened after that?'

'She called my wife from Moncreiffe Wood. Bridget called me, and I waited by the entrance in the car. I dropped them both off at home.'

'What did you do with Finlay?'

'You have to understand that I did what I thought was right at the time. I knew what it looked like. I knew both of my girls would come under suspicion and I was trying to protect them.'

'I understand,' Jessie lied. How could she understand that?

'I walked up the track and found my wife and daughter in a horrible state.' He closed his eyes and shivered as he recalled the moment. 'Finlay wasn't moving.' He paused, the words struggling to come out. 'Bridget arranged for Theresa to be seen as an emergency. She was admitted to hospital for assessment that day.'

'What did you do then?' Jessie probed. She needed him to tell her.

'We put him back in Theresa's rucksack, and covered the bag with gravel and some twigs and stones. I know what we've done is wrong.'

'You have to underst—' Jessie began.

Phil raised his hand in front of him. 'Please, let me finish.'

'Sure, carry on.' She nodded.

'What we did, Bridget and me, we didn't feel we had any choice. We thought Theresa had murdered Finlay. We couldn't, we just didn't know what else to do.' He paused. 'Are you a parent?'

Jessie shook her head, but she was really, in her heart. Ryan would always be part of her. That would never change.

'No, I'm not.'

'You can't understand the need, the overwhelming need, to protect them. It's unexplainable. Indescribable. Prison would kill Theresa.'

'But you know now that she didn't kill Finlay?'

'Darren told me what the post-mortem said.' Phil bowed his head and kept his eyes on the table.

'That must have been difficult to hear, after what happened.'

'The only comfort was the fact that Finlay didn't suffer.'

On that they were both agreed.

'You're right,' she said. 'So why didn't you come and tell us, or even just call me and say what happened that day?'

'It had gone too far for that. Paul McKinnon knew, and you were asking him all sorts of questions by that time. Confession gave Bridget so much comfort. She's devastated about Paul's death.'

'Did she confess?' Jessie was curious.

'She did. That first day. I was so angry that she had been so stupid. We had – I had – done something awful to protect Theresa, and she went and told *him*.'

For the first time Jessie spotted a darker side emerge. Phil's fists clenched before he placed them onto his lap. Was this man capable of the savagery Jessie saw inflicted on Paul McKinnon's body?

'I had to stop him talking to you. I know all about the sanctity of the confessional, but you were determined to find the truth. I had to stop it. If he told you, then Theresa would be in danger and I couldn't live with that. So I killed him.'

'But you could live with the pain Claire and Darren were going through?'

'I don't expect you to understand.' He sighed. 'What's going to happen to me?'

'Can I just clear something up first?'

Phil frowned. 'I've told you everything that happened. Please promise me Theresa won't get into any trouble. She didn't kill him. You said that yourself.'

'Your daughter has been involved in the concealment of a dead body, Mr Moran, not to mention obstruction. As have you and your wife.'

Phil shuffled uncomfortably in his chair, fearing this confession had all been in vain. 'But Theresa isn't well. She didn't know what she was doing.'

'Your loyalty is admirable,' Jessie told him, and that wasn't a lie. He was prepared to go to prison for his daughter. She knew for a fact that her own father would never do that for her. She wasn't sure whether to feel envious of Theresa or not. 'I would just like to clarify one last thing before we finish, and then I'll explain what's going to happen next.'

'OK. If I can help, obviously I will. You know that.'

'Can you confirm how many times you stabbed Paul McKinnon?'

'What? Why does that matter?' He shuffled back in his chair and glanced sideways, whether to avoid Jessie's eyes or seek guidance from Michael Rogers was unclear. 'I told you. I killed him, and I know that was wrong, but I, erm, I thought it was the right thing to do at the time.'

'Please, how many times? For the record. Tell me exactly what happened.'

'I, erm, took the…' He coughed and then ran his fingers across his brow. 'The, erm, knife – from the kitchen.'

'Your own knife?'

'Yes, yes that's right. Then I drove to Paul's and could see him in his office window. He saw me and waved me to come inside, so I did. He met me in the hallway and offered me a whisky.' Phil hesitated and scratched his head. 'I followed him back into the study and watched him pour two drinks from the bottle of single malt.' He paused.

'So you were in the study?' Jessie encouraged him to continue. It was becoming clear he didn't know Jessie had been first on the scene.

Phil nodded. 'Yes. Then I asked him about Bridget and what she'd told him, and then I can't remember exactly what happened next. I can only remember standing over him with the knife in my hand. He was on the floor holding his chest. Then I ran.'

'You stabbed Father McKinnon once in the chest, then left, is that what you're saying?'

'Yes. I'm sorry, I really am. He was a good man.'

Jessie stared at Phil Moran, wondering exactly how big of an idiot he thought she really was.

CHAPTER SEVENTY-THREE

Jessie had never wanted to scream bullshit more in her police career than she did when she listened to Phil Moran claim to have murdered Paul McKinnon. She knew he hadn't done it. Perhaps it was admirable that he'd tried to protect his family, but the best thing he could have done for them was to call the police as soon as Theresa reached out to them for help. It would have been better for everyone, including Claire and Darren. The sight of Paul McKinnon lying in a pool of his own blood still haunted her. It had been a while since a case had crept into Jessie's dreams, but this one had the night before. Not surprising when she'd spent all evening chewing over Phil's confession.

Why would Phil Moran come clean about the concealment but lie about Paul's murder? Did he really believe his wife was capable of murdering Paul McKinnon? But why would she? She understood the sanctity of the confessional. Wasn't that why she went there? To unburden herself, safe in the knowledge he couldn't tell anyone? They were all up to their necks in it anyway. Was it really simply a case of protecting them? Jessie was glad to have the office to herself for a change this morning – it gave her some space to think.

Isla Wilde's digging into Lisa McKinnon's finances had shown some interesting changes in her spending patterns recently, and rapidly growing debts, so Jessie had sent the young PC and Dylan to her hotel to find out more. Lisa did seem genuinely upset by Paul's death, but it played on Jessie's mind that the police hadn't been the ones to tell her. Perhaps Gertrude Laing had called her. She needed Dylan and Wilde to check on that, too. Gertrude had been unquestionably upset when her statement had been taken, and there was never any suggestion in Jessie's mind that the old lady was involved. Gertrude was clearly very fond of Father McKinnon, and had even explained exactly how Paul liked his tea: strong, with just a splash of milk and no sugar. He only drank coffee on special occasions, and even then it had to be good-quality beans and not cheap supermarket brands.

It's the little things, Gertrude had said. That's what she was going to miss the most. Gertrude was also concerned about what was going to happen to all of Paul's antique books, some of which were already fragile. She hated the thought of having them moved.

Jessie's phone buzzed with a text, snapping her out of her thoughts. She was delighted to see it was from David Lyndhurst, the pathologist. She'd been worried about him and was glad to read that he was recovering well, but perplexed as to why he had examined Finlay Lucas's post-mortem results, which seemed to be the main reason for the text. He should be resting, but he said he needed her to meet him – now.

CHAPTER SEVENTY-FOUR

Given the woman had severe financial problems, it was odd that Lisa McKinnon was staying in such an expensive hotel. *This is no Travelodge*, Dylan thought as he pulled into the car park of The Parklands Hotel.

A few minutes later, Lisa placed her cup down by the kettle when she heard the knock at her room door. DI Blake had told her that her colleagues would be arriving some time that morning to ask her some questions. She glanced at herself in the mirror above the antique pine dresser and checked her lipstick, then flicked her fingers through her hair, which she realised she probably should have washed.

'Come in, I've been expecting you.' She forced a smile and held the door wide open.

'Please sit,' Lisa pointed to the two armchairs in the corner as she stood by the window and looked out across the hotel garden, that was filled with yellow and blood-red dogwood shrubs, as well as a selection of forsythia and winter-flowering clematis. 'What can I do for you? Has there been a development?' She directed her question towards Dylan.

'Not exactly. We just have a few things we would like you to clarify for us.'

'If I can.' Lisa felt nervous all of a sudden. She didn't enjoy the way the young female police officer was gazing at her leather jacket, which was hanging from the handle of the wardrobe door.

'Nice jacket, is it Gucci?'

Wilde's question surprised Dylan.

'What? Erm, no,' Lisa stammered. 'It's an Armani.'

'It's lovely,' she smiled.

Dylan's eyes drifted from the jacket back to Wilde, who smiled at him then tried to shrug without catching Lisa McKinnon's attention.

'OK, so it's come to our attention that you have had a few financial difficulties very recently. Can—' Dylan was interrupted before he could continue.

'I beg your pardon?' Lisa exclaimed. 'What business is that of yours?'

'Miss McKinnon,' Wilde intervened. 'When someone becomes the victim of a brutal attack, like your uncle, the police have to consider every possibility in order to eliminate all the wrong ones, thus leaving only the truth. Do you understand?'

Dylan was stunned. Wilde was damn good at this interviewing thing. She would make a great detective one day, if she chose that route. He watched Lisa hesitate then swallow hard before answering.

'Yes, well, it's private, and I would rather not discuss it with you.'

'Can you at least confirm that you and your husband have suffered a considerable financial loss?' Dylan took the baton and ran with it, then paused to give her time to answer.

'He's not my husband, and…' Lisa hesitated and pursed her lips. 'OK, yes, Anders has a gambling addiction. He's in treatment but he spent pretty much everything we had, well, *I* had.' She slumped down on the corner of the kingsize bed. 'I was really here to ask Paul for money, not to visit friends.'

'Mm,' Dylan responded.

'"Mm"? What's that supposed to mean?' Lisa snapped.

Dylan lifted a hand. 'My apologies. I didn't mean to offend.'

Lisa sighed. 'Good.'

'Where were you two days ago between three and five o'clock?' Wilde asked abruptly.

'Are you two serious?' Lisa blasted, and stood to walk towards the door. 'I want you both to leave.'

'Could you please just confirm for us where you were?' Wilde repeated as she stood.

'I was here,' Lisa boomed. 'Arguing with my addict boyfriend on the phone. Telling him our wedding will not happen until he proves to me he can be trusted. Telling him how much he has broken my heart. Here' – she pulled up the call log on her phone and showed them the relevant entry – 'is that enough for you?'

'Thank you, Miss McKinnon, you've been very helpful,' Dylan told her on his way out the door.

'Thank you,' Wilde said too, as the door was slammed, almost hitting her back.

'Wow. Remind me not to get on the wrong side of you, Officer. Wilde by name, wild by nature. I thought Jess was a bulldog.'

Her heart had been racing the whole time, but Isla wasn't about to admit that to him. She liked that Dylan saw how strong she could be – she knew that sometimes a woman has to be twice as fierce as her male colleagues to succeed. Jessie Blake had taught her that much already. Maybe she would look into a career as a detective. It wasn't something she had considered until a couple of days ago, but Jessie was becoming a bit of an inspiration.

'You're a lucky man, though.' She grinned.

'How's that?'

'You've got two strong women to take care of you.'

'Oi, I can take care of myself.' Dylan laughed as he patted his pockets. 'Erm, do you know what I did with the car keys?'

CHAPTER SEVENTY-FIVE

'Are you sure?' Jessie's head spun at the news.

The sombre nod of David Lyndhurst's head was like a punch in the gut. The only comfort in the whole case was that Finlay Lucas had passed peacefully, but that outcome was now in tatters.

'You see these tiny red pinprick marks under his eyelids, and the two in the whites of his eyes? It's much harder to spot them in such a young baby.' David glanced at Benito, then moved back so Jessie could lean right down to see. 'I'm afraid they mean he was suffocated.'

With Benito standing nearby Jessie felt terrible about asking questions, but how the hell had he missed that?

'But time of death is still the same, right?' Jessie asked.

'I'm so sorry,' Benito spoke up from behind them. 'I just didn't see them.' He grabbed a pile of folders from the worktop and left the room, Jessie and David still standing next to Finlay's body.

'It *was* easy to miss them. Like I said, with such young babies it's difficult,' David pointed out. 'But Benito's giving himself a hard time.'

Jessie didn't know what to say. She had to focus on how this changed the investigation.

'But there's no evidence of bruising on his face or neck, so what does this mean?'

'My experience is telling me this was a tragic accident,' David explained.

'Accidental suffocation?' Jessie suggested. 'But how?'

'It's much easier than you think. Co-sleeping, for example. Adults rolling or leaning on a sleeping infant.'

Jessie shook her head. 'No, that's not possible. He was in his cot. I know that for sure.' She fidgeted with her hair tie. A nervous tic. 'Well, at least I thought I did. I feel like I don't know anything any more.'

David shrugged. 'I'm sorry, but I guess you're going to have to figure that one out. Was Finlay a fussy baby who cried a lot?' he probed.

'I don't think so.'

'What about the parents. What are they like?' David asked. 'Don't you always look at them in situations like this?'

'We did, until Benito gave us his findings.' She paused to stop herself shouting out how angry she was that he'd messed it up so badly. 'Thanks, David. Let me know if you find out anything else. And it's good to see you. You had me worried there.'

David covered Finlay's body and moved away from the cold steel table to wash his hands.

'I scared myself, if I'm honest. Makes you think about your own mortality even more than being surrounded by death every day like I am. Cheryl was fussing something chronic, as you can imagine. Thankfully it was just a scare. Nothing else. Cardiac arrhythmia. They're going to keep an eye on it, but you know me. Take more than that to topple me off my perch.' He grinned. 'She's on at me now to retire, though, Jessie, and I'm beginning to think she's right. Twenty-five years I've been doing this. Did you know that? I suppose part of me knew time was running out. It's kind of why I hired Benito.' David stopped before he said any more.

Jessie couldn't blame Cheryl, Lyndhurst's wife. It must have been terrifying to see a big man like David reduced to helplessness like that.

'If you do retire, I'll miss you and your big smiling face looking at me over a corpse,' Jessie teased.

'You say the sweetest things, Jessie Blake.'

Jessie's mind was in turmoil as she shoved her shoulder into the double swing doors. She turned her head quickly when she heard her name being called from an open office door.

'I have to go, I'm sorry,' she told Benito, whose sombre expression told her exactly how sorry he was about everything.

'OK.' She heard his answer just as her phone buzzed in her pocket. She didn't have time for his self-pity. She had to figure out who had suffocated Finlay Lucas. This case was becoming more and more confusing by the day. 'Hey Dylan, how did you get on?'

Jessie allowed the hint of a smile to grow while she listened to Dylan describing Isla's interview technique; she felt a flush of pride on hearing how far her protégée had progressed in such a short time. It didn't take long for her thoughts to return to the memory of Finlay's little body, though, lying there battered and broken. Perhaps it was an accident, as David suggested. She stopped in her tracks and told Dylan she would meet them in the office, before running back into the mortuary, almost crashing into Benito.

'Hug me,' she said to him. 'Comfort me as if I'm crying. I'm crying so hard and you're desperate to stop the noise.'

'What?'

'Just do it and do it hard.'

Benito moved forward in a state of total confusion and wrapped his arms around her. Jessie nestled her face into his chest, and had to admit her experiment wasn't completely unpleasant.

'Squeeze harder,' her muffled voice rose from his chest. Benito's grip tightened, and Jessie began to struggle to find air. 'Harder,' she stuttered, her words muffled in his chest until Benito's arms pulled away.

'What are you two playing at?' David Lyndhurst shouted after hearing a commotion in the hallway.

'Thank you, Ben, you've been a huge help,' Jessie announced before running out of the door towards the car park.

Benito glanced at David and shrugged. 'I have no idea.'

Jessie's head was spinning. Finlay's death had evolved from natural causes – a tragic event – to murder, or manslaughter at best. But who was responsible?

CHAPTER SEVENTY-SIX

Tim McCabe's entire body was covered in sweat despite the freezing temperatures. He'd struggled to sleep since he'd been asked to do it. Tim hadn't dared tell his brother Peter what he was up to; he would be so angry that someone knew their secret. He had no option but to confess. Like poor Father McKinnon said, confession was good for the soul, and he had felt better for telling him.

Tim was different to his brother; Peter seemed so confident and sure of himself, able to compartmentalise his life. Tim had tried to tell Peter they shouldn't get involved, and especially not to use the garage, but his brother didn't want to hear it. It would be fine, he'd said, and anyway, it wasn't for long. Not to mention the amount they'd been paid for their trouble.

Tim walked towards the station door, startled by the siren that started abruptly from behind him. His heart raced dangerously fast. He couldn't do it. He couldn't tell that detective. He had too much to lose. Peter would kill him if he found out. The blackmail probably hadn't even been necessary. Not really. But bringing up Theresa like they did tugged at his heart anyway. He hadn't realised until recently how much she still meant to him. He owed it to her to go and see her. That's what he would do. That detective didn't need to know. He hadn't done anything really, had he?

With all of these thoughts whizzing around his brain, he hadn't even realised that he'd turned away from the police station door and was walking back towards his car.

He tugged the collar of his fleece further up over his neck against the biting wind. He glanced back once at the two officers coming out of the police station entrance, smiling a greeting at them as they passed before getting into his car. He blew warmth into his cold fingers and started the engine before turning the heat up as high as he could get it to go, the fan blasting the warm air in his face. He slammed into reverse, glad that he hadn't messed things up for him and his brother just because he had a guilty conscience. Peter would never have forgiven him, and Tim couldn't cope with losing another part of his family. Not for this.

CHAPTER SEVENTY-SEVEN

'Jeez, that changes things then,' Dylan commented. 'What now?'

Jessie stared at the board that hung behind her desk. Finlay's smiling face was right at the centre of it, which is where he should be. It was this defenceless six-month-old who was the focus of her attention, plain and simple. Someone, whether deliberately or as a result of a tragic accident, had ended his young life. Being squeezed by Benito was horrible. The sense of helplessness at your body being overpowered was frightening enough for Jessie. It was sickening to think of a baby in that position. He must have fought for his life with what little strength he had.

'Now we have to figure out who could be capable of this.'

'Are we looking at Claire, do you think?' Dylan took a cup of coffee from Isla, who had just joined them. 'Thanks.'

'Aye, thanks,' Jessie smiled. 'What do you guys think? You've both spent time with her. Wilde – you were first on the scene of his disappearance.'

PC Wilde recalled Darren's desperate expression when he'd opened the door to her. Claire was more subdued, which she did think odd at the time, but as she got to know the couple, Claire's medical problems could explain her behaviour. She took a small sip, accidentally spilling coffee on her chin. She blushed at Dylan's grin. Thankfully Jessie was looking away from her, and had missed her making a fool of herself.

'I don't know. Did she do it to stop him crying? Does she even know she's done it? What about Theresa?' Wilde suggested. 'Could she have smothered him before shaking him?'

'The sister's got mental health issues too, but time of death puts Finlay already dead by the time she gets there, though,' Dylan commented. 'Concealment, aye, but the actual killing? I don't see it.'

Jessie glanced from Finlay's picture to Paul McKinnon's. Were they really connected?

'What did you two make of Lisa McKinnon, then?'

'She's broke, but I don't think she's capable of murder. She loved her uncle and I don't think she would have it in her to kill him,' Dylan told her.

'I disagree,' Wilde chipped in. 'What's the expression? The lady doth protest too much, or something like that. Her temper was quick to turn on us: if Paul McKinnon said no to her request for money… Well, I don't know, anything's possible. The supposed phone call to her fiancé doesn't prove much in itself – we need to check the hotel's CCTV. And we still don't know how she found out Paul McKinnon was dead.'

'Right.' Jessie took command. 'You two go and bring in Claire and Darren. It's time we got some straight answers from this family. Take two cars. They don't travel together and keep them separate when they get here.'

Both Wilde and Dylan reached for their keys in sync, and Jessie watched them from her window as they crossed the station car park until she heard her name being called from the doorway.

'Sorry to bother you, ma'am, but could you come down to Custody? There's a guy been brought in drunk and disorderly, and aggravated assault. The guy he was fighting doesn't want to press charges now, though.'

'Why do you need me? I'm in the middle of an important case. Can't it wait?'

'He says he's your husband.'

CHAPTER SEVENTY-EIGHT

The pounding stress headache grew quickly from a dull ache to a throbbing pain in her temples as she walked downstairs to the cells. How dare he? Hadn't he already caused her enough grief? Given his history, this was the last place he should want to be. Jessie's stomach lurched at the sight of Dan Holland, dishevelled and slumped on the bed in the cells. The angry aura oozed from him. She'd seen that so many times before. The knees of his jeans were filthy and wet where he had clearly fallen. There were grazes on his knuckles and a purple bruise was forming under his right eye. Blood around his split lip had already dried. Jessie thanked the custody officer when he opened the cell door and left them to it. Dan struggled to focus as she stood in the doorway, unwilling to get too close.

'Jessie,' Dan slurred. 'I'm sorry but I didn't know what else to do. He just wound me up. Thank you. I knew you'd come.'

Jessie took a step back as he approached.

'I don't know what you expect me to say or indeed do for you, Dan. You're a grown man and you'll have to accept the consequences.' She turned to leave, her heart racing and the pain in her head pounding. Dan leaped towards her before she could leave. He grabbed her arm and was so close to her she could smell the whisky on his breath. His nostrils flared and his eyes changed to black, the way they used to. Like a reflex, she covered her head the way she always did all those years ago, allowing a whisper of a squeal to escape her lips. Before he could hit her with the fist he'd balled up, two officers tackled him to the ground. Jessie fell backwards into the wall opposite the cell, struggling to keep her footing. Her heart raced and her legs trembled underneath her, threatening to give way. She watched in horror as Dan fought with the officers, spitting and screaming in their faces even after another two joined their colleagues in wrestling him to the ground. Dan's anger seemed to give him much more strength than his simple, small frame warranted.

Dan had known exactly what he was doing by saying he was her husband. No matter how hard Jessie had tried to keep her past a secret, Dan had ruined that. How many more ways was he going to use to destroy her? Jessie struggled to control her breathing. No matter how hard she tried, no amount of gasping could get enough oxygen into her to stop the panic. She wanted to be sick. She wanted to cry. She didn't know which to do first. But most of all she wanted to run. She wanted to escape.

'DI Blake, are you OK?' One of the women from the admin department had witnessed what had happened and her words drifted into Jessie's thoughts. She knew she'd said something to her but couldn't quite make out her words. Jessie had to get as far away from there as possible. This was all wrong. She hadn't worked so hard to get him out of her head for this to happen. *Why can't he just leave me alone?* She had to get out. She had to clear her head.

CHAPTER SEVENTY-NINE

Dylan locked up his car and winced at the biting wind. He walked towards Claire and Darren's house, pleasantly surprised that he had arrived before PC Wilde. He lifted a hand and waved with a wide grin when he spotted her pull in behind him.

'OK, Lewis Hamilton, I didn't realise this was a race.' She locked up and walked towards him over the slippery ground, almost losing her balance before quickly righting herself.

Dylan was really enjoying working with the young PC. He remembered meeting her sister, also a police officer, briefly in Inverlochty. Her sense of humour complemented Jessie's perfectly, and he had to admit she wasn't difficult to look at either. Not that he would ever betray his wife's trust.

'Come on, let's go get them. Which one do you want?' Dylan asked.

'I'll take Claire,' Wilde suggested. 'You'd better take the easy one,' she added as she walked on ahead of him, leaving him processing her insult for a minute.

The two detectives could see that Claire was sleeping on the sofa as Dylan knocked on the door. They heard footsteps echo from the hallway.

'Hang on,' Darren called out as the key turned in the lock. 'Come in, Detectives.'

Dylan and Wilde both wiped their snow-covered feet and followed him inside.

'What's happening?' he asked.

'I need you to come to the station and answer a few questions, Darren,' Dylan told him.

'What?'

'There are a few things we need to clear up.' Dylan stepped forward, but Darren took a step back.

'Questions, what kind of questions?'

'I can explain everything to you at the station,' Dylan told him.

'Explain to me now,' Darren demanded. 'Have you found out who dumped Finlay's body? Because it certainly wasn't me, if that's what this is about. Stop wasting your time.'

'Look, Darren, it's come to our attention that Finlay may not have died the way we thought before.' Dylan began, trying to be as diplomatic as possible.

'What the hell does that mean?' Darren blasted. 'How did he die, then?'

So the in-laws haven't been in touch. One of our lot should have, though, Wilde thought. She stepped forward and kept her voice low. 'Darren, come on. The sooner you come with us, the sooner you can get home, OK?'

'No, I want to know.' Darren stepped back and shook his head. 'I want that Detective Inspector here, right now.'

'Darren,' Wilde persevered. 'Come on.'

Dylan watched him open his mouth to protest, until Wilde raised her eyebrows.

Darren lifted up his hands and scratched at his head. 'I'll go and get my trainers on, wait a minute.'

Dylan looked at Wilde, impressed with her negotiation technique. He was just about to tell her as much when Claire walked into the hall, a frown framing her pale features.

'What's happened? Where's Darren going?' She gestured through the open front door.

Before Dylan and Wilde could react, Darren's car spat gravel across his driveway as he drove quickly away from the house.

'Shit, I'll call it in.' Dylan rushed out the door with his phone close to his ear.

'What's going on?' Claire asked.

'We need you to come in and answer a few questions, Claire. Are you happy to come with me?'

Claire stared at her in an attempt to comprehend what was happening.

'Yes, of course, I'll go and get my jacket,' she said eventually, and wandered through to the kitchen.

Wilde spotted a jacket slung over one of the kitchen chairs and lifted it up. 'Is this it?'

'What? Yes, thanks.' She picked up her house keys from a bowl on top of the fridge and slipped her feet out of her slippers and into a pair of black suede boots sitting under the kitchen table. 'Right, let's go. Get this over with.'

CHAPTER EIGHTY

'Can I get you a cup of tea or coffee, Claire?' Wilde smiled while she showed her into an interview room. 'Your solicitor is on his way.'

Claire spun quickly. 'Why do I need a solicitor? Where is Darren? I need to speak to Darren.'

'We're looking for him now, I promise. Try not to worry.'

'I don't understand what's happening,' Claire pleaded. 'I thought I'd been through all your questions before. What more can I tell you? I don't remember anything.'

Claire slumped down onto a chair and rested her head on the table.

'I'll go and get you a tea. I won't be long.'

PC Wilde really wished she could answer both Claire's questions, and hoped Dylan would join them soon with good news. Jessie was not going to be pleased that they had only managed to bring one of the Lucases in. That was, if she ever turned up, too. A friend had told her what had happened down in the cells – the force grapevine could be quick – and she was worried about her new boss. Not to mention stunned. Jessie Blake was married? That really was a surprise. There had been rumours that Jessie and that young pathologist were very friendly. PC Wilde wondered if Dylan knew about Dan, the ex-husband, and, if he did, how much he knew about their obviously frosty relationship.

*

Darren's foot pressed hard on the accelerator, his speed increasing with every second. Metallica roared out of his speakers, but it wasn't loud enough to drown out the grief that threatened to overwhelm him. His vision was obscured by the tears that filled his eyes. He hammered his palm on the steering wheel and screamed in torment at his loss.

He slammed on the brakes and banged his fist on the horn as he rounded a bend to find a bus in front of him. His frustration threatened to boil over. 'Get out of my way!' He was almost bumper-to-bumper with the lumbering vehicle. As rage bubbled up inside him, he tugged his steering wheel right and squeezed the accelerator down hard to overtake. The bus driver could see an oncoming Land Rover, though, and banged his hand on the horn to try and stop the imminent collision. Darren could see it too, and didn't care. He kept his foot down, the collision looking inevitable, but at the very last moment a lay-by appeared and Darren squeezed into it, pressing his brakes with force, causing his Ford Focus to come to a halt close to a gate into a field that ran alongside the road. Darren's heart raced. The car had stalled. The Land Rover drove on, and Darren felt the eyes of the driver and passengers on him as the bus continued on its route.

He staggered out and vomited into the long grass. He had never felt pain like this in his life. Losing his mum was bad – it hurt like hell – but this… This was too much. Wherever he looked, wherever he went, he couldn't escape this grief. And now the police wanted to question him again. He'd told them everything. It wasn't him – they were wasting their time. Darren straightened up, spat vomit-streaked saliva from his mouth and wiped his lips with the back of his hand. His throat ached from retching. He'd almost died; his recklessness had almost taken the life of an innocent stranger. Darren would have had to live with that for the rest of his life. *Like father, like son.*

The pain of his grief gripped his stomach again and Darren cried out into the air, startling a flock of crows that had gathered in the field. He watched them fly away and sniffed back his tears.

The strong, chill wind blew through his mop of brown hair and he rubbed warmth into his bare forearms before getting back into the car. He rested his head back onto the driver's seat and closed his eyes.

What kind of hell was this? He grabbed his phone from his jeans pocket and rubbed his face clean, the tears making his skin raw to the touch. He had to reach out to someone, and she was the only one who seemed able to help him right now. Darren knew it was wrong, but he was desperate.

CHAPTER EIGHTY-ONE

All those years. All that distance. All that hard work in counselling. It meant nothing. In that moment, for those few brief seconds when Dan had his hands on Jessie, she felt like nothing had changed. Even though he had been swept away from her before he could do any physical damage, the psychological hurt was there. It was like he still had the power. It didn't seem to matter how many years had passed.

She had to gather the chaotic thoughts crashing through her brain. She had to refocus. She'd got as far as her car before realising her keys were still in her office, along with her jacket and gloves – all left behind in her rush to flee. An aimless walk around the block had followed, and now she was back outside the station, rubbing her hands together against the freezing air. This was crazy. Jessie knew that better than anyone. Dan was in her past, and she was determined to leave him there.

'Come on, pull yourself together,' Jessie murmured and blew out a huge breath, the trembling in her legs decreasing finally. It was the shock, that's all. In trying to reassure herself, she hadn't noticed the footsteps approach from behind her.

'Jessie, are you OK?'

She turned to see Benito striding across the car park towards her, his eyes narrowed. It was then she realised how odd she must look, standing out in sub-zero temperatures with only a thin blouse and skinny black trousers. Jessie hated the thought of anyone seeing her like this, let alone him. She looked weak, and she hated that.

'Yes thanks, I'm fine, don't worry,' she lied. Jessie was far from fine.

'Are you sure?' he persisted, catching her gaze with his large brown eyes, his brow furrowed in genuine concern.

In a moment of weakness, Jessie began to cry. She had been strong for so long; too long. She should never have stopped the counselling, but she just didn't feel she had time for it. Now look at her. Standing, freezing in the station car park, she wiped away the mess of tears on her cheeks.

'No, Ben, I'm not,' she whispered.

He didn't speak, didn't offer empty platitudes. He stepped forward and hugged her, and Jessie took the chance to cling on to the support she should have sought long before now, and it felt so good. Good to share her fear; her pain. A calmness drifted over her from inside his arms. A feeling that seemed alien to Jessie. She pulled away.

'Thank you.' She smiled, a little embarrassed, but so very grateful.

'You're very welcome, but this hugging thing between us is becoming a bit of a habit, huh?' He laughed to break the tension.

'Yes, I'm sorry about that earlier.'

'No problem. You had David baffled for a minute, but we get it. You think he was accidentally suffocated, don't you?'

Jessie was relieved the topic of conversation hadn't parked on her meltdown.

'Yes, but by who?' Jessie rubbed her freezing-cold arms as she shivered. 'Claire? Theresa? I mean, how long had she really been there? Or Darren, he can't be ruled out either.'

Benito removed his leather jacket and draped it over her shoulders. 'Come on, let's get a coffee. It's bloody freezing out here.'

'Good idea,' she said, and walked on ahead of him.

CHAPTER EIGHTY-TWO

Claire didn't understand why they wanted to talk to her again, and her confusion deepened with the speed at which the interview was terminated. It seemed that telling them she couldn't remember brought everything to a standstill. But she wasn't lying. She couldn't remember anything about that day. Why couldn't she remember?

It had been kind of her solicitor to drop her home. He seemed as confused by all this as Claire was. She pulled her door key from her pocket and lifted it to the lock, but her feet just wouldn't take her inside. Instead, she stared along the hall and called out for Darren. When her call went unanswered, she slammed the door shut again and walked back across her drive and away from her home. She didn't know where she was going, but this felt like a better idea than going home to an empty house.

Claire slid part of the way down the slope that led to the path along Deich Burn. She passed the thick clumps of yellow and red dogwood that lined the bank. A golden retriever barked at her from across the water as he raced to the corner of his garden, which backed onto the burn. Claire slipped again on the glistening mud that had frozen over in the extreme cold. She stared into the water, also frozen on the surface, and could see a trickle running freely underneath the layer of ice. She wondered where it got its energy from. Where did its drive to flow and survive come from? There seemed to be an invisible force pushing it forward. Claire wanted one of those.

She tugged her scarf tighter over her mouth and nose as the bitter wind snapped at her skin, and carried on along the path, past the skeletal spindles of the bramble hedge that had been heavy with fruit six months ago. Her mum's bramble jelly was a hit with the church ladies' scone teas, with most of the harvest being provided free by the plants that now lay bare. Claire stopped by a huge rowan tree that stood on the edge of the open patch of grass that became a football pitch in the summer months, but was now encased in thick, deep snow, with only the footprints of foxes and birds trailing through it. She wandered through the virgin snow, leaving behind the first human prints, and stopped by the burn's edge. She wondered at the determination of the beavers, whose dams on this stretch of water had been dismantled several times by disgruntled homeowners, who claimed their homes were at risk of flooding. Claire didn't care. Her house could be swallowed by the water. She was already drowning in her grief.

*

Dianne Davidson was startled by a loud bang from outside her kitchen window, almost spilling her cup of tea as she sat at her kitchen table. She grabbed a cloth from the sink then peered outside, but couldn't see whose footsteps she'd heard crunching the gravel on Claire's drive. They had managed to get away before she reached the window.

She opened the fridge and took out the milk. She poured the remnants of the teapot and recoiled at the sight of the curdled milk that fell into her mug, horrified that she had just drunk that in her first mug of tea. She'd get some more. She stepped into her faux-fur-lined boots and snuggled inside her duffle coat – Colin teased that it made her look like Paddington Bear – then lifted her purse from the worktop. She checked to make sure she had enough change. The fresh air would do her good. Some of the nausea that remained after taking all those pills still lingered and her throat stung from retching.

Dianne felt guilty about leaving Benson behind, but she hated tying him up outside the shop. 'I won't be long, you silly thing.' She rubbed him behind his ears and promised him a treat when she got back, before pulling the front door shut behind her. She was sure it had become even colder in the past few hours. She smiled to the elderly couple with the bichon frise that she could never remember the name of. *Henry? Harry?* His little coat made her smile in any case.

She turned the corner onto the path along the burn, which was a short cut to the shop, and spotted the outline of someone sitting in the snow by the water's edge. She was horrified to see that it was Claire. The water wasn't deep but it must be freezing cold, and Claire's legs were dangling close to the icy surface. A lump grew in her throat at the sight.

'Hello Claire, it's good to see you.'

Claire turned towards Dianne's voice without smiling. 'Hey Dianne.' She turned her gaze back to the water.

'Is it OK if I join you?' Dianne asked.

'Sure.' Claire shrugged.

Dianne moved slowly through the snow, tugging her coat tighter as she moved. She lowered herself and tried to get comfortable next to Claire.

'How are you doing?' Dianne stretched her arm around Claire's shoulders, knowing that was a ridiculous question.

Claire shrugged again without answering, then gently rested her head on Dianne's shoulder. Dianne swallowed hard. The memory of the pain of Stacey's death pushed forward in her mind. The quiet trickle of the burn under the frozen surface was the only sound for a moment, until Claire spoke without lifting her head.

'What if I did it?'

Dianne was unsure how to respond.

'Erm, I…' Dianne muttered.

'I don't remember doing anything.' Claire finally lifted her head and looked Dianne in the eye. 'The police can't decide. If I can't remember…' She paused. 'That must mean I didn't do it. I didn't do anything to him, did I?'

Dianne looked away and allowed her eyes to scan the burn's bank as far as she could see, then pulled Claire close and laid a gentle kiss on the top of her young neighbour's head. 'I'm so sorry, darling.'

CHAPTER EIGHTY-THREE

Darren had driven back into the village and reached Maggie's place in a blur. Nausea stalked his stomach the whole way. His phone had buzzed several times with calls – from that detective, he guessed. Sure he shouldn't have run out like that, but he felt cornered. Why, he didn't understand. He just did. Like everything was slipping from his grasp. Darren indicated to pull into the car park at Maggie's block and parked in the last space next to her green Mini, relieved not to see Calum's car. She'd told him Calum was out, but it was a relief all the same.

Maggie had been excited to see Darren's number show up when her phone buzzed. She'd missed him so much she ached. She wondered if this would be a good time to tell him about the flat. Her application had been accepted and she could pick up the keys at the end of the week. Maggie was so excited about this new chapter in both their lives. She would help Darren recover. Get him through his grief. She ran a hand over her stomach. They both would. She rummaged in her make-up bag for the black mascara to try to do something to fix her tired eyes. She wasn't sleeping well, and her eyes couldn't hide that fact. The morning sickness wasn't helping. Claire had told her how horrible it was, but Maggie hadn't believed her until now. It was constant. She didn't know why they called it morning sickness because she felt the nausea from the minute she woke up until she fell asleep. Even when she had to get up to pee her stomach churned. That was one of the things Calum fussed over. Her diet. She was sure he'd downloaded every available new parent's guide onto his iPad. Calum was so excited about this baby. Guilt should have been Maggie's overriding feeling, but it wasn't. The fact this baby might be Darren's was all she could think about. She hated the pain he was going through. And that Claire was going through, of course.

The rumble of Darren's engine got louder, the hole in the centre silencer of the exhaust making it so recognisable. Of course he hadn't had time to do anything about it. Maggie glanced over at the clock – Calum wouldn't be home for two hours. She knew that for sure, because she had spoken to his client herself when he called to ask for an extra hour tonight. Calum apologised and promised he would bring home takeaway so she didn't have to cook. Part of her thought she should be grateful, but it was Darren who occupied her mind, not Calum.

'Hey you.' Maggie wrapped her arms around Darren's neck and kissed him passionately on the lips. 'I've missed you,' she murmured, and led him by the hand away from the front door.

'You know I can't stay.' Darren pressed his lips against Maggie's before standing to slip his T-shirt over his head. 'Calum will be home soon, anyway.'

Maggie grabbed for his arm when he tried to walk away. 'Don't go. Stay with me, please.'

'I couldn't, even if he wasn't coming home. I have to go to the station to make a statement or something.'

'Again?' Maggie was confused.

'Yes, I don't know what else they expect me to say.' He dropped down onto the edge of her bed. 'My son is still dead. What the hell else can I tell them?'

'I'm sorry, Darren. I'm sorry you're going through this.' Maggie released her grip on his arm and caressed his shoulder. 'Have they said when you can arrange his funeral?'

'Jesus, his funeral. Nobody should have to think about their own kid's funeral.' He snatched his keys from her bedside table and walked away without looking at her. 'I have to go. I'll call you.'

Maggie wished she could take this pain from him. It was all such a mess. Maggie hadn't planned any of this. Everything had got out of her control. She was terrified that she wouldn't ever get that back. She watched him climb into his car then waited by the window until the dull roar of his engine faded. If she had known how complicated this would become that first night, after that first kiss…

CHAPTER EIGHTY-FOUR

Jessie sat at her desk and sipped the lukewarm coffee she should have finished fifteen minutes ago when it was brought in to her piping hot. She'd devoured the cheese and pickle sandwich she'd been looking forward to, wiping crumbs and a small piece of pickle that landed on her shirt. Her enquiries into the McCabes were stalling – it seemed the company van had a legitimate reason to be on Kintillo Road that day. Peter McCabe had called to say they'd been called out by a woman who lived not far from Claire and Darren's. Her car had refused to start. McCabe had provided the customer's details, telling the officer he'd spoken with to 'tell that lovely PC Wilde no' to bother herself aboot it'.

The customer had duly confirmed the call-out, but that didn't stop Jessie getting bad vibes from the brothers, Peter McCabe in particular. His arrogance annoyed her. It didn't help her mood to discover that Dan had been released without charge. She might have wanted to forget about the incident, but she'd hoped the man he attacked would change his mind and press charges. At least that way Dan might face more time behind bars. It had taken several hours to get over the shock of his lunge at her. Ben had been so sweet, and if she wasn't careful she could come to enjoy the comfort he offered. The custody sergeant had been kind enough to let her know Dan was back on the street at least. Forewarned is forearmed. Jessie didn't think he would dare approach her now, but at the same time she couldn't trust him to simply disappear no matter how much she prayed he would.

Dylan tapped briefly on her office door before walking in.

'Jessie, you are not going to believe this,' Dylan's huge grin was the best thing Jessie had seen all day.

'What is it? Don't keep me in suspense.' She smiled and sipped the coffee again before screwing up her face and quickly placing the cup back down.

'The Morans intend to plead guilty to concealment of a dead body and obstruction.'

'No way,' Jessie beamed. She balled her hand into a fist and punched the air in front of her. 'Fantastic news.' Then she reflected on what this would mean for Claire. This was no victory for her or Darren.

*

'I'm Darren Lucas, I'm here to see DI Blake.'

'Sure, take a seat over there. I'll give her a call and let her know you're here,' the desk sergeant told him.

'Cheers,' he replied with a huge sigh, and sank into the last chair in the row of black plastic seats in what he supposed passed as a waiting area. His eyes flicked across a board of notices and a folder of leaflets about home security. He could smell Maggie on his skin. He shouldn't have spent time with her today, but it had stopped him thinking about Finlay briefly, and those thoughts were crushing him. Maggie helped him stop thinking about everything, and if he didn't have that, he feared he would go crazy. Finlay's funeral. God, when was that going to happen?

'Hi Darren, thanks for coming in. Come on through with me.' Jessie held open the door into the heart of the station. She punched in the code to unlock the interview room door halfway along the corridor and switched on the light. 'Bear with me two minutes, will you.'

Darren nodded and watched her leave, allowing the room door to swing shut slowly by itself. He tilted his head back after taking a seat and, with closed eyes, inhaled a long breath before blowing it out, hard, as his head dropped into his hands. What the hell was the hold-up? He stood and pushed the chair into the table then walked up and down while he waited, his patience growing thinner with each second. He turned to see the door open once again.

'I'm sorry about that. We'd scheduled time to have a chat with you earlier, but that didn't happen, of course.' Jessie smiled and was followed this time by PC Wilde, who nodded a greeting without talking.

'What's this about? I'm sorry I took off earlier, but I've told you everything, DI Blake.'

'I know, I just want to clarify a couple of things. You're not under arrest, so—'

'I should hope not!' Darren roared. 'This is becoming harassment. You do realise that?'

'Can you remind me where you were on the afternoon Finlay died?'

'I already told you, I was with someone I shouldn't have been. I'm not proud of that, but that's what happened.' Darren was struggling to control his frustration and avoided her eyes. 'It was Maggie McBride, Claire's friend.'

'We'd worked that out already. It's not our place to judge. We need the facts, nothing more.' Jessie tried to reassure him. 'Can you tell me: how did Claire seem to you when you got home? Before you discovered Finlay was missing?'

Darren frowned and shrugged. 'Her usual self, I suppose. Slouching on the sofa where I left her in the morning.'

'She didn't seem different in any way, at all, in your opinion?' Jessie persisted. 'To the best of your recollection.'

Darren slumped in the chair. 'To the best of my recollection everything about my life was the same until I didn't see my beautiful boy in his cot.'

Jessie could hear his voice quiver under the strain.

'I'm sorry you're going through this.'

Darren didn't answer. It didn't matter how sorry she said she was; she could never take this pain away from him. Suddenly, the pressure of the past few days was released, and Darren talked. He really talked. He opened up about everything, and Jessie wondered if he was ever going to stop.

CHAPTER EIGHTY-FIVE

'It's getting late, Jess,' Dylan pointed out.

'I'm fine, you get home to Shelly and Jack. Give that gorgeous boy a big kiss from me, will you, and give Shelly a break. She must be knackered just now. That wee one must be ready to pop any day.'

Dylan offered a playful salute before snatching his jacket from the hook. 'I'll tell her you said that. See you in the morning.' Before he left, Dylan spotted PC Wilde carrying two mugs from the kitchen. 'Ladies.'

'You get off too, if you like. You don't have to stay, but thanks for this,' Jessie told Isla as she took the proffered mug.

'I want to stay. If you don't mind, that is.' Wilde corrected herself when she heard how pushy she sounded, but if she was honest she had nothing really to go home to. She'd been so happy when Jessie offered her the chance to help out on this investigation, which had become more complicated every day. It was rare that a uniformed officer was asked to join an investigation – in fact, she'd never heard of it happening before. The relationship she'd built initially with Darren and Claire had given Jessie the idea of bringing her on board, she knew that, but even so, the DI must have had to pull some strings.

Isla's sister Molly had suggested this was a great opportunity for her and she should grab it. She definitely wasn't in a rush to get back to what was now an empty home. Especially after the way things had ended with John, her ex-boyfriend. It was still weird to think of him as her ex. She hadn't thought about him for a few days, which was just as well, because Jessie Blake didn't need a broken-hearted basket case on her team. But watching him walk out of their flat with his rucksack had been horrible. Isla would never forget the look on his face.

'Your social life is as packed as mine, then?' Jessie teased, as if she'd been listening in on Isla's thoughts.

Isla laughed a little. 'You have no idea how true that is. Not that I mean you have no social life, of course.' Wilde blushed.

Jessie really liked this tough little blonde who sometimes said the wrong thing. She reminded her of herself in many ways.

'I think this all comes down to basic motive and opportunity,' Wilde suggested. 'Claire really is the only one. Darren was with his fancy piece, which we've corroborated, haven't we?'

'Not officially. We just have to take their word for it, but I believe him. I can see the guilt he feels about it.' Jessie scribbled on her notepad.

'Time of death clears Theresa of killing him, but she did conceal his body, we know that from Phil's statement. I hear he's going to plead guilty,' PC Wilde added.

'Aye, thank God. Bridget, too. We're still assessing the best way to proceed with Theresa's case, given her illness. And then there's the Paul McKinnon murder. Bridget's saying she knows nothing about it, and I'm certain Phil's confession is bullshit. So what about Lisa McKinnon? Can you see her killing him?' Jessie was curious about what she thought. 'For the money? Or did Bridget want to keep him quiet?'

'Honestly, I don't know. Both of these women had motive and opportunity. Lisa's phoned the station to ask about Father McKinnon's body – she seems in a hurry to arrange a funeral, and has asked for access to the house to locate her uncle's will. That's another thing I came to discuss with you – I've gone back through Lisa McKinnon's credit card activity and spoken to the hotel and airline – looks like she arrived two days before he died, not the day after.'

CHAPTER EIGHTY-SIX

Jessie knew that Claire was going to need a full psychiatric evaluation. It was time to stop all this running around, chasing their tails. This case was so complicated. Not to mention Father McKinnon's death on top of it. Claire had killed her son. Most likely by accident. That seemed by far the strongest hypothesis now. It couldn't have been easy for Darren to open up about their lives and Claire's post-natal depression the way he had. She was right about the guilt eating him up. His angry outbursts weren't just the grief talking. He'd regretted being with Maggie that day, and Jessie appreciated his honesty. His pain was palpable. Jessie felt she was close to the truth, but struggled to feel happy about it, knowing what that truth was likely to be. She would go alone in the morning to pick Claire up.

She parked up and could see Smokey in the living room window, pacing up and down the ledge after hearing her car pull in. She smiled as a text arrived from Ben. She could tell how awful he felt about his mistake when they last spoke. It had hit him hard, especially in such a sensitive case. On top of that he was so desperate to impress David Lyndhurst. He was asking her out for a coffee. She tapped her fingers on the steering wheel and read it again. Her finger hovered over reply three times before finally deciding it was just coffee. What harm could it do?

Sure, that would be nice.

She locked her car before slowly crunching through the snow that lay thick on the path towards her block. She jumped at an unexpected cracking sound that echoed loudly from behind. She spun quickly and peered into the road, scanning up and down. Nothing. *Why can't the council fix that damn flickering light at the end of the path?* she thought, irritated more than anything else. Her encounter with Dan in the cells had shaken her and she feared he was watching her; waiting for an opportunity to do it again.

Nobody had said anything to her yet. About Dan. But she figured it wouldn't be long. Jessie sure as hell wasn't going to volunteer the information. She dropped her post onto the sofa and picked Smokey up as she moved towards the living room window to close the curtains. The sky was heavy with snow again. Movement in the corner of her eye focused her attention to the end of her drive. She frowned and leaned down to allow Smokey to leap out of her arms. She screwed up her eyes and stared, sure she'd seen something, then shook her head.

*

Dan crouched behind the car, startled by Jessie's sudden appearance at the window. He hadn't anticipated that, but he didn't think he'd been seen. Blowing on his hands to keep warm, he glanced at his watch. Ten more minutes, then he would head back to the hostel. Tomorrow he would remember to bring gloves, and maybe a flask of hot coffee.

CHAPTER EIGHTY-SEVEN

Darren's head spun. The post-mortem. Phil and Bridget. Theresa. He'd been stunned into silence by what DI Blake had told him. Claire. He needed to speak to Claire. He wanted to try and understand. Make sense of what was happening around him. He feared he was losing his mind. DI Blake said that Claire was to be examined by the psychiatrist before they took things further. This was such a mess. Not only was he grieving for his son; he had also lost most of his family. His phone buzzed again for the fourth time, or it may have been fifth, Darren didn't know. He'd ignored every one of the calls. He had to focus. He couldn't crack the way his dad had. The pain was too much for his dad, and he crumbled. Darren couldn't do that to Finlay's memory. He needed Darren to be strong. There was a funeral to arrange. Darren wouldn't let his boy down.

Darren picked up the toys and clothes that lay scattered on Finlay's bedroom floor. He hung his little dungarees on a coat hanger and tidied his plastic bricks into their tub. A present from Dianne. *Dianne.* Darren and Claire owed her so much. He lifted the picture book that lay open and had slipped just under Finlay's bedside table. He smiled at the brightly coloured elephant Finlay loved so much. *The Elephant That couldn't Trumpet*, it was called. Finlay giggled every time Darren pressed the button to make the trumpeting sound. He pressed the button. It was then the tears began to trickle down Darren's face, pooling on his jaw before dropping onto the elephant's smiling face. Darren's legs trembled.

The tears wouldn't stop. The pain in his stomach was like nothing he'd ever felt. He fell to his knees and cried out Finlay's name over and over until he was hoarse. His gorgeous boy was gone for ever. The sound of his phone buzzing again broke into his grief. He snatched it from his pocket. It was Maggie.

'Maggie,' he answered through his tears. 'It's Claire. They've arrested her.' He blurted out before she could speak.

'I don't understand,' Maggie began to say, until Darren hung up the call and threw his phone across the room.

CHAPTER EIGHTY-EIGHT

Dr Christine Hunter showed her ID to the desk sergeant and pushed her large black glasses further up her nose. Her short, greying bobbed hair framed her pixie features perfectly: Celtic green eyes and small features, with a dimple on her chin that she feared made her look like a child despite her forty-six years of age. She followed the officer then introduced herself to the frail, pale young woman who sat hunched over the table, her thin hair tousled and greasy.

'Hello, Claire. My name is Dr Hunter. Detective Inspector Blake has asked me to come and have a chat with you this morning. Would that be OK?'

Claire looked up without answering the greeting. That detective had said someone would be coming to speak to her. A doctor.

Dr Hunter unbuttoned her navy raincoat and peeled her arms out before taking her seat. Claire glanced past her to avoid her gaze, nodding only very slightly to acknowledge her. Claire felt defeated; broken even. They thought she killed him, but she couldn't remember. It was all so blurry.

'They think I killed him,' Claire muttered with her head still down. 'But I don't remember.'

'How were you feeling the day you lost your son?' Christine wasn't there to establish Claire's guilt or innocence.

'What does that mean?' Claire finally peeled her eyes up from the floor.

'You're being treated for post-natal depression. Is that right?'

'Yes, that's right. It was hard for me, you know, after Finlay was born. Everything was falling down on me. Crushing me. It was scary and I was tired all the time.' Claire took a long, slow breath. 'It wasn't an easy birth. I lost a lot of blood, they said.'

'I'm sorry to hear that. That must have been very difficult for you and your husband. Darren, isn't it?' Dr Hunter paused to check her notes. 'Can you describe how you felt that day? Or now? How do you feel now? Can you describe that?'

Claire had to think for a moment before answering.

'Heavy. No – empty.' She corrected herself. 'Maybe even cloudy. If that's even possible.'

'And that day?'

Claire sighed. 'Tired.'

'OK.' The doctor acknowledged her answer.

'Finlay wouldn't stop crying.' Claire tucked her hair behind her ears.

'Mm.' Christine nodded. 'Were you able to soothe him?'

'Finlay didn't like being with me, and Dianne wasn't there. He liked Dianne.' A small smile grew on her lips. 'Dianne loved him.'

'Dianne is your neighbour, is that right?' Christine glanced down at her notes again. 'She's been very supportive of you, hasn't she?'

'Dianne has been so amazing. I couldn't have managed without her.'

'You've been very lucky. Not everyone has someone like Dianne to rely on.'

Claire's eyes filled with fresh tears.

'But that day I picked him up then held him close to my chest and he looked up at me. He really looked at me, and for the first time I saw him. I really saw him. We connected, but now he's gone. I laid him down and he was still looking at me. I didn't kill him. I couldn't have. He was still looking at me, I think. It's all so blurry. He drifted off to sleep, then I must have fallen asleep again, back in the living room. I didn't kill him.'

'Describe what you mean by you saw him,' Christine encouraged.

'It was like' – Claire paused to search for the right word. She glanced around the room – 'it was like I'd just woken up.' She frowned. 'Sounds stupid, doesn't it?'

Christine shook her head while she made a quick note on her pad. 'No, not stupid at all. It makes perfect sense. I've heard that many times from women suffering from post-natal depression. It's a very common expression to describe that emotion, and it can take many weeks even after that "waking up" moment to recover more fully.'

Claire shrugged. 'Doesn't matter now, though, does it?' she whispered.

The remainder of Christine Hunter's assessment led her to the conclusion that Claire was suffering from post-natal depression and crushing grief, just as Jessie suspected, but the doctor wouldn't be drawn on her guilt or otherwise. That wasn't her job. She was, however, fit and competent to be charged, if DI Blake so wished.

CHAPTER EIGHTY-NINE

Darren's garbled statement scared Maggie. He was all she could think about. She slipped her feet into her trainers and grabbed her car keys. With Claire out of the way now, they could be together. The flat was ready for them. The deposit and first month's rent was paid. She'd only packed the basics in her bag, but would come back for more of her things later. She left a short note for Calum. Perhaps she was a coward, but she couldn't face him. His breaking heart would be horrible to see. He was so excited about this baby, and Maggie was stealing it from him and giving it to another man. The one she was deeply in love with. In time, she hoped he would understand. Calum was a good man, and he would meet someone else. A woman who could treat him better than she did. Someone who wouldn't betray him. With his best friend.

In her haste, she pulled her green Mini into the path of an oncoming van, whose driver held his hand on the horn longer than was necessary. She frowned and turned onto the main road, and was soon turning off it again and onto Darren's street, her tyres skidding on the icy road surface. Her heart leaped to see his car in the driveway. This could be the start of the rest of their lives together. This hadn't been the plan, exactly, but circumstances had evolved. Faster than she'd anticipated.

*

Darren's attention was caught by the skidding tyres on his gravel drive. He was confused to see Maggie striding towards his back door, with a large black sports bag slung over her shoulder. He went out to meet her.

'Maggie, what a surprise.' He looked behind her to see if Calum was with her, and saw Dianne Davidson taking some rubbish out, easily within earshot and eyeing Maggie curiously. 'What are you doing here?' Even now he was trying to keep up appearances.

'What do you mean, what am I doing here? Of course I was going to come.' Maggie paused and stared into the house. 'Now that Claire's gone.'

'OK.' Darren's confusion deepened. 'I don't know what you think is happening here, but—'

Maggie pushed past him and into the house, making her way to his bedroom. 'You're not even packed. You can't expect me to live *here*, can you?' She shook her head at him and stroked her stomach. 'That wouldn't be right, not really. You must see that.' Maggie reached for his hand.

Darren was horrified. 'Have you been drinking?'

'Of course I've not been drinking, you idiot. I wouldn't do anything to risk our baby, would I?'

He stared at her until she reached for him again. Maggie took his hands in hers and leaned in to kiss him. He pushed her away, perplexed by her behaviour.

'Wait! What are you doing, Maggie?' He lifted his hands up and tried to move away. 'I-I can't leave,' he stuttered. 'I can't just go away with you. Certainly not right now – I have responsibilities. Funerals and court cases and who knows what else. When did I ever agree to this? And this baby could be Calum's.'

'I know it's yours, Darren. I know our child can't replace Finlay, but—'

Darren couldn't believe she'd just said that. 'Maggie, you need to go. Claire needs me, and I need to understand what happened.'

'*Claire* needs you?' Maggie yelled. 'After everything I've done to be with you!'

It was then that Darren's guilt about betraying his best friend hit him.

'Calum doesn't have to know about us. You can still save your marriage,' he shouted back. 'You and Calum can have the family I've just lost.'

'But you haven't lost me,' Maggie begged. 'I love you, Darren. I need you. This baby needs you.'

'Well, I don't love *you*!' Darren roared in her face. 'I love Claire. Don't you get it? Are you stupid?' He tapped her forehead with his finger.

Maggie was stunned. 'But I don't understand. You said if it wasn't for Finlay and Claire we could be together.'

Darren stepped back a little and frowned.

'When did I say that, Maggie? Hmm? When?' Darren grabbed hold of her arms and shook her. 'I never said that, did I?'

Maggie struggled to speak. Every time she opened her mouth nothing would come out. Nothing that made any sense, anyway.

'Please go.' Darren released her from his grip and walked towards the back door. He lifted her sports bag and held it out to her. 'Please go home to Calum. I don't know if this baby is mine, but please just let Calum be the father. He deserves to be happy.'

Maggie pulled her bag to her chest and moved closer to the door. 'I was here that day,' she muttered, keeping her voice low and slow, but Darren's head snapped up in response.

'What do you mean, you were here?' Darren pleaded. 'When?'

'After you left me. I went for a run to clear my head.' Maggie glanced down to the floor and sighed, hoping Darren would take pity on her. 'What you said hurt me, deeply.'

'I don't understand.'

'I told you I wanted— No, that's not true. I *needed* more.' She paused and reached out to touch his cheek. 'I love you. Couldn't you see that?'

'Maggie, you knew what we were doing could never go any-where. Surely you must have realised it. I didn't have to spell it out for you.' Darren's frustration was increasing. 'We were just—'

'We were just what?' Maggie's eyes widened. 'A dirty secret, is that it?'

'Now you're being crazy!' Darren blasted.

'Yes, well, this "dirty secret" was going to tell her – tell her everything.' Maggie's heart raced. 'But Claire was sleeping. I looked in on Finlay because he was crying – he was crying, Darren, and Claire was ignoring him, like she always did.' Maggie pressed her finger hard into Darren's chest, forcing him to take a step back.

'Stop, just stop, don't talk about her that way. Get out, Maggie.' Darren knew if Claire had done something to Finlay it was because she wasn't in her right mind. The things that DI Blake had said made him realise that. He pulled the front door open.

'I picked him up and held him,' Maggie continued. 'I tried to soothe him, Darren.'

'Stop,' Darren covered his ears. 'Stop. I don't want to hear this. I said, get out.'

'I didn't mean— I didn't know.'

Darren stopped dead, attempting to calm the chaos of his thoughts.

'What have you done?' he whispered, closing the door again. He grabbed Maggie and pushed her against the wall. 'What did you do?' he screamed, recoiling from her.

'It was an accident. He wouldn't stop crying, Darren. All I did was hold him,' she pleaded. 'I stopped his suffering. Claire didn't love him. You must have known that.' Maggie moved forward and reached out to touch him. 'But I did it for us. Don't you understand?' she smiled. 'We can be together now.'

The fog of confusion lifted quickly for Darren. Her smile sickened him, but he needed to hear it all, just to be clear.

'What do you mean, Maggie?' Darren swallowed hard. 'You did what for us?'

'I'm sorry, I know this is all so confusing for you, and I didn't know someone was going to take him away. I just didn't see that coming at all.'

Darren grabbed hold of Maggie's shoulder and shook her.

'Darren! You're hurting me, let go!' Maggie cried out.

'It was you.' He pushed her away from him and clasped his hands behind his head. 'You were going to let Claire take the blame.'

Darren wanted to throw up. Nausea rose in the pit of his stomach and burned into his throat. He could taste the vomit before it struck. He barely made it to the kitchen sink before it burst from his mouth. Maggie followed him and pressed her fingers into his back.

'But don't you see? It's just you and me now, and our baby, of course,' she explained.

Darren's confusion and disbelief turned to anger, before morphing into blind rage. He slammed Maggie back into the fridge, hard, sending the bowl of keys toppling to the floor. She was a stranger to him. An evil stranger, who had stolen the two things he loved most in the world.

It was only the echo of Colin Davidson's shouting that woke him from his daze. Darren looked down at the motionless body at his feet, then at the blood oozing from his knuckles. By the look of the wall, it would seem it had taken most of his anger, but with Maggie slumped at his feet he couldn't be sure exactly what he'd done.

'Darren, get back. I need to check if she's breathing,' Colin pleaded from behind him.

Darren stepped back and stared from his hands to the floor. As soon as he moved, Colin dropped to his knees, relieved to find a pulse quickly. He grabbed his phone from his pocket to dial for help. He turned to stare at Darren.

'What the hell have you done?'

Darren couldn't speak. He glanced from Colin to Dianne, who stood in the doorway, aghast at the sight of Maggie's slumped body.

'I can't do this,' he muttered. He shoved past Dianne and out onto the drive. He snatched his car keys from his jeans pocket and started the engine before skidding on the gravel in his bid to escape. With no coat, he was freezing, shivering in the cold, but he had to run from what he'd done. What he'd learned. He had no idea where he was going but he couldn't stay there. Not now that he knew the truth – that it was all his fault his son was dead. Darren would never be able to forgive himself for what had happened.

Before he knew it, Darren was on the slip road to the M90 heading south.

CHAPTER NINETY

Jessie arrived at the Forth Road Bridge as quickly as her old car would take her. Dianne Davidson's call had stunned her, even given the roller coaster that was this case. Sure, Darren was struggling with everything that had happened, and Jessie knew grief did strange things to people, but she was shocked he'd launched such a vicious attack on Maggie. According to Colin and Dianne, they had no idea why he would do such a terrible thing to Claire's best friend, but Jessie figured the couple knew nothing of Maggie and Darren's illicit relationship. Jessie wondered if he'd been drinking heavily before the assault.

Now this. He must be in great pain to consider this as an option. As Jessie parked at the edge of the blocked-off area, the look on the face of the PC who greeted her was one of pure relief. A member of the public had made a frantic 999 call when they'd seen Darren sitting on the barrier, his legs dangling precariously towards the freezing Firth of Forth beneath. In Gaelic the river is called Abhainn Dubh, meaning black river, and today Jessie could see why. The angry current swirled below them. Heights were not on her list of favourite things, but she edged forward past more officers, who stepped back and nodded to her ID when she lifted it towards them. From their position so far above the choppy body of water, the wind was fierce.

'Please don't come any closer,' Darren called out to her without turning round.

Jessie was struck by the calmness of his tone.

'OK, I won't, if that's what you want,' she replied, and pulled her gloves from her pocket to warm her icy-cold hands. 'But could you bring your legs back over, Darren, so we can talk? It's going to be difficult to have a proper talk at this distance if you're facing away from me. Especially in this wind.'

Darren stared down into the raging current below. It would be so easy to just lean forward and let go. As soon as he was swallowed into her icy grip, then all the pain would be gone. All of his mistakes would be paid for. Claire had her parents to take care of her, and they would take good care of her, despite what they'd done. They loved their daughter. She even had Theresa to support her, and of course Dianne. Darren owed Dianne so much for what she'd done these past few months. He was sorry he'd got so angry when the police took her in to question her, but he was hurting and scared, not knowing what had happened to Finlay. Finlay, his precious boy. The police had told him he hadn't suffered, but that wasn't true. That lie ate Darren up inside. The pain was physical. He'd even blamed Claire. How could he do that to her? She didn't deserve that. But the truth? The agony of the truth was too much to bear, and it was all his fault. Finlay died because of his sordid, secret, stolen moments with Maggie. She was so still when he left her lying there. What if he'd killed her and her baby? That baby would be another innocent victim.

'Maggie is going to be fine,' Jessie explained. 'She's going to be sore for a while, but she's OK, Darren.'

Darren turned to face her. 'And the baby?'

'I'm sorry, I don't know anything about her baby, but Calum is with her.' Jessie paused as she watched him turn away and stare back down to the water below. Her stomach lurched. 'You don't have to do this. Please – come back over this side.' Jessie exhaled. 'I can see you're hurting, and I want to help you.' She paused. 'You and Claire.'

Darren spoke without turning back this time. 'Where is Claire?'

'She's still at the station answering some questions, but I can take you to her. Please, Darren, I can help you.'

'Claire didn't do anything, DI Blake.'

'OK.' Jessie's heart almost stopped with fright when Darren shuffled forward. She stretched her arms out in front of her and her body ran cold. 'Please, Darren, don't do this. Claire needs you. Your dad needs you – please.'

'Claire will never forgive me.' Darren shook his head then rubbed his palm roughly over his eyes to rub away the tears. 'And I can't blame her. What I did was...' He dropped his head into his hands as he teetered on the edge. 'I am so sorry. Tell her I am so sorry.'

Jessie was horrified as he shuffled further forward.

'Darren! No! Move back. Let's talk. You don't have to do this.'

'I can't expect forgiveness for this, for causing all this.'

'Of course she'll forgive you. It might take time. Whatever it is, Claire loves you.' Jessie pleaded with him. 'Come on – please. Come back over this side.'

A huge gust of wind ripped through Jessie, chilling her to the bone.

'Not this, she won't. She can't. My weakness caused all this suffering, and this is the right thing to do. An eye for an eye.'

Jessie thought her heart would stop when she saw him move again. Darren was now standing on the outside of the footpath that ran along the vast structure, barely holding on with one hand.

'No, Darren. Nothing is unforgivable.' Jessie searched desperately for the right thing to say. Then she just blurted it out. 'I've lost a son. A long time ago. I know the pain you're going through.'

Jessie's words seemed to hit Darren hard. He glanced at her, frowning. 'I'm sorry, I didn't know that.'

'Yes, it's still hard some days to think of Ryan.' Jessie could feel tears straining to burst out, but this was not the time or the place to lose control. 'You won't stop loving Finlay, or stop missing him, and you certainly won't ever forget him, but we do find a way to live with our loss over time.'

Darren's shoulders straightened as he braced himself. Then he exhaled, turned and climbed back over the barrier.

'It was Maggie,' he whispered. 'She killed Finlay.'

It took Jessie a moment to process Darren's shocking revelation, but she couldn't dive in with questions straight away. 'I'm sorry, Darren, but you can't blame yourself for that. You can't control what other people do. None of this is your fault, so please, come with me. I'll take you back to Claire, and you can explain what happened with Maggie on the way.'

Darren's eyes searched Jessie's for the help he craved. He wiped his arm across his face to clean himself up.

'Thank you,' he whimpered.

Jessie took hold of one of his arms and smiled, then led him back towards her car.

Watching Darren and Claire reunite brought a lump to Jessie's throat. She wasn't lying when she told him that she understood his grief. She understood it completely. After she'd taken Darren's statement, she left them in an interview room to talk in private, and caught up with Dylan.

'Here you go, Jess,' Dylan handed her a mug of coffee and a Kit Kat. 'Thought you might need a chocolate hit as well. You certainly deserve it.'

Jessie didn't feel like a hero. She was utterly drained, physically and mentally. Battling against the freezing temperatures hadn't helped the situation either.

'Cheers, but we can't sit back for long. We need to get to the hospital again. I feel like I've never been away frae that place recently.'

'I know. Maggie McBride. Bit flipping *Fatal Attraction*, isn't it?' Dylan suggested. 'I've spoken to Maggie like you asked. While you were on your way back with Darren.' He took a breath. 'She did it. And she's lost her baby in the attack by Darren. When she was told that she broke down again, said she was being punished for killing Finlay. She told me everything, Jess, but we'll need to talk to her formally once she's been discharged. She's bruised, but nothing's broken at least. This case. What a mess, eh? Obsession turned to murder, I guess.'

'Aye, that's one explanation, I suppose. Like you say, we need her in as soon as she's fit to be discharged,' Jessie added. She was too exhausted to discuss it much more.

'I don't envy the person who has to tell Maggie's husband, and I wouldn't want to be in Darren's shoes when Calum finds out he's been screwing his wife. Christ, he's going to lose it big time. He's a flipping big lad, too.'

Jessie sighed. 'Aye, well, we'll try to avoid that, but Darren's made his bed and will have to lie in it. With Claire, too, when she finds out, because she will have to live with it, as well. He could be telling her now. I feel so sorry for her.'

Jessie's mind drifted back to Father Paul McKinnon. It seemed they now knew what had happened to Finlay – smothered by Maggie, then his tiny body shaken and spirited away by a distraught, distressed Theresa. Now they had to figure out why someone thought they needed to kill Father McKinnon, and whether that had anything to do with Finlay Lucas at all.

CHAPTER NINETY-ONE

Jessie woke with a start. Smokey was standing on the bottom of her bed, hissing, with his back arched. She ran her hand down her soaking-wet nightshirt then through her damp hair. It was just a nightmare, she reassured herself, but it had felt so real. The images were as vivid as if they were happening in real time. The pain in her stomach felt genuine, too, and the blood. Jessie could even smell the blood when it had oozed out from her body. Dan had been standing over her, his fist clenched, with his other hand tugging on a large clump of her hair, pinching the edge of her hairline at the back of her neck. Jessie allowed her fingers to slide around to the spot, and she pressed down her hair. *It wasn't real*, she repeated to herself. *It wasn't real*.

'Come here.' She reached out to Smokey, who curled himself onto her chest and purred. Jessie realised she must have screamed out, startling him. 'I'm sorry, wee man.' She pulled him closer and nestled his smooth grey fur close to her chin, inhaling his smell, letting it soothe her racing pulse. She felt his heart beat next to hers and smiled. No other living thing on this planet meant as much to Jessie as he did, and she hoped the feeling was mutual. After all, they'd been through her marriage to Dan together.

It had been a while since she'd had a dream like that, but talking about Ryan probably triggered it. Losing Ryan was something Jessie would never get over, but she had to find a way to live with her grief, and she'd been doing fine until recently. Finlay's death and Dan's unwanted attention didn't help. *Dan. Why can't he just accept that it's over?* They'd been divorced for a long time. His drunken lunge outside his cell had scared her. It was a terrifying reminder of what her life once was. If she'd stayed with him, how long would it have been before Jessie's mother would have been burying her? *Is it even me he misses*, Jessie wondered, *or is it having someone to control and bully?*

She was pleased to have another couple of hours before she had to get up. It was going to be a long day. The doctors had told her that Maggie McBride was lucky. Her injuries were only minor, despite the beating she clearly took. It had saddened Jessie to hear about the loss of her pregnancy. The baby might have been Calum's, but what state their marriage was in right now Jessie didn't know. She had court in the morning, too. It was Phil and Bridget Moran's day before the judge, and although she'd been told they intended to plead guilty, Jessie wouldn't believe it until she saw it with her own eyes. Theresa was yet to be assessed by the psychiatrist, so Jessie had to wait for that outcome.

She couldn't get back to sleep, and this time it was Father Paul McKinnon's face that kept creeping into her mind. Not just his face, but the numerous stab wounds to his chest. She was certain Phil had claimed responsibility in the belief that he was shielding his wife, but the more she thought on it, the harder Jessie found it to believe that Bridget had killed McKinnon to keep him quiet – she knew he wouldn't betray the sanctity of the confessional, surely. Jessie was only now truly looking past her feelings towards the bitter, unpleasant woman. Something Wilde had said jumped into Jessie's thoughts. Why was Lisa McKinnon in such a hurry to bury her uncle? And why had she lied about how long she'd been in Scotland? That thread was hanging loose after the chaos of the previous day. Paul must have refused her the money she so desperately needed, because she'd also asked for permission to search the house for a will and apparently was not happy when told she'd have to wait. Not happy at all.

Jessie reached for her phone and noticed an unread text from Ben. He was persistent, she'd give him that. His text had been sent at 1 a.m., and she wondered if he'd been drinking. His mistake had crushed his confidence immensely, and he wanted to remind Jessie how sorry he was – and that he was looking forward to meeting her for coffee. Jessie liked Ben. She couldn't deny she was attracted to his tall, dark, handsome and brooding Latin looks. She didn't text him back though, hoping he was asleep at this time. She put her phone back down and snuggled under her duvet with Smokey curled up close to her, his body warming her against the cold of her bedroom. The sound of her neighbour Dave's motorbike drifted into her mind as she dozed. If that was him leaving for an early shift, Jessie still had another ninety minutes to snooze.

CHAPTER NINETY-TWO

Jessie sat in the High Court in Perth and watched as Bridget admitted her part in concealing her grandson's body. Jessie respected the strength it must have taken for Bridget to plead guilty, knowing her like she did. Then again, she had no choice if she wanted to avoid a lengthy custodial sentence. Jessie and Dylan didn't wait around to find out what punishment the Morans would face. It was enough for her to know they'd pled guilty. There were no winners here. How the family was ever going to heal after such a trauma Jessie had no idea. She'd given Darren details of a counsellor for both him and Claire to use. She really hoped they could make it work. Darren wasn't a bad person – he'd made the mistake thousands of people make all over the world every day, and he seemed genuinely sorry for it. Sorry enough to sacrifice his life, although others may have called that running away from his guilt. Leaving Claire alone in her grief. He, too, would have his day in court over the assault on Maggie.

'What did you make of that?' Dylan asked as they headed towards Jessie's car.

'I admire her for it.'

'What?' Dylan was unable to hide his surprise.

'Bridget Moran.' Jessie clarified. 'Couldn't have been easy, when you consider the way she is.'

'Aye, but it was either that or go to jail for who knows how long,' Dylan pointed out.

'I know, but still. She knew we were sitting there watching her. She clocked me as soon as I sat down. I know how she feels about me. Poking around in her family's business. Picking through their secrets and dirty laundry.' Jessie waved a hand, as if dismissing Bridget Moran for now. 'Come on, we have a date with Lisa McKinnon. She didn't take too kindly to being refused access to her uncle's house. She wanted to look for a will, and is extremely keen to organise a funeral – claims she needs to get back to work.'

'What about Maggie McBride?' Dylan asked. 'What's the score with her this morning?'

'She's being discharged later today, all being well. I called the ward early this morning. She's being brought straight to the station.'

'I've said it before and I'll say it again. It's so *Fatal Attraction*, isn't it?' Dylan scratched at his stubbly chin.

'Surely you're a bit young to remember that film?' Jessie tapped him playfully on the arm. 'Even I am. I was only nine when it came out.'

Dylan grinned. 'It's a classic. Everyone knows that movie.'

'Aye, well, this story ends in much more tragic circumstances.'

CHAPTER NINETY-THREE

Jessie was surprised to be greeted in the hotel doorway by Lisa McKinnon.

'I saw you through the dining room window, Detectives,' the young woman said, evidently interpreting Jessie's look. 'While I was trying to have a late breakfast,' she added pointedly.

'Good morning. We have one or two more questions for you. We can talk here, or would you prefer to come to the station? It's your choice.'

That didn't sound like much of a choice to Lisa, exactly. More a veiled threat.

'Of course.' She forced a smile. 'We can talk in my room, Detective.'

Lisa slid the key card in and invited Jessie and Dylan inside. She lifted the clothes from the chairs by the window. 'Sorry about the mess. Please sit down. What else is it you need to know?'

Jessie unzipped her jacket in the heat of the room. 'Thank you. My colleague informed me that you're very keen to get into the chapel house. Why is that?'

Lisa perched herself on the edge of her bed and stared from Jessie to Dylan and back again, then dropped her head.

'I'm not going to lie to you. I was hoping to find my uncle Paul's will.'

'I see.' Jessie nodded. 'I'm sorry, but the house is still an active crime scene at the moment.'

'I know, I know. I don't expect either of you to understand, but I told you about my financial difficulties. I just needed to know whether I would inherit or not.'

Jessie was shocked at her honesty. Impressed, but shocked. 'Like I said—'

'I've found it, though, the will,' Lisa added, her face serious, a single tear teetering on the edge of her eye. 'Bishop Menzies contacted me to express his condolences, and said there was a will and he had it, or rather that it was with a solicitor for the Church.'

Jessie knew nothing about this. 'Have you read it yet?'

The sombre nod of Lisa's head told Jessie that the contents did not please her.

'He's left pretty much all of it to a homeless charity he set up a few years back, and the rest...' She hesitated, attempting to control her tears. 'I'm sorry. I guess he figured I didn't need it.'

'Don't worry,' Dylan tried to be sympathetic. *Poor woman*, he thought. Grieving and bankrupt. Can't be easy, on top of finding out her husband-to-be had been lying to her.

'Miss McKinnon, that doesn't explain why you lied about your arrival in Scotland. We know you were here when he was killed,' Jessie said, boldly.

Lisa's tears flowed more freely now. 'I know what you both think of me,' she continued, once she'd composed herself. 'Yes, I came here to ask for money, and he turned me down, he said until Anders straightens himself out. Well, what Uncle Paul actually said was something like "fights the demons inside him".' She scoffed. 'He said that he prays, and suggested we should pray together.' She gave a short laugh at the memory.

'I didn't leave him on good terms – I said some things I regretted,' she went on, unburdening herself. 'I decided to apologise, and yes – beg once more for help, but it was too late. I went round there and there was police tape everywhere, and the neighbours talking about what had happened. I was scared someone had heard us arguing and how that would look, so I panicked and went straight to the police station, acting like I'd just arrived. It was stupid, I know. But I did not kill my uncle for his money. I'm guilty of lots of things, but murder is not one of them. I've already shown you my call log – I was talking to – well, pleading with – Anders on the phone, like I said. Arguing, perhaps, is more accurate. He was threatening to leave the rehab unit, you see. He says he can't hack it. The hotel should be able to confirm I was in my room, and can't you pinpoint my phone signal location, or something?'

'It's possible,' Jessie said. 'I'm sorry, but you said most of the money was left to charity. Who else benefited as a result of your uncle's death?'

'She hasn't told you?' Lisa said, taken aback. 'Gertrude Laing.'

CHAPTER NINETY-FOUR

Darren handed Claire the mug and hoped that she would end the horrible silence between them. He needed her, and was desperate for her to understand that he was grieving, too. He didn't blame her for being angry and was relieved that she had agreed to stay, after initially packing her bags. *Where can I go anyway?* she'd blasted. She'd been betrayed by everyone she loved. Claire's entire world was disintegrating around her. Her husband. Her best friend. Her sister and her parents. Every person she had ever trusted had let her down; badly. Well, not exactly everyone. Dianne Davidson. She'd been with Claire through it all. Like some kind of guardian angel. She was more of a mother to Claire than Bridget ever was. Claire knew how much she'd disappointed her good Christian mother by getting pregnant out of wedlock. But the police had even tried to blame Dianne.

Claire took the mug of tea and moved away from Darren. She headed out of the kitchen into the living room, with Darren following close behind.

'Claire, please. Can we talk?' he begged. In truth, Darren would have done anything to stop her hurting.

Instead of acknowledging his pleas, Claire turned and took her tea into the bedroom and shut the door in his face before he could join her.

She perched on the edge of the bed and picked up the photo frame from her bedside table. Finlay was ten minutes old in the picture and the new parents looked so happy. It was the happiest day of her life. Post-natal depression had stolen those precious bonding moments not long after. She kissed the tips of two of her fingers and pressed them onto Finlay's tiny body and sighed. They'd tried to convince her she had done that awful thing to her beautiful baby boy. Part of Claire had started to believe them, too. Her mind was so confused by grief but the fog was lifting, and she could see the reality of the situation. It wasn't pretty. Now she would have to arrange Finlay's funeral. He needed her, and Claire would do her best for her son.

'Claire,' Darren tapped on the door. 'Can I come in?'

Despite ignoring his request, Claire caught sight of the door opening slowly before his head poked round it.

'We can't go on like this,' he whispered. 'We need to talk about it.'

Claire's anger had turned to disgust in such a short time. It shocked her with its intensity. The idea that Darren would cheat on her hadn't ever entered Claire's head. Let alone with her best friend.

'I'm not ready to talk to you yet,' she said without looking up, because the sight of him made her sick. 'Leave me alone. I can't even look at you right now.'

'No, I won't.' Darren stood his ground. 'I can't change what's happened, but if we're going to get through this we need to be there for each other.'

Claire's head snapped up.

'Like you were there for me when I needed you? No, that's right, you were screwing Maggie, my so-called best friend who, guess what, decided to kill our son,' she screamed, causing Darren's eyes to widen with fright. 'What did she think was going to happen, Darren? I would go to prison for it and you would be free to be with her? I must have been mad to think I could stay here with you.'

Claire shot up from the bed, spilling her tea over the bedside cabinet, and snatched at the bag she'd already packed. She grabbed

Finlay's photo and wiped the tea splashes from it before placing it in the bag. She slid the contents of her dressing table in after them, then shoved her way past Darren. He didn't attempt to stop her. He knew when he was defeated. Claire forced her feet into her boots and lifted the car keys from the bowl. Her recent seizures meant she wasn't allowed to drive for at least a year, but that couldn't stop her. She grabbed her handbag from the back of one of the kitchen chairs and checked how much money she had. Ten pounds in cash wouldn't get her far, but her debit card would get her a room in the Travelodge for tonight at least. That was if Darren hadn't taken that from her too.

*

Dianne looked up from rinsing her mug under the kitchen tap when she heard the Lucases' back door slam shut. It was done with such force that even Benson jumped up from his bed and offered one long, deep bark at the noise. She watched Claire storm towards her car and drop her bag on the ground while she wrestled with the lock. She looked so sad, sitting there in the driver's seat with tears streaming down her face. Dianne couldn't leave her like that. She put down the mug she was rinsing and dried her hands.

'You stay there, lad,' she instructed Benson, who got up to follow her.

*

Claire hadn't heard Dianne's footsteps on the gravel drive – she'd turned her radio up so loud she couldn't hear the sound of her own tears. Dianne hunched her shoulders against the driving, freezing rain that had recently replaced the driving snow. She had to tap her knuckles on the window twice before Claire noticed her. The two women greeted each other with a gentle smile without saying a word. Claire switched off the engine and got out of the car. Dianne held out a hand to her, which Claire took, then the pair silently walked back into Dianne's. If anyone understood Claire's pain, it was Dianne.

'Where were you going in such a hurry?' Dianne asked while she filled the kettle. She smiled at Claire struggling to control Benson's over-affectionate greeting. 'Go on, you big oaf. Go to your bed.'

'He's fine.' Claire answered and scratched him behind his ears. 'He's a lovely dog, isn't he? It feels like such a long time since I've seen him. Since I've seen anyone or anything.'

A tear slid down her cheek unhindered. Claire made no attempt to halt its progress. Instead, she permitted it to reach her chin then drip onto her T-shirt.

'There you go.' Dianne placed a mug of tea next to her on the kitchen table then took the seat opposite her. 'You didn't say where it was you were going.'

The ghost of a smile grew on Claire's lips. 'Honestly, I have no idea. I just had to get out. Get away from Darren.' She took a single sip. 'I can't look at him after what he's done.'

'This is a horrible time for the both of you, I know.' Dianne tried to comfort her. 'But you'll get through it, together.'

'I don't think so.' Claire sipped. 'Did you know about him and Maggie?' she asked.

Dianne almost spat out her tea. 'What, your pal Maggie? Her and Darren? No, surely not.' Dianne was appalled. 'Are you sure?'

Dianne feared Claire was still quite unwell. Paranoid even, until Claire continued. She listened in disbelief as Claire explained exactly what had happened to Finlay. Darren's betrayal. The crushing pain her parents had caused. She said she didn't blame Theresa, and that her sister would need her support even more now.

'So, what's going to happen to them? Your mum and dad, I mean.'

Colin was going to be devastated to hear about Phil and Bridget. Phil was his friend as well as his partner in the renovation at the back of the burn path. Chances are he would go to prison for something so awful.

Claire shrugged.

'I don't know, but that bitch Maggie will burn in hell for what she's done.' Claire's composure slipped. 'Darren and Finlay were my world. I loved him, both of them, and she's stolen both of them from me – because Darren is not the man I married. He's a stranger to me now. A dark, lying stranger. I will never, ever trust him again.' She rubbed away her tears as Dianne handed her a tissue. 'But I need to focus on Finlay's funeral, because that detective said they would be releasing his body. But I have no idea what to do. How do you arrange a baby's funeral?'

This was something Dianne knew all about, sadly.

'I can help you.' The words caught in Dianne's throat and she reached for Claire's hand. 'I'll help you.'

CHAPTER NINETY-FIVE

Jessie was angry that Gertrude Laing's alibi hadn't been corroborated properly, more so with herself than with Wilde or Dylan. She had been so blinded by Finlay's death. Jessie should know better by now. She'd also been duped by the caring housekeeper stereotype, and it all amounted to her missing the revelation that Gertrude Laing was in line to inherit a small fortune after Paul McKinnon's death. His will should have been more of a priority. Now Gertrude was in the wind – nobody had seen or heard from her for two days, and her car was missing from her cottage.

'I've told you, my mum isn't here, Detective.' Gertrude's son followed Jessie into his kitchen, his ample beer belly jiggling as he moved quickly. 'What is this about? I haven't spoken to my mum for a few days.'

Jessie's eyes darted around the room for clues as to whether a woman was staying with him, just to be sure. A little digging meant she knew him to live alone, after the death of his wife.

'Did she tell you about Father McKinnon?'

'What about him?' he asked.

'Did you know about the will?' Jessie continued.

Gertrude's son frowned. 'What will? What are you talking about?'

After a quick look into Gertrude Laing's bank account, it was immediately apparent the ageing housekeeper was living well beyond her means. It seemed Lisa McKinnon wasn't the only person close to Father McKinnon who urgently needed money.

After taking out a second mortgage on her sixteenth-century cottage to pay for renovation work, Gertrude had fallen vastly behind on her payments and was being threatened with repossession. It would have broken her heart to lose the home she'd raised her son and his two sisters in. On top of that, it seemed she'd been too proud to ask any of them for help. She had claimed years of thrifty saving had paid for the renovation, and her children never asked any questions. Jessie had to tell her son everything.

'Do you know where she could be?' Jessie persevered. 'It's really important I speak to her.'

Gertrude's son fell back into an armchair in shock. He had no idea about any of it. Jessie took a seat on his sofa and stared out the window at his stunning view over Perth. Gertrude must be out there somewhere, hiding from what she'd done.

'She's a vulnerable woman, Detective, and she's missing. Neither of my sisters have heard from her for a couple of days – that's not all that unusual, to be honest, but still.' He covered his mouth with his hand. 'My mum adored Paul McKinnon. I can't believe for one minute she would do anything to harm him. How could she? She's only five foot, for goodness' sake, and there's hardly a picking on her.' He shook his head. 'No, you've got this wrong, so wrong. In fact, this conversation is ridiculous.'

Jessie felt sorry for him as she left. He was genuinely shocked by the revelations. At least they had Gertrude Laing's car registration number – she wouldn't be missing for long. And she had a lot of explaining to do.

CHAPTER NINETY-SIX

Gertrude Laing noticed that her petrol gauge read just less than a quarter of a tank.

'Bother,' she whispered. She switched her CD off and indicated to pull in at the petrol station a few hundred yards ahead.

That was careless, she thought to herself. She checked her bag for her purse before getting out to fill up. She smiled at the hefty driver of the white van at the pump next to hers. He nodded back before pulling his large frame into his seat. The cold wind that whipped through the garage forecourt made Gertrude shiver, and the driving rain hadn't halted in the past half hour. She hoped it wouldn't affect her journey to Aberdeen. It shouldn't take her more than two hours if the roads were clear, but she feared the snow gates might be shut at Glenshee because of the weather. She would just have to deal with that if it happened. She replaced the nozzle and walked inside to pay. She took her change from the overweight girl behind the till, whose sullen face did nothing to endear her to the customers, Gertrude decided. She put the sandwich and flapjack she had also bought into her bag and headed back outside.

Now she was back on the road, she checked the time. Her thoughts drifted back to her last conversation with Father McKinnon. He was a good man. That was his problem. She'd loved working for him – he'd been so easy to get on with. That niece of his wasn't like him. She may have looked like Paul, but her manner was brusque and there was something about her Gertrude disliked immensely. She had heard what she'd asked Paul for. As far as Gertrude was concerned, she'd made her bed and had to lie in it. Father McKinnon's death was devastating to Gertrude. She would miss him, but there was no time to be sentimental.

A flashing blue light appeared in her rear-view mirror.

'I wonder where he's off to in such a hurry,' she murmured, then leaned down to switch her CD back on. Nathan Carter. A favourite of Paul McKinnon's, too. Gertrude hummed along to the song then frowned when the police car seemed reluctant to overtake her. She peered down at her speedometer. She wasn't going more than thirty miles an hour. She turned the volume down on her radio and stared into her mirror to see the young officer point to the left. He was asking her to pull over. Gertrude felt sick. She'd never been pulled over before. She flicked her indicator on and stopped in a lay-by. The young officer got out of his vehicle and put on his hat. Gertrude's body felt chilled all over as he approached. She opened her window and smiled at him when he leaned down to speak to her.

'Hello, madam, do you have any idea why I've asked you to stop?'

Despite the trembling in her legs, Gertrude answered, 'No, I'm sorry. I have no idea, Officer.'

CHAPTER NINETY-SEVEN

Calum didn't understand fully his reasons for being there. By rights, he should hate Maggie. Finding out about the flat, quite by accident, was bad enough. But this? He locked his car and walked, head down, into the police station. His entire world had just been turned upside down. Two days ago he was looking forward to becoming a father and planning for the life he'd mapped out for himself and Maggie and their family. Perhaps they would have added two or three more children later. Now, not only was the baby gone, but he'd learned he might not have been the father; that hurt, but nothing was more crushing than knowing the truth, the whole truth. An affair he could forgive, but Maggie had done the unthinkable. Unforgivable, even. He wanted answers, so that he could begin to process the information.

'What can I do for you?' the desk sergeant asked.

Calum stared at the middle-aged man, whose uniform appeared to be straining across his stomach. He didn't know what to say now that he was there. What did he want? Could this police officer explain why his wife had betrayed him?

'Erm… I…' Calum stammered and swallowed hard. 'I'm...' He took a deep breath and leaned on the front desk to steady himself.

'You're…?' the desk sergeant questioned him. 'Do you have a problem that I can help you with, sir?'

'My wife, she was brought in here a little earlier, from the hospital. Maggie McBride. Can I see her?'

'Take a seat over there.' The officer nodded to the other side of the station entrance. 'I'll call and see what I can arrange for you.'

Calum tried to smile his thanks and did as he was told. He lowered himself onto one of the uncomfortable-looking chairs and waited. His heart was racing erratically.

*

PC Wilde picked up the phone. 'I'm not sure, hang on.' She held the receiver away from her ear. 'Dylan, can you take this?'

Dylan glanced up from the mountain of paperwork Jessie had generously donated to him and wheeled his chair closer and took the phone.

'Dylan Logan.' He sighed while he nibbled the inside of his cheek, mulling over Calum McBride's request. What would Jessie do? 'Aye, he can have five minutes. I'll come and get him.'

Dylan hung up.

'Do you think that's a good idea? Letting him see her?' Wilde asked.

'I'll be with them. It'll be fine. Might help keep her calm, knowing he's supporting her. She might be more likely to be cooperative. I hope so, anyway.'

She shook her head as she watched him leave, then got back onto her portion of the paperwork. The downside of detective work. But Isla could live with that.

*

Maggie stood up as soon as Calum walked into the room. He moved forward, took a seat opposite her and coughed to clear the tightness that was stalking from his chest to his throat. He regretted coming here as soon as he saw her. She looked different. He knew she was bruised, but her eyes were black; emotionless. Like all the feelings she once had had been sucked out of her. This wasn't his Maggie.

'I'm glad you came.' She spoke so softly Calum could barely hear her.

Calum took a long, slow breath and stared at her without talking.

'Please say something.' Her voice now a mere whisper. 'Calum.'

Dylan could feel the tension in the small interview room. It was suffocating, and he feared it might erupt at any moment. Perhaps this had been a bad idea after all.

'Why?' Calum asked, without taking his eyes off her. 'That's all I want to know. That's why I came here today, to ask you why.'

Maggie dropped her face into her hands. 'I don't know.'

'Didn't I make you happy? Wasn't what we had enough for you?'

She shook her head as the tears started. 'I'm sorry. He just got into my head and I couldn't stop myself.'

'I know about the flat in Perth,' Calum announced. 'There was a message on the answering machine from the letting agent. When were you going to tell me?'

Maggie continued to cover her face. 'Don't do this.'

'How long had it been going on?' Calum hammered his fist on the table. That made Maggie lift her face finally. Her eyes widened.

'Calm down, or you'll have to leave.' Dylan was firm. 'You hear me?'

Calum glanced across at him and raised a hand. 'I'm sorry, I'm sorry.'

'As long as we're clear. I'm doing you a favour here, all right?' Dylan took a quick look at his watch. 'Five minutes.'

Calum looked at Maggie again – the emotionless gaze was back. 'I don't need them.'

He'd seen enough. His head was still spinning as he made his way down the long corridor and out the station exit, back to his car. He sat and stared at his reflection in the rear-view mirror before slamming the car into reverse. He wasn't going to keep so calm when he visited Darren, that was for sure.

CHAPTER NINETY-EIGHT

Gertrude Laing's car had been spotted with a back light out, and been pulled over quite by chance outside a primary school, Jessie was told. When the young traffic officer discovered that the woman he'd pulled over was wanted in connection with a murder, he hadn't hesitated to contact Jessie, who was now on her way to the road that linked the centre of Perth to Scone – the home of Scone Palace and crowning place of the Scottish kings. Keir Street was also home to the block of sheltered residential homes for the elderly where Gertrude's ninety-six-year-old mother still lived. Jessie figured that must have been Gertrude's destination, and was grateful she'd been intercepted before she made it there. Arresting her in front of a frail elderly woman would have been uncomfortable for both of them. Not to mention devastating for her mother. Jessie didn't want to be responsible for causing a heart attack in an elderly woman, which might well be a consequence of such a shock. That would have been awful.

Jessie gave a wry smile at the circumstances that had led to Gertrude's apprehension. It was like something from the movies. The killer is trapped by a simple traffic violation. It didn't matter how, though. Gertrude had been located and that was what mattered.

'Do you think she'll admit it?' Dylan asked as Jessie pulled her car in across the road from Gertrude's.

'I suppose we'll find out soon enough.' Jessie switched off her engine.

'She's a tiny pip of a thing though, Jess,' Dylan said. 'Could she really do something so brutal?'

'Desperate people do desperate things. We know that now better than ever,' Jessie answered, and made her way across the street.

*

Gertrude Laing was angry with herself for being so careless. Her attention to detail was usually so precise. It was one of the qualities that made her job with Father McKinnon work so well; she maintained order over his untidiness. Maybe if she hadn't stopped for petrol when she did? Gertrude sighed. She was normally so careful about checking her car was in order – if there was a bulb needed fixing she got her son to change it for her – but she'd had a lot on her mind recently.

That could probably be seen as an understatement. She couldn't believe everything had got so out of control. This was not her. She'd been living on her nerves these past few days. Part of her was relieved she'd been stopped. The smart young officer was kind. He said she would have to go with him, and she probably should; but not yet. She wanted to explain. She needed to tell that nice young detective inspector first. She wanted to explain, on her own terms, before coming in. It was important to Gertrude that the young detective understood first.

CHAPTER NINETY-NINE

Darren jumped with fright when the first bangs landed on the back door, even before he recognised the voice of his angry visitor. He had been expecting him. Maybe he should have gone to see Calum himself, but he was here now. It was time to face him.

'Open this door, you piece of shit,' Calum roared, kicking the door hard as he yelled. 'Or I'll break it down. You hear me?'

The ten-minute drive from Perth Police Station back to Bridge of Earn was more than enough time for Calum's rage to reach boiling point, especially after seeing the state of Maggie.

'Open the damn door, or I swear I'm going to kick it in.'

Calum didn't hear Dianne's front door open, or Claire come running towards him.

'Calum! Stop!' she screamed. 'This won't help anything.'

He spun and held up his hands to keep her back. 'Stay out of this, Claire, please. Go back inside. This is between me and him.'

The anger in his eyes scared Claire.

'Claire, come on back,' Dianne called out from her doorway when Calum resumed hammering and kicking the door. 'I'll call the police.'

When Claire didn't return, Dianne rushed over and pulled her away to protect her. Calum was out of control. She pushed Claire inside and locked the door.

'Darren – I'm coming in whether you open this door or not.' Droplets of spit flew from his mouth. Chips began appearing in the wood at the bottom of the door. 'Darren, I mean it. You don't want to test me, you really don't.'

Darren stood at the end of the hall and watched his friend's progress. He was relentless. His rage would soon remove the barrier between them. He wondered if that would really be a bad thing. He deserved what he had coming.

Then it happened – Calum's foot broke through the bottom of the door.

'I'm going to kill you!' Calum yelled, and kicked and hammered even harder. 'When I get in there, you are a dead man.'

When Calum finally swept the last part of the door aside, Darren realised he no longer felt scared. He watched the shattered, ragged pieces of the door scatter into a heap on the carpet.

Calum stopped just inside the doorway, sweat lashing from his face and neck. He gasped to catch his breath. This was his chance. He'd never done anything like this in his life before. Never even had a fight in school. But right now he wanted to kill Darren Lucas. The best man at his wedding. His best friend. The man who had slept with his wife. The man whose illicit affair with Maggie had driven her to do the unthinkable. The anger built in him like nothing he'd ever felt, and it was growing with every breath.

Darren stood still and waited. He didn't run. He didn't hide. Instead, he took a breath just before the first punch slammed into his cheek. It didn't knock him down, but only because he braced himself against his bedroom door frame. He winced with the pain of what he figured was a broken cheekbone, and spat the blood from his split lip. He faced Calum again, without fighting back. This wouldn't bring Finlay back, but he deserved every one of the blows that rained down on him.

The strength of Calum had shocked him, despite his size. The pain and the rage powered into him, and Calum kept on punching until the police officer's words drifted into the fog that surrounded him. He was yanked backwards by three of them.

'Get off me,' he yelled, and fought against the officers who struggled to get control of him. 'Let me go. This is between me and him.'

Claire watched Calum being restrained and then marched towards the waiting police van, his fists covered in Darren's blood. She winced. His anger made him a stranger to her. She turned her head as the paramedics lifted her husband into the back of the ambulance, his face covered with an oxygen mask. His pain didn't give her any satisfaction, even after everything he'd done to her. Dianne wrapped her arm around her shoulders and led her back inside.

CHAPTER ONE HUNDRED

A cordon had been put in place before Jessie arrived. The confused onlookers were all moved back from the road outside the village bowling club. The school kids were long gone, but not before some had managed to snap pictures on their phones, which Jessie assumed were already on Snapchat, Instagram and Twitter. She wished she'd considered that possibility and fixed her lipstick before getting out of her car. Or at least run a brush through her hair. She turned and smiled at Dylan, who winked and mouthed to her that she had this. She wished she had his confidence as the driving rain battered her cold cheeks, dripping down her soaking-wet hair. *Typical*, Jessie thought to herself. *Why don't these things happen on a steamy hot summer day instead of a manky, wet, cold winter one?* She noticed that Gertrude was watching her approach her car in her wing mirror. When she got closer, the driver's window opened a little more than a crack, but not much.

'Hello, DI Blake.' Gertrude's voice was barely audible over the sound of the heavy rain battering off the car roof.

'Gertrude,' Jessie answered, and wiped her wet face with her palm. 'Could you at least open the window a bit more so we can talk? I can hardly hear you in this rain.'

Gertrude hesitated then narrowed her eyes and looked her up and down.

'Get in,' Gertrude said unexpectedly, as Jessie heard the passenger door unlock.

Jessie looked back to where Dylan and the other officers had gathered, and licked her lips nervously. She became aware of a headache growing across her temples from straining her eyes against the rain.

'Well, what are you waiting for, lass? Get in out of the rain,' Gertrude repeated. 'I won't do anything stupid, don't worry.'

Dylan watched in horror as Jessie walked around the car and opened the passenger door. He dialled her number.

'Come on, pick up, pick up. What are you doing, woman?' When it went to voicemail he tried again. 'Bloody hell, Jessie, don't be a hero.' He anxiously scratched at the back of his hair then got out of the car, pacing back and forth and considering marching across the road to bring her back. He should have gone in her place. He watched her close Gertrude's passenger door behind her. He hammered his finger on Jessie's number again and listened to it ring out. 'What the hell are you doing?' He tugged open the car door and threw his phone onto the seat in frustration, before getting in and slamming the door shut.

Jessie was soaked. Her hair dripped onto her jacket and dribbled down her face and neck. She was so cold.

'Here.' Gertrude passed her a handful of tissues from a packet in the driver's door pocket. 'That should help you get dried. A wee bit at least.'

'Thank you.' Jessie was genuinely grateful. Her wet hair made her feel even colder and she noticed her teeth were chattering. Then the enormity of what she'd done slammed into her – she'd just got into a car with a murder suspect. She could soon be a hostage. For all she knew, Gertrude could have a knife or any other kind of weapon in her bag or anywhere in the car. The glove box, perhaps. Or in her coat pocket. Jessie glanced back towards her own car to see Dylan anxiously staring back at her.

'I expect you're wondering why I wanted to talk to you, Detective Inspector?'

Jessie wanted to say that she wondered a hell of a lot more than that.

'Yes, I'm definitely curious,' Jessie answered. 'Why did you disappear like that? What are you trying to run away from, Gertrude?'

Gertrude turned her body to face Jessie and her sudden move made Jessie jump. Then Gertrude shrugged.

'Honestly, I don't know. It was a stupid thing for a woman of my years to be doing.'

'It was unexpected, I'll give you that.'

A wry smile crossed Gertrude's lips. 'I'm just a silly old fool.'

'I know about the money you lost and what you owe.' Jessie was confused by the growing frown. 'And the will.'

'What will? What are you talking about?'

The look of confusion that grew on Gertrude's face perplexed Jessie.

'Come on, Gertrude. You don't have to lie to me. Not any more. I know everything. You killed Father McKinnon because you found out about his will. That you were to be one of his beneficiaries.'

Gertrude gripped the steering wheel and wept. Jessie waited and watched. She seemed genuinely upset and surprised.

'Paul left me money?' she asked, and wiped at her eyes.

'You're telling me you didn't know?' Jessie shook her head. 'Forgive me if I don't believe you.'

'On the life of my children and my mother and as God is my witness, I did not know anything about Paul's will.'

Jessie sat back and tilted her head to stare at the car roof. Coming from Gertrude, that oath carried weight.

'Then why?' Jessie waited while a silence settled between them. She watched Gertrude's expression soften. This little slip of a woman didn't seem capable of such brutality.

'Why did I kill him?' Gertrude asked.

'Yes, if you didn't know about the money. Why would you do that?'

Gertrude clasped her cold hands together and blew warm breath into them, then faced Jessie. 'Do you have faith, Detective?'

That question really made her think. What did she believe in? She shrugged and searched for an answer.

'I guess I do, yes. I believe in doing the right thing.'

Gertrude nodded and smiled at Jessie's answer. 'Paul believed that, too. That's why he was torn between his faith and doing what was right. I heard him talking to Bishop Menzies about it. He was getting so upset and angry.'

'About what?' Jessie asked.

'Bridget Moran and her confession.'

'Could you hear what they were saying? Paul and the Bishop?'

Gertrude nodded once again. 'Oh, I heard, and I couldn't let him do that. I couldn't let Paul betray the sanctity of the confessional. You know what they do to priests that do that, don't you? I couldn't have that, could I?' She paused, then carried on without looking at Jessie. 'But of course, I did try to get someone to do it for me first. When blackmail didn't work, I had to do the job myself.'

Jessie was genuinely confused. She couldn't think of anyone Gertrude could possibly coerce into murder. 'Who?'

'That lad was never going to amount to much anyway. Not the way he's been carrying on.' Gertrude continued as if she hadn't heard Jessie's question. 'So sad. He'd been such a lovely wee boy.'

Jessie still struggled to figure out who she was referring to and her frustration with Gertrude's reluctance to tell her was growing. 'What lad are you talking about?' She found her voice had risen an octave in a bid to get the truth.

Gertrude briefly glanced at her own reflection in the rear-view mirror and finally turned to face Jessie.

'Does it really matter now?' Gertrude sighed, her voice echoing the defeat she felt.

'Yes, I'm afraid it does, Gertrude, because he knew what you had planned.' Jessie informed her. 'Who was it?'

Gertrude sighed again. 'Will he get into trouble, Detective Inspector? Because he didn't do anything. Not really.'

'I can't promise that. You must know that.' Jessie was running out of patience. 'Who was it?'

Gertrude pulled a tissue from her jacket pocket, wiped her nose and shook her head.

'I overheard young Tim McCabe talking to Paul about something he and his no-good brother had done.'

Jessie narrowed her eyes as Gertrude paused. 'Oh yes, what was that?'

'They have a gun. A gun that's been involved in an armed robbery. They're keeping it at the garage for someone. I didn't hear who, though.'

'And you told him you would tell the police if he didn't help you?' Jessie suggested.

'Aye, but he got cold feet, didn't he? Probably for the best in the end. Told me not to do it and it wasn't too late to change my mind.' She sighed in resignation. 'This way, at least he's got a chance to have a life. He made the right choice.' She gave a wry smile. 'He had more strength than I gave him credit for. I have to admire him for that.'

Jessie watched Gertrude Laing being guided into the back of the police car, her hands in handcuffs, pondering the bizarre rainbow that streaked across the sky above them. Jessie had been adamant that Theresa and Claire held the key to solving both Finlay Lucas and Father Paul McKinnon's deaths, but the truth was that neither of the sisters were to blame. Instead, Theresa and Claire became victims, too. Jessie felt guilty.

The sound of Dylan's voice woke Jessie from her trance. He draped a tartan blanket around her shoulders to stop her shivering.

'Hot cup of coffee, Jess? I'm buying.' He grinned.

'Damn right you're buying.'

Dylan smiled and tightened the blanket around her shoulders. 'I think we can both agree that was the bravest and stupidest thing you've ever done, Detective Inspector Blake.'

'Hey, remember who you're talking to, young man.' Jessie shivered until Dylan draped his arm round her shoulder and led her back to her car. 'I expect a Kit Kat to go with my coffee at the very least.'

'Whatever you say, boss.'

CHAPTER
ONE HUNDRED AND ONE

Dan Holland felt more settled than he had for a very long time. He hung up his phone and punched the air with delight, then corrected himself when he realised the council housing officer had seen him. But she grinned.

'Good news, I'm guessing?' she asked, pulling a pen from her bag.

'Yes.' He coughed to compose himself. 'I had a job interview yesterday. Not much, just a kitchen porter position, but that was them.' He shrugged. 'I got the job.'

'Wow, that's good news. I'm really happy for you.' She laid the tenancy agreement on the window ledge in the flat's kitchen, music from the upstairs neighbour drifting into the room.

'Yes, I'm finally getting my life together. It's been a long time coming.' He sighed. 'But I'm getting there.' Dan held the pretty young woman's green eyes, then looked away.

'Well, there you go, Mr Holland.' She handed Dan three keys that all looked the same, and a larger one. 'The big one is your shed key. The numbers are on the doors. You'll find it easy enough. OK, well, if there's nothing else, enjoy your new home.' She zipped up her bag and slung it across her arm. 'If you have any questions, my number is on the back of your copy of the agreement.'

'Thanks a lot. I really appreciate your help.'

'No problem. Good luck with the new job, as well,' she added before closing the front door behind her.

Dan stood with his back to the door. He pulled his phone from his pocket and pressed the number next to the letter J. He listened to it ring out then hung up.

EPILOGUE

Three weeks later

Jessie couldn't stop her right knee from trembling, she was so nervous. So much that it was difficult to walk without drawing attention to the wobble. Or so Jessie thought. She had no need to be anxious, she chastised herself. Benito was a lovely guy. He wasn't Dan. Anyway, this was just coffee. The coffee she owed him for his kindness, after all.

'He's already here,' she muttered under her breath and smiled to where he waved from the corner of Willow's coffee shop, in the café quarter on King Edward Street.

Benito stood to greet her, placing a soft kiss of welcome on Jessie's cheek. He smelled good. Benito Capello always smelled good. Jessie wasn't sure exactly what it was but it was really nice.

'You look lovely,' he commented and pulled a chair out for her.

'Thanks.' Jessie wasn't sure what to say to that. She was wearing her usual skinny jeans and leather jacket. Her day off clothes.

Jessie wasn't the only one off duty – she had just called to congratulate Dylan and Shelly on the birth of their daughter, slightly earlier than anticipated after a fifty-minute labour that had left the couple stunned and exhausted. They were going to call her Katie. Jessie loved that name. Jack and Katie. Two lovely, traditional names. She planned to go baby gift shopping after coffee with Ben. Dylan had also decided, while Shelly was in labour, that he wanted to take his detective sergeant's exams. Jessie had been pleased to hear that. Hell, maybe she could even persuade Isla to transfer to CID now. They made a great team, and Isla confessed she'd had a blast working with them. Then she'd blushed, realising she might have said the wrong thing again.

'What can I get you?' the waitress appeared behind Jessie as soon as she sat down.

Jessie uncurled her scarf and smiled. 'A latte please, thank you.'

'Cappuccino for me, thanks,' Ben told her.

'Is that everything?'

Jessie nodded before their waitress wandered back towards the kitchen. The silence between the pair was awkward, until Ben spoke.

'How have you been?' His eyes held hers.

'Aye, good thanks,' she answered. 'And you?'

'Good, yes. I've just got back. I was visiting family in Naples.'

'Sounds lovely.'

'If you enjoy sharing a small house with three hot-headed sisters, a crazy brother and Mamma and Papà, of course. As well as three dogs, two cats and lots of chickens.' He laughed. 'It was Mamma's sixtieth birthday, so I kind of had to go. They wanted to move back home when Papà retired.'

Jessie enjoyed the way he talked about his family.

'Must have been nice. Coming from a big family.'

Before Ben could answer, the waitress arrived with their coffees.

'Grazie,' Ben said.

'Thanks,' Jessie told her.

'You would think so, maybe, but' – Ben shook his head – 'Italian women are loud and passionate. My sisters especially.' He tipped a packet of brown sugar into his cup and stirred. 'What about you? Do you have brothers and sisters?'

'I have one sister, Freya. I don't see her all that often these days.'

'I'm sorry to hear that.'

'It's fine. We're OK with it. Heck, I'm too busy anyway.' Jessie laughed.

She'd begun to relax without realising it. He was so easy to talk to. He made her smile. No, that wasn't true. He made her *laugh*. She thought everyone would benefit from having a Benito Capello in their lives.

*

Dan stood with his back resting on the wall of St John's Kirk, right across the cobbled road from Willow's coffee shop. Jessie had ignored all of his letters of apology and phone calls, so he'd begun to keep tabs on what she was doing and where she was going. Looking for the right opportunity to talk to her. If she would just listen to what he had to say, she would understand that he was sorry about what happened. He'd made a mistake. Fallen off the wagon. He stared into the window at the couple sat talking and laughing in the corner booth just inside the door. How could she just move on like that?

The sound of a bin lorry roaring along the cobbles drew his attention away from Jessie, before obscuring his view of her.

Jessie glanced out of the window briefly as the bin lorry drew up, then returned to what Ben was saying. He'd been offered a job in Edinburgh, and she agreed he would be mad not to take it. He told her he would like to keep in touch with her. She liked that. It caused butterflies in her tummy that she'd not felt for a seriously long time.

The bin lorry rolled away after consuming the contents of the café's wheelie bin. Dan tugged the baseball cap he was wearing down over his eyes and pulled up the collar of his jacket, then walked away, his body obscured by the slow-moving vehicle until he turned the corner on to George Street and on towards his flat.

A moment later, Jessie caught sight of the sun peeking over the top of St John's Kirk, and smiled.

A LETTER FROM KERRY

For those of you returning to Jessie after reading *Heartlands*, thank you, and I'm so glad you loved her enough to come back. To those who are meeting her for the first time, welcome and thank you for choosing this book. I hope you've enjoyed getting to know her.

Jessie doesn't claim to be perfect, but she tries to do the right thing. To stand up for those that can't stand up for themselves, and for that I admire her immensely. She's faced enormous challenges in her life, and that has made her the strong woman she is today.

If you want to keep up to date with all my latest releases, just sign up at the following link. Your email address will never be shared and you can unsubscribe at any time.

www.bookouture.com/kerry-watts

I hope that you've enjoyed this book. I would really appreciate it if you would leave a review on Goodreads and Amazon, and perhaps tell your friends about Detective Inspector Jessie Blake. I love to hear from readers on social media, and I can be found on both Facebook and Twitter. I look forward to hearing from you.

Thank you,
Kerry

KerryWattsAuthor

@Denmanisfab

ACKNOWLEDGEMENTS

First, I want to thank Helen Jenner and Bookouture for their awesome support and enthusiasm. Thank you, Helen, for helping me shape Jessie into the wonderful character she has become. I mean that sincerely.

Thank you, Kim Nash and Noelle Holten, for all your hard work, words of advice and wisdom. Your help and encouragement mean a lot to me. I hope you both know that.

My sincere thanks also go to Fraser Crichton. Where would this book be without you?

The support of my family throughout all of this is appreciated beyond words. Mark, for your copious amounts of tea and quiet optimism, thank you. Hannah, for your endless words of encouragement, and Flynn, for making me giggle every day. Dad, for asking 'How are you getting on with your book?' every week over our Thursday lattes at the theatre. Denise, for telling her friends she has a famous writer sister. Not to forget Domino and Buttercup, of course. Thank you. All of you.

As always I am so grateful to have a fantastic bunch of supporters on Facebook. Susan Hunter, Dee Williams, Craig Gillan, Livia Sbarbaro and Norma Ormond. Thank you, all of you, for always cheering me on.

For crime fiction lovers, your love of the genre makes writing such a pleasure. To the members of the UK Crime Book Club and Crime Fiction Addict – thank you. You are all amazing.